P

ope

She stood there for a moment, then her mouth just dropped open. She raised her arm and pointed, but no words came out. Then she slowly moved toward Patricia until she stood behind her. Her fingers slowly combed through Patricia's hair, feeling it and looking at it. Pinky stared over her shoulder into the mirror.

"What have you done?"

"*Nothing!* I woke up and there it was."

Paul ran to the open bathroom door and stared. He saw a strange woman standing naked in the bathroom with Pinky.

She turned slowly toward him.

Patricia looked as surprised as Paul felt. They both froze.

Then he felt something he'd never felt in regard to Patricia. He felt a pure heated rush of arousal.

"She's blonde," he said. "All over."

"Macpherson succeeds in creating . . . romance that stands out from the pack."

Publishers Weekly

By Suzanne Macpherson

Hysterical BLONDENESS

SUZANNE MACPHERSON

AVON BOOKS
An Imprint of HarperCollins*Publishers*

AVON BOOKS
An Imprint of Harper Collins*Publishers*
10 East 53rd Street
New York, New York 10022-5299

ISBN-13: 978-0-06-077500-1
ISBN-10: 0-06-077500-9
www.avonromance.com

First Avon Books paperback printing: September 2006

Printed in the U.S.A.

10 9 8 7 6 5 4 3 2 1

To all my favorite blondes,
Christie Ridgway, Kim, Pipper, Jenny G.,
and most of all, Miss Mary Kathryn.

Acknowledgments

Special acknowledgment to Natalia Ilyin for her amazing work of non-fiction, *Blonde Like Me: The Roots of the Blonde Myth in Our Culture,* which added that special touch of blonde wisdom to my entire book.

Chapter One

Friendship is constant in all other things
Save in the office and affairs of love.
William Shakespeare

Patricia Stillwell watched as the curvaceous blonde made her way down the aisle of the company lunchroom. A tiny hot pink handbag dangled from one wrist. It matched the blonde's hot pink lips and her hot pink knit top. The hot pink top brimmed over with a cleavage that seemed almost real. In her slender arms she balanced a salad in a clear plastic box as if it were a gift.

"Look at that. Look how she *moves*! It's like

Jell-O on springs," Pinky McGee hissed across the table to her friend Patricia.

As soon as the woman passed by, Patricia twisted herself backward and watched with fascination as the men in the lunchroom respond in a mass-hysteric Pavlovian response wave.

"Those aren't *real*." Patricia gave her best friend Pinky a roll-eyed look. "It's *silicone* on springs, not Jell-O."

As Patricia continued to watch the passing parade, she saw every guy in the cafeteria develop a snap-action Ken doll head as the blonde and beautiful Lizbeth Summers from the lingerie department passed by their long tables.

"Unbelievable. You'd think she was a T-bone steak and they were starving dogs," Pinky said. "Look at them drool." Pinky pushed her black-rimmed glasses back up in disdain.

"So what? She's a blonde," Patricia said. "She's Marilyn Monroe and we're Jack Lemmon and Tony Curtis. Or in our case, more like Geraldine and Daphne, their female alter egos."

"Just find me Osgood Fielding the Third and you're on." Pinky smirked and batted her eyes.

"You are impossible." Patricia took a bite of her

sandwich and ignored her friend. The subject of blondes vs. brunettes was not a new one in the Nordquist Department Store's employee lunchroom.

"You use that same obscure movie reference every time I yammer about some bimbo blonde from the lingerie department making all the boys go ga-ga." Pinky crossed her arms and stared, unblinking. Patricia gazed upon her best friend. Pinky's brown eyes looked bigger because of the way her glasses magnified them. Her Mary McFadden bobbed hairdo set the whole picture off. Pinky always made her smile and drove her nuts at the same time.

Patricia finished her bite before she set her friend straight. "*Some Like It Hot* is not obscure. It's a classic. And besides, Paulie knows what I mean. Who cares about anyone else but you, me, and our honorable landlord and third musketeer, Paulie?" Patricia slumped over her sandwich. She was in a mood. She sucked her diet Coke through a straw and hid her face from Pinky so her blonde envy wouldn't show. The truth was, she wished she could be as beautiful as Lizbeth.

If she had been the pretty sister instead of the plain one, would she be here working at Nordquist in the catalogue department? Or would she be engaged to an Orthodontic Greek God like her sister Carol, or maybe teaching Russian and Romantic literature to a room full of attentive college students focused on her striking appearance yet still soaking in the wonder of Dostoyevsky's *Crime and Punishment*?

"We need new movie references; modern movies, beyond the sixties. We're just getting so inbred; so predictable. Isn't that the same thing you ate last Tuesday?" Pinky asked.

"What's wrong with leftovers?"

"It's the meatloaf Tuesday thing. Every Monday Paulie makes meatloaf. Every Tuesday you eat a meatloaf sandwich."

"So I'm economical."

"No, Patricia, you are in a rut! We are in a rut."

"Okay. I'm in a rut. I admit it. What shall we do, take a cruise to Fiji? Enroll in a knitting class? Go river rafting? Learn to ride a bike again?"

"You're a very pretty girl, you know." Pinky tapped her short unpainted fingernails on the bare woodlike tabletop. "You haven't had a serious relationship in over four years. You should be dating."

"Are you hitting on me?"

"*Fesso.*" Pinky reached over and swatted Patricia's hand. Good thing she'd put down the sandwich.

"Ouch. What's that mean?"

"Idiot in Italian. Paulie is teaching me Italian."

"So what's your point? Under this plain exterior we're both living dolls? We're not. We are the plain-brown-wrapper girls. We are Barbie's best friend whazzername. See? We can't even remember Barbie's best friend's name. And do you know *why*? Because she was a brunette like us. She probably had a degree in some obscure literature."

"Like you?" Pinky smiled.

"Yes, and that's why we don't know her name, because she's twenty-eight, working in the catalogue department of Nordquist, underutilizing her education, and not even getting a decent employee discount because she doesn't quite have what it takes to be on the sales floor. She's at Nordquist getting the second-tier discount. Sad, isn't it?"

"She was a redhead sometimes. I remember that. But I had her with brown hair. She was probably an Irish Catholic girl from Brooklyn," Pinky mused.

"Like you?" Patricia took another bite of her sandwich. Eating with Pinky always made eating somewhat difficult and slow due to their joint tendency to philosophize over lunch instead of chew.

"Yeah, like me. You think this Northwest land of Norwegians and fish is so great. These Scandhoovians have no idea what do to with food. Did I ever tell you about the food in New York? People out here just don't get it. What is with the bagels here in Seattle? Just stupid." Pinky made a very weird face and gestured in the air.

Patricia laughed. "Let's see, did you *and* Paulie ever tell me about the food in New York? Only about a thousand times a week. Shall I just flop over and expire of hysterics right here? We've been searching for the perfect bagel in this city for five years, Pinky. Talk about predictable!" She snorted in response to her friend.

Pinky made a mean face at her, which abruptly changed to a happier configuration. "Oh, look, here comes Osgood Fielding the Third."

Patricia turned completely around to see what

Pinky was staring at. Just like the blonde moment, a hush fell over the lunchroom as their new store manager, Brett Nordquist, son of the owner, made his gorgeous way down the aisle.

Patricia felt herself flush with a strange, unnerving desire to throw herself at Brett's lean beautiful body and declare her love. Her lips parted and she breathed in his scent as he passed. She'd spent an hour at the man-scent counter on the first floor figuring out what cologne he used. It was Eau Sauvage by Dior. Intoxicatingly animal.

On so many levels the beautiful Brett was the male counterpart to Lizbeth Summers. She wondered if Brett and Lizbeth knew they were destined to create genetically perfect children together. She wondered if she could possess Lizbeth's body and take her place for that union—a surrogate Lizbeth, so to speak.

Brett stopped to talk to Lizbeth. Perhaps he had an inkling of his fate after all. He was doing that casual kind of hands-in-the-pants-pocket-of-a-great-suit thing. Lizbeth looked perturbed at him. Silly woman, Patricia thought. Wake up, Lizbeth; look up at the bronzed blonde, godlike creature, almost kneeling at your feet and recognize your preordained path!

"How could Lizbeth be dissing Osgood like that?" Pinky mused.

"Brett Nordquist is so, so beyond Osgood." Patricia sighed.

"That's going to be our new saying. Beyond Osgood."

"I'm in love with him."

"Beyond Osgood? Really?"

"Yeah, Beyond Osgood. Pathetic, isn't it?" Patricia started to laugh and snort at the same time; a bad and strange habit that overcame her on occasions when the laughter was tainted with embarrassment, thereby compounding the problem twofold. "Deeply, hopelessly in love."

Paul Costello walked up behind Patricia and put his hands on her shoulders. She jumped at least an inch off her chair, startled, he guessed. He winked at Pinky across the table. Her short brown hair parted to reveal her thick glasses and a large grin directed his way.

Patricia looked up at him with her less-thick gold-rimmed glasses. She had that whole Marion the Librarian look down pat. But she was pretty, too, like Marion. He stared at her lovely features for a moment.

"What's going on here? I hear snorting. You girls know what happens when you snort-laugh and try and drink diet Coke at the same time. It is just not pretty." He pulled out a chair beside Patricia and studied his two best friends. They both had their hands over their mouths in a lame attempt to stop the inevitable blurt of gossip and free-form hysterics that occasionally came upon them.

"You're gonna blow, you know. Just don't mess up the suit." Paul held up his hands in a fake protective manner and cringed against the wall.

They blew, then started gossiping about unnamed blondes. It was loud and somewhat embarrassing, although it took a whole lot to embarrass him these days.

After all, he was the assistant buyer of "ladies' better handbags" for Nordquist Department Store. For a living, even. Sure, the money was actually quite good, and he traveled to all his favorite places. But when you said what your job was, the eyebrow almost always raised up. He hated the eyebrow.

So hanging out with these two was harsh at times, but not that bad. His family could always top it. Just take his Sunday visits with his Seattle-transplanted Bronx Italian family where his brothers would make with the jokes. "Oh, *Paulie*, you forgot your *purse*!" His youngest brother Mitchell would make some excuse to do *that* little joke every time. Then Nick would laugh his head off.

So what could two off-the-wall broads do that his two brothers couldn't top in a heartbeat? Besides, they were *his* off-the-wall broads, living in the lower half of his house, and he loved them both. He adjusted his glasses and gave them both a look.

"Stifle it, ladies. I'm here slumming with you underlings, so show some respect," he said.

They quieted and apologized for their childish behavior, then gave him huge doses of crap for his slumming comment. He knew perfectly well the whole Buyers-mingling-with-the-riff-raff thing would never fly—he just had to poke the anthill once in a while for fun.

The truth was, he was a happy man with his interesting, quirky housemates. Sometimes he wondered what could ever lead him to change the way things were. *And yet,* little things did lead him. Which reminded him of his mission.

"I brought chocolate," he announced.

"Oh, oh, we promise to behave." Patricia grabbed his arm and made tiny jumps in her seat.

"You two are like Chihuahua dogs. I'll refrain from making you roll over or beg."

"Hand over the chocolate and no one gets hurt," Pinky said.

Paul opened the tiny gold Godiva bag he'd brought with him and pulled out one glazed apricot dipped in dark chocolate for Pinky, and one espresso truffle for Patricia, each one wrapped in a bit of waxed paper. He knew what they liked. Both girls swooned and made a great drama of accepting their heavenly treats.

"Oh, Paulie, have we told you how much we love you?" Pinky nibbled on her apricot.

Patricia gave him a somewhat wet kiss on the cheek. "You are a god among men, Paulie. You've spoiled us for all others. Nordquist's is lucky to have an assistant handbag buyer such as yourself."

The place where her lips touched his cheek had probably left a ketchup splotch from her meatloaf sandwich. He borrowed her napkin and blotted. Yes, indeed, ketchup. She was so funny. Her kiss felt good, though. Patricia had a special place in his heart.

"Keep your panties on, ladies, there's a price to pay."

"Ooo, I just knew it." Pinky's eyebrow tweaked high on her forehead as she looked sharply at Paul. "I'm such a *fesso*."

"That's her new word for today. It's Italian . . ." Patricia said as she bit into her truffle. Paul watched her lick her lips with pleasure.

". . . for idiot," Paul said. "I know. It's a little on the fancy side as usage goes." He paused, then went ahead and threw himself to the she-wolves. "I need a few hours alone tonight."

"As in an actual date alone? As in make the moves on some poor unsuspecting girl? Why? Wouldn't she love to meet your charming house-mates? What is she, antisocial?" Patricia asked.

"No, she's social. She's very social."

"Is she a werewolf and you don't want us to see her change into a horrible fanged hairy beast when the full autumn moon rises?" Pinky asked.

"No, she's not a werewolf as far as I know."

"Well, then, what is she, chopped liver? Princess Mononoke? The bride of Frankenstein?" Pinky leaned over the table, arms extended, and said that fairly loudly.

"No, she's . . . she's . . . blonde."

A collective groan passed between Patricia and Pinky. Pinky slapped the table. Patricia smacked Paul on the back of the head.

"Fesso!" she hissed.

Chapter Two

What fools these mortals be!
Shakespeare

The coast was clear, or so it seemed. Paul noticed his blue striped necktie hung on the doorknob of their front door like how his old frat house buddies used to signal the room was "in use." So amusing. He removed the tie and stuffed it in the pocket of his leather jacket. It would just get wet out here.

He was glad he'd bought this place. It was perfect for him. Two blocks from Lake Union so he could kayak whenever he wanted to, close to work, and so affordable with his two housemates.

He'd thought about shedding his two bosom buddies and getting some real privacy, but they were so much fun and their rent kept the property taxes paid. He had to admit he'd miss their crazy ways if he put them out in the cold.

A light Seattle rain drizzled over the edges of the porch roof as it sheltered him and his date, the lovely Danielle Wylie from Accessories.

"What a terrific place you have, Paul."

"Thank you, Dani, I was lucky to have found it before the market exploded. It was a fixer-upper, though." A moth fluttered around the arts and crafts porch light he and the girls had picked out and installed together. He glanced through the small stained-glass window into the house just in case some odd forms resembling his housemates came dancing out of the shadows through the colored glass light.

He put his key in the lock and twisted the deadbolt back, then swung the door open for his guest. He flicked on the hall light. "Welcome." He gestured for her to go ahead of him.

Danielle Wylie moved herself with the style

and grace that came from finishing school, or money, or both. If he could bottle it, he'd make a fortune. He wondered at the amazingness that was her back end as she swayed ahead of him. Her long blonde hair swished like a horse's tail. Swish. Swish. He was mesmerized.

"Let me take your coat," he said, approaching her.

She offered herself backward, and he slid her black coat off her bare arms. She certainly had the right stuff, back and front. He'd been a little surprised when she'd agreed to have dinner with him—twice, even.

"Can I get you a glass of wine?" he offered.

"That would be lovely," she replied.

It wasn't like he didn't know the rituals. It had been a while, but he knew his way around a woman.

Hanging Dani's coat in the small closet by the door, he noticed Patricia's Burberry plaid raincoat with its matching umbrella she'd nabbed on super sale. Gosh, did she forget to take it today? He had a vision of her all wet and huddled in a doorway somewhere with a soggy cat in her arms like Audrey Hepburn in *Breakfast at Tiffany's*.

Wait, that was ridiculous. He knew perfectly well she and Pinky had gone to a double feature at the Grand Illusion Theater—a *Thin Man* festival. Patricia fancied herself very Myrna Loy. She called certain dresses she owned her plus-size Myrna Loy dresses. He learned all these names from being forced to watch old movies every Friday night for the last five years.

"Love the lunch boxes. Yours?" Dani gestured to the hall display of over thirty vintage lunch boxes that greeted them as they came in the entry. Patricia had put the Dudley Do-Right lunch box, his favorite, in a place of honor so he would see it every time he entered the house.

"Pinky's. We all help her look for them now. It helps to have a purpose when you go into one of those giant antique malls. And on eBay, of course."

"Cute," she commented. Dani lightly touched each lunch box on the midlevel shelves with one finger as she passed. Then she walked into their living room and made herself comfortable on the sofa.

"It's too bad about the rain. Otherwise we could go out on the deck. October is usually our best weather around here." Paul walked to the open kitchen and pulled out the bottle of Vouvray he'd put in to chill before he'd left for work. There was a sticky note attached to the label:

Va-va-va Vouvray! Go for it, Stud.

He ripped it off and stuffed it in his jeans pocket.

"Oh, this is cozy. October in Los Angeles is so boring. Just sun, sun, and more sun."

"What a drag," Paul said, hoping she wouldn't notice his slightly sarcastic tone.

"Who took all the great photographs?"

"That would be Patricia, housemate number two." Paul moved to show her the sepia-tinted photos hung on one wall of the living room. "These are her Pioneer Square photos. I love how she makes them look as if they could have been taken fifty years ago. She documents buildings that are going to be demolished, too, like this one, the triangle building under the monorail they tore down to build Westlake Center.

"Patricia has quite an eye. I've always told her she should become a photojournalist. She's sold quite a few of her photos, too." Paul realized he'd gone on about Patricia's photographs just a little too much. But he was very proud of her creative efforts and loved to show them off to company.

He looked over to see Dani's foot jumping like an impatient kid in a waiting room. She uncrossed her legs and looked up at him.

"Your place has such a man's touch, Paul, with all the wood and earthy colors and all. I suppose that's okay with your housemates since they live downstairs, right? Upstairs is the manly part, downstairs must be the girl stuff. Well, partly, I guess, with the photos and lunch boxes and all that jazz." Dani seemed to have lost her train of thought. "I mean, I knew right away you were straight even with your job and all," she blathered, but no eyebrow, which he appreciated. "Because you are so *guy*—you know what I mean? You aren't, like—sleeping with the downstairs girls, are you?"

He returned from the kitchen and poured wine into two glasses. He wasn't sure how to reply to her comments. "I assure you nothing out of the ordinary is going on here. My housemates are just friends. I live my life up here, they live their life down there, happy as clams."

Of course, he didn't mention how their lives

had become a very intermingled affair and that his downstairs girls ate most of their meals with him as cook, and that their own downstairs mini-kitchen had probably grown cobwebs except for the microwave and the coffeepot. No, he didn't mention any of that.

She took her wine glass and smiled brightly at him. Paul took a gulp of his wine on that note and took up the other end of the sofa. Dani was certainly friendly. He hadn't thought to make any moves on her this early, but maybe he should try a less subtle approach in his dating technique and break his dry spell.

Asta, their very huge Maine coon cat, sauntered in from downstairs. He'd probably been sleeping in one of the girls' rooms. He jumped on the sofa and tried to make nice to the guest. Paul knew that was just a precursor to biting her. "*Scram*, Asta."

"Oh, what a cute kitty, and so huge," Dani proclaimed, but didn't attempt to touch Asta. A wise move, Paul thought.

"So how did you get to be a buyer's assistant anyway?" she asked. The cat jumped off in a huff without biting anyone.

"It all comes from speaking Italian and my

grandfather back in New York being in the garment business. I'd taken a summer job in the men's department of Nordquist's after college, you know, in between finding a real job?"

"M-hm," she mumbled as she sipped wine.

"They've had this same buyer for years and he doesn't speak Italian. He'd always had an assistant, but the woman in that position had gotten married and left the company. So they put out a job posting on the bulletin board and I figured I'd get a free trip to Italy out of it, and I did." Paul took his glasses off and cleaned them with his sweater vest, a habit, he realized, connected to his tendency to sink into retrospective thought.

"And you liked it so much you stayed?"

"More like I liked the paychecks. But over the years I've come to really enjoy the buying trips, and I get to see my grandparents back East so often. Henri is a good guy to work with, too. I have a degree in liberal arts, English, fiction writing, that sort of thing. It helps with all the levels of communication I find myself involved in."

"How old are you, Paul?"

"Thirty."

Somehow he felt the dark cloud of judgment descending upon him. He supposed it didn't sound like he was uber-ambitious. The creeping feeling of someone taking note that you're not the top executive in some corporation, nor do you intend to become one—the expected fast track for guys you see in movies but not real life—worked its way up from his gut to his head. It left rather a stale taste in his mouth. He liked his job. Was that such a problem?

During their two dinners they'd spent most of the time talking about her: what schools she'd attended, what her goals were. All her life she'd wanted to become a buyer and work in the fashion business. She'd gotten a degree in fashion merchandising along with a four-year degree in something else. Paul couldn't remember what. Business, maybe? So, hey, she could be some high-powered CEO herself.

Anything he said at this point would just sound like an excuse. There was nothing wrong with his job. It was cool traveling all over the place, and he felt a sort of kinship with his grandfather as he went about his business. He was a smart buyer, too. His department was in a terrific profit upswing and the company loved that.

He'd spent a total of no more than six hours with this woman, and suddenly he had serious doubts about his continuing with the evening. Sure, the short black skirt and glowing sunlit blonde mane had been major motivators. She was pretty. She smelled good, like expensive perfume and salon-done hair.

But he didn't feel much like seducing her anymore. He was having a little argument in his head. It was like Pinky and Patricia had gotten in there and were chiding him for going for someone with "the look" instead of a "kindred spirit," as they put it. Where was his sense of character? Where was his brain?

In his pants, no doubt. But now it was shifting back to his head. What a pity. A guy should make his head shut up sometimes.

"You're very cute, you know. Talk Italian to me."

"Just randomly? Or in context?"

Oh, God, he sounded like Pinky now. What fool would talk himself out of a girl's advances, no matter what her motivation was? They were both sober, consenting adults, after all.

Something was nagging at him besides the ghost of his two housemates' lectures. Did Dani, in the back of that blonde head of hers, think that he could advance her chances of being made buyer? Surely she couldn't be that misguided, could she?

"Paul, I've applied for a job as a ladies' shoe buyer. We could end up going to Italy together. Wouldn't that be cool?"

"Say, you don't think dating me could actually improve your chances of getting that job as a buyer, do you? Because you've got what it takes already. You don't need me."

"Well, it wouldn't hurt for you to give me a good recommendation, now, would it?" She gave him a pouty-lipped blue-eyed stare. Then she set her wine glass down—and his, too. She rolled right on over to him and ran her hand up his neck, maneuvering herself into a very body-oriented kiss. His glasses fogged up from her wine-scented breath.

As he endured her kiss he considered his options and hoped it would end fairly soon so he could offer her a nice Oreo or something.

"Oh, I shouldn't have done that." She paused. Her nose was just millimeters away from his. She looked cross-eyed from this angle. Like Asta when he came and sat on Paul's chest in the morning.

Now is your chance, boy, just say, *Oh, yes, oh,*

yes, let's go for it! I'll give you a recommendation!

"Um, would you like an Oreo with your wine?" Paul accidentally thumped his knee against hers as he moved slightly out of her grasp. She awkwardly withdrew her lovely body from his side and glared at him.

"I think we might be moving a wee bit fast." Oh, a classic, *classic* line. The exit-this-way line.

"Are you, like, serious? Because you are a very sexy guy, Paul. You've got that whole Colin Firth thing going on, you know?"

"I'm just a very conservative fellow." He swooped up his wine and cooled himself off with a hearty swig. "The old-fashioned type, I guess. I like to take things slowly." I'm obviously a giant idiot, too, he thought. *Fesso,* as Pinky would say.

She brightened up. "Well, that's sweet." She patted his leg. "And I'd love an Oreo with my wine." She scooted herself back into the comfort of the sofa of many colors.

That's what the girls called it—the sofa of many colors, because it had four different colors of chenille decorating the thing. He'd objected, but they'd pushed it off as very brown and eclectic and masculine with its wooden trim. Craftsman style, they'd said.

Now, why did he think about things like that in the middle of times like this? Was he descending into domestic hell? It was all the fault of those two crazy girls. He shuddered and jumped up to get the Oreos.

Oreos, Oreos, let's hope those two chocolate monsters hadn't consumed them all. Wasn't Patricia back on a diet? Paul rummaged in the junk drawer—home of all bad evil *junk* food. Score. He plated up a half dozen and tried to show some class to his guest. Although Oreos hardly qualified.

Oh, yes. Sitting on his sofa, eating Oreos with the hot girl. Smooth.

"Yum." She munched her cookie. "Wicked, aren't they?"

Paul twisted his open and scraped the white *guts,* as he and the girls called them, against his teeth. "Wicked," he replied, consuming the innards of his Oreo.

Maybe he could talk himself back into some shallow sex with Dani Wylie. But tragically, he actually *was* the old-fashioned type. He had to be in love with a woman to take her to bed. And the naked truth was, he wasn't even slightly in love with Dani Wylie.

She grinned at him. She had Oreo in her teeth.

"Moooooooon River, blah blah blah blah blah," he heard a long drawn-out duet like two cats mating outside on his front porch. He sat up rod-straight. Those . . . those bitches! They'd promised him at least four hours.

There was a long, silent pause, some obviously hushed conversation, then the turning of the lock. *The turning of the lock!*

He jumped up and stalked toward the entryway, cutting them off at the pass before they assaulted his date, which he knew they would. "*What* are you *doing* here?" he demanded in a low voice.

"Our double feature was canceled. We saw *Breakfast at Tiffany's* instead." Pinky started crooning "Moon River" again. They appeared rather drunk.

"Patricia forgot her raincoat."

"Wow, that's so weird," Paul said, "because I had a whole Audrey-Hepburn-and-her-soggy-cat moment when I saw Patricia's coat in the closet."

"I'm sorry, Paul. We ran out of money and places to go. Have we ruined your hot date?"

Patricia sort of yowled. Her shoulder-length brown hair was dripping water

"Shuten ze uppen and shuten ze door." Paul used his German commando voice, which they knew must be obeyed. Pinky hung up her tan London Fog in the coat closet, then reached in and retrieved the small towel from Paul's golf club bag. She threw it to Patricia.

"Ooh la la, she's still here. Look, last season's Chanel, the one with the black and white checkered piping." Pinky held out the coat for Patricia to see.

"Oops, we sort of screwed up, didn't we?" Patricia said. She dried her hair with the small towel, then handed the towel back to Paul, dripping wet.

"Yeah, you got that right," Paul said. "Just be polite to Dani and then make yourselves scarce, okay? Down the stairs you go." Paul threw the towel in the closet, then headed back to his date with the cookie bits in her teeth.

"That'll get all mildewy in there if you leave it like that," Pinky said quietly.

"Shudd*up*," Paul answered.

Pinky and Patricia walked right behind him.

* * *

Patricia took it slow, but Pinky headed straight for the goods on the sofa. A very spandexy Dani Wylie from the accessories department was perched on their sofa of many colors, eating *their* Oreos.

"Oh, hello, we're Paul's pesky housemates. We're so sorry to interrupt your evening. Our event was canceled. We were going to see a double feature, *The Thin Man* and *After the Thin Man*. That's the first two films of the six. They were supposed to show two each weekend. But the film didn't arrive in time, so they showed *Breakfast at Tiffany's* for the hundredth time, but we didn't mind. Don't you just love that movie anyway? Sort of high camp and tragically odd at the same time." Pinky went rolling along.

"Gosh I've never seen it."

"What?" Pinky's arms went up in the air. Paul undoubtedly knew what was coming, so he hooked Pinky by the arm and said, "Excuse us for a minute." He dragged her to the kitchen, which was rather open, so they could hear him hiss at her and send her to her room.

"But . . . who hasn't see that?" Pinky protested. More hissing went on.

Patricia was left with Dani Wylie. "Hello."

Patricia circled the sofa. "How was your dinner?"

"Just yummy. We went out for Italian and Paul knew how to pronounce everything."

"Like, spa-ghett-*i*?" Patricia asked dryly.

Dani looked at her blankly, then laughed. "Oh, you are so funny, just like Paul said you were. Patricia, isn't it?"

"It is."

"You work in catalogue, right? You're the department that's always nabbing our stock before we get it on the floor."

"Gotta fill those orders, you know." Patricia sat across from her in the mission-style chair.

"Well, they should keep the numbers up when it's in the catalogue. That's the buyer's fault."

"Those damn buyers."

"When I'm a buyer I'll remember that," Dani said.

"Are you going to be a buyer?" Patricia asked.

"Yes, I applied for the ladies' shoe buyer position, and Paul is going to give me a good recommendation."

Patricia noticed Dani had black stuff between her teeth.

"Another Oreo?" she asked.

"Why not?"

"I can't eat them, myself. I have one of those sluggish metabolisms that turn Oreos into fat thighs. Might be my thyroid."

"Oh, you poor thing."

Paul reappeared, shooting daggers out of his eyeballs at Patricia and jerking his head to one side to indicate she should make like a tree and leave, as they liked to say.

"I'm off to my room, then, and it was so nice to meet you, Dani." Patricia stood up and shook Dani's hand.

"Likewise, I'm sure," Dani said, with her Oreo teeth.

Patricia passed by Paul and gave him a kiss on the cheek. A sort of sexy, slow one. "Good night, Paulie, honey."

She headed straight for the "junk" drawer and snatched the opened Oreo package. Then she stole the bottle of white wine Paul had opened, grabbed two jelly glasses from the cupboard, and ditched down the stairway.

Patricia burst into Pinky's room. Poor Pinky was still ranting out loud.

"What kind of sociological Neanderthal doesn't absorb the cinematic history of her times? She could learn a whole lot from that movie. Rats and super rats."

Patricia closed the bedroom door after Asta cat made his entrance. She set down her cookies and wine, put her finger across her lips, and shushed Pinky.

"Shhh. We need to develop a more understanding nature," Patricia hushed her.

"Why?"

"She's got Oreo teeth."

"Good grief, let's say a small prayer for her. No one deserves that fate. Shall we light a candle?" Pinky asked. She bounced onto her vintage white chenille bedspread and positioned her rear on one of the large turquoise flowers in the design.

"Nah, maybe later. Your wicks are getting low." She nodded toward Pinky's collection of Immaculate Heart of Mary candles displayed on the white painted dresser. Patricia poured them each a jelly glass full of white wine and handed one to Pinky. She climbed on the bed carefully, wine and cookies in tow, and took her own place over a large pink flower. Asta joined them, draped himself over Pinky's lap, and purred.

"Pass me an Oreo." Pinky held out her hand.

Patricia handed two cookies to Pinky and kept two for herself. "Pinky, my mouse, I think we are getting way too shallow. Working at Chez Nordquist has thrown us into the shallow end of the pool. We're being unfairly judgmental.

"Just because someone is born blonde doesn't mean she's a ditzoid. It is not a genetically exclusive trait to be a bimbette because you are blonde. Look at Ingrid Bergman. She spoke five languages," Patricia argued.

"I don't think Ingrid was a true blonde. Her early photos show a tendency toward natural auburn." Pinky lolled against the old painted metal headboard, sipping her wine.

"See? Your immediate response proves my point. Now, we are intelligent brunettes. We need to be accepting of our fellow women, no matter what color their hair is," Patricia said.

"I read something that said only seventeen percent of women are actually blonde. The rest are drugstore blondes. They are brunettes in disguise."

"Pretty nice disguise." Patricia let that slip.

Pinky gasped and clutched her chest. "Are you professing blonde envy? You know brunettes are the superior species. We discuss current events.

You take artful, amazing photographs. We see foreign films and read obscure novels. We write *poetry*, for pity sakes."

"Blondes write poetry. Sylvia Plath was a blonde."

"Look where that got her. She stuck her head in an oven."

"She wrote stunningly good poetry before that. You said you'd move her biography up to the top of your to-be-read pile."

"I read it. Poor thing. But I've moved on from realistic fiction. I'm currently on an Isaac Asimov kick. I'm reading *Black Widower*."

"Ooo, dark but compelling."

"It's my autumn think-a-thon. What are you reading?"

Patricia kicked at a chenille flower. "I've been reading Victor Hugo."

"Well, no wonder. What are you now, this tragic heroine? The unrequited love of Brett Nordquist driving you to wander the streets in a state of love-induced insanity?"

"Hopefully not the tragic heroine." Patricia sighed. "I suppose it is just too much of a hassle becoming artificially blonde. Imagine the whole double-processing deal. What a nightmare. But . . ." Patricia toyed with the chenille bumps on the bedspread. "I have to confess to you, my best friend, whom I know will never, ever repeat this, that I have fantasized about being a slimmer, more attractive me, and in that fantasy I had just maybe the hint of blonde highlights."

"Is this about your crush on Brett Nordquist? The poster boy for Scandinavian genetics? Silly Patty, don't you know that those Norse god types prefer dark, mysterious women so the public contrast is more striking? You're perfect the way you are already."

"Then why is he chasing Lizbeth Summers?" Patricia thumped the bed with her fist. Her wine threatened to spill, so she chugged the rest of it down and set the glass on the bedside table. She pushed her glasses back up her nose.

"Because he doesn't know you are alive. Do you really want to climb Mount Olympus for a shot with Brett? Is that your true heart's desire?" Pinky reached over and clicked on the monkey-on-a-palm-tree bedside lamp.

Patricia flung herself backward on the bed and moaned. "Sadly, I think it *is* my heart's desire.

I want to be set free of the Nordquist catalogue department forever. I want to bask in a lounge chair on the brick palazzo of the Nordquist family compound.

"I can picture myself with a batch of little towheaded Nordquists and their nanny playing badminton on the expansive lawn." Patricia sighed dramatically. "I want my biggest decision to be which shoes to wear to the charity function. Is that wrong?"

"Yes, Patricia, that is wrong. You can't become a rich socialite snob. You've been poor. You've eaten popcorn for dinner before Paul took us in and fed us properly. You have a conscience. Besides, where would that leave me?"

"You could be my personal assistant and dressmaker."

"Jolly."

"Okay, so I'd be the volunteer queen of the Bellevue Highlands. How's that? Every noble charity would have me at their beck and call. Now can I have him? He makes my heart thump." Patricia waved her hand in the air and let it fall back on her chest. "He has the bluest eyes. And his teeth are like . . . like sunshine."

"Wow, I never knew what a bad poet you were. I take that whole poetry-writing thing back. If you feel like that, of course you should have him. It would do him good to have a girl like you instead of some blonde bubblehead like Lizbeth Summers. Why, I can make it my personal mission to make the planet a better place by maneuvering a socially responsible person like you into a position of wealth and power through an advantageous marriage to the stinkingly rich Brett Nordquist! I *like* it," Pinky declared.

"Good, now where do we start?" Patricia asked from her prone position.

Pinky grabbed the Oreo bag. "Right here. You're going to lose some of that padding. Rich girls are thin. They fit into tennis outfits."

"Oh crap. I hate this already." Patricia untwisted herself and sat up.

"South Beach, Slim·Fast, spandex, and *exercise.*"

Patricia grabbed a round pink pillow and screamed into it.

"Hey, no pain, no Brett. But I draw the line at dyeing your hair. He's got to like the basic package. And you have to dump him if he is too hideous. No amount of money can make up for him being a jerk-wad."

"Give me my last Oreo," Patricia demanded. "And refill that glass with my last wine. Even if I don't get Brett, I'll end up a better brunette. Here's to love." Patricia took her refilled glass from Pinky.

"Is that what this is?" Pinky looked at her with a hard look. "How about here's to personal improvement and social advancement?"

"Whatever. How about here's to the next Mrs. Brett Nordquist: me, me, me!" Patricia clinked her jelly glass against Pinky's.

"Good grief, woman, snap out of yourself." Pinky drank her wine in a very aggressive gulp.

Paul had taken a bathroom break and he paused briefly as he passed by the stairs on his way back to his guest. The voices of the girls carried up through the hallway and he heard them toasting. Brett Nordquist? This was Patricia's goal in life? To marry Brett Nordquist?

Oh man, that was just stupid. Paul felt himself actually get angry. How could Pinky let her wallow in that fantasy? Brett was all wrong for

Patricia. Patricia was bright and quirky and full of very strange, creative ideas. Brett was a corporate drone whose rich daddy gave him a fat position in the company. Hardly her intellectual equal.

Paul stomped back down the hall to the living room, then on to the closet. He slid the door open, grabbed his jacket and Dani's coat. "Dani, let me get you home. We've got a break in the rain. Now is our chance."

Now he was pissed. Sometimes he just wanted to shake Patricia and get her to realize what a wonderful woman she was. She was a very special woman with deep insight and creative talent and she was damned pretty under those wire-rimmed glasses!

Oh brother, now he was all worked up. Wouldn't you know that somehow those two devil housemates of his would squash his mood and ruin his date? Well, the Oreo teeth of Dani sort of added to it. He was going to have to rethink his appetizer choices next time.

And he was going to have to have a talk with Patricia. Maybe over breakfast. The sooner the better.

Chapter Three

I have no other but a woman's reason.
Shakespeare

Patricia folded up the newspaper advertisement she'd torn out of the *Seattle Weekly*. Room 203, the Feltzengraad study. She looked at her watch, one-fifteen. She rubbed her hands together briefly and turned the doorknob.

A makeshift waiting room took up one corner of the room. Behind a counter sat a perky-looking girl of about twenty wearing a bright orange, cropped sweater. Midriff girls, Pinky called them.

Pinky would kill her if she knew what she was doing.

"Patricia Stillwell," she blurted out. She pushed her glasses up.

"Oh yes, you're right on time. Have a seat, Patricia. Dr. Bender will be with you in a moment." Midriff girl snapped her gum.

Before she even had a chance to plant her rear end in a chair, Dr. Bender came out from behind a frosted glass room divider. His hair was Einstein-wild; his glasses were Buddy Holly fifties horn-rims. They made his eyes look very big, kind of like Pinky's glasses did.

"Come on back, Miss Stillwell. We'll get you all fixed up."

Oh, the ominous tone of that phrase! Patricia rose and followed Dr. Bender like a foolish sheep led astray by the greener grass over the hill, closer to the wolf.

Her next hour was spent being charted, prodded, poked, and . . . weighed, damn them. Medical scales were never as kind as the one in her own bathroom that she'd adjusted back five pounds.

When it was all over, Patricia sat across the

desk from Dr. Bender and his Buddy Holly glasses and set her signature to a document that relieved New Frontier Pharmaceuticals from any legal liability regarding her consumption of their experimental weight-loss drug.

With each swirl of her signature *P* and *S* on each duplicate copy, Patricia kept reminding herself how much she hated dieting, hated exercise, and would do anything to sharpen up her look for the potential title of Mrs. Brett Nordquist. She was a woman with a purpose. And really, if she turned green or keeled over dead, Pinky would feed the cat.

Besides, after half a lifetime of grueling no-carb dieting, power walking till her toes hurt, and using a huge rubber band to stretch herself to the breaking point, Patricia knew perfectly well what the consequences would be as she attempted yet another go-around. She'd be on the yo-yo track again. Down ten pounds, up ten pounds, like some crazy ride at the county fair. Her fat-o-meter was obviously busted. Stuck. Unmovable. Incapable of doing anything but driving her to the edge of insanity.

Drastic was the only answer. It was part one of her two-part plan: one, get thinner; two, get noticed. That was as far as she'd gotten in her plan to meet and marry Brett Nordquist.

"Here you go, Miss Stillwell." Dr. Bender handed her a brown bottle of mystery capsules. Lord help her. "Remember to follow all the directions we gave you. Keep your charts filled out daily. We're counting on you."

"Thanks." Patricia took her life in her hands and accepted the experimental diet drug bottle as she rose to leave.

Well, hell, they'd tried it on rats and none of them had died. Some were even thinner rats now.

Her footsteps had a tennis shoe squeaky sound as she tried to walk quietly out of the room. She felt like a big, obvious lab rat. She didn't want anyone to know what she was up to. Hopefully she could just become a statistical success marker on New Frontier's Feltzengraad data compilation without Pinky finding out. Pinky wasn't keen on experimental drugs.

Good grief, she sure hoped she wasn't in the placebo group getting a sugar pill instead of the world's next miracle reducing drug. That would be a complete bummer.

A hot October wind rushed at her as she

opened the outside doors. She picked up her pace and jogged through the scattered leaves.

"Where did you get off to at lunch?" Pinky stared at her cut-too-short fingernails, then lifted her gaze directly to Patricia's shifty hazel eyes. She noted a visible squirm on the part of her friend.

"I had some personal business. Hey, I'm working here, see? Don't you have an inseam to measure or a hem to take up or something?"

"I'm on a break. And, gee, it looks to me like the buttons on your phone are pretty nonactive at the moment. No blinking, no buzz, and, hmm, is this your order stack?" Pinky rifled through a small pile of papers. "So, where *did* you go, because you look guilty. Watson's Chocolates? Elsie's for a piece of pie?"

"I did not do anything that will add a single pound to my body. No dessert items or bread-related items passed through these lips."

"Darn, I was hoping you'd brought something back for me. So why do you look so guilty?"

"It must be my upbringing. The spurts of Catholicism my mother subjected us to overlaid with my agnostic father's new age karmic insight.

Between the two of them I turned out pretty confused." Patricia shuffled papers.

Pinky leaned back in the crappy chair that barely fit in Patricia's cubicle of a workspace. She lolled her head backward. She threw her leg over one arm of the chair and let her sensible loafer slip off her heel and dangle in midair. She threw her arm over the back of the chair so her body draped like a boneless dummy.

Patricia was hiding something and she was going to wait it out. "Boy, this is a tiny office. I'd be claustrophobic in here. Stuffy, too. Can you turn on that fan?" She continued to imitate a rag doll.

"What do you want from my life?" Patricia stood up and flicked on the small white fan clipped to her catalogue shelf. It kicked up the order forms she'd just restacked.

"Pattycakes, there is no such thing as *personal business* between us. There is only total and complete sharing of every last ever-lovin' detail. If you want me to help you become Mrs. B.N., you're going to have to be completely honest with me."

"Oh, shit, you are just such a nosy Nellie." Patricia crossed her arms.

"I'm w-a-i-t-i-n-g," she drawled. She heard

Patricia's stomach growl. Wow, whatever it was, she skipped lunch for it. This could be good. Patti looked so brown today—brown sweater, brown hair, hazel brown eyes. They were the brown girls; that was for sure.

"I signed up for an experimental drug that is supposed to make you lose ten pounds in one week. I've already taken my first pill, which did not kill me. I also had to take a gallon of water with it because apparently it's like swallowing a sponge and if you don't get it all the way down your stomach it blows up like a blowfish in your esophageal area and renders you unable to scream, 'Help.' There, are you happy now?"

Pinky snapped herself upright. "You *what*?"

"Oh, we both know I will never be able to lose weight the regular way. You've seen me try. Well, I need some quicker results this time. Then I can do the long-term thing."

"I have to say, that was brave of you. And the thing went down your gullet okay? Let me see them."

Patricia opened her desk drawer and brought out a large brown bottle of pills. Pinky popped the lid and stared. "Wow, big suckers."

"You're not going to yell at me?"

Pinky shrugged. "You're a big girl."

"Yeah, that's my problem. I'm a big girl."

"I completely disapprove, of course. There is only one true way to lose weight, and that involves sweat and salmon."

"You should talk, bird woman of Brooklyn. Your ancestors gave you a small butt."

"My ancestors gave me a time-released butt. By the time I'm forty-five I'll be hard-pressed to find a chair I can get in and out of gracefully. We McGee women have that whole Irish waif thing going until we hit midlife, then we turn into matronly pears in brown tweed dirndl skirts."

"Well, my butt has a head start on your butt," Patricia pointed out. "Now get out of here. I have to send twenty Pucci scarves down to shipping before five. Who'd figure this color would be back?" She held up a lime green paisley scarf with brown accents. "Lime is the new beige, you know." She held the scarf up to her face like a model and made a puckered up face at Pinky.

"That actually looks fabulous on you. Get yourself one. Now, after you've magically dropped ten pounds and you've turned lime green from this crazy drug, what are we going to do to make your Brett dreams come true? Trip him as he walks by? Run naked through the housewares department?"

Patricia fanned herself with the scarf, then let it drift down to her desk like an autumn leaf. "I had an idea. You know that Christmas party the Nordquists' throw for all the buyers and managers?"

"The one we peons are never invited to?"

"That's the one. I was thinking Paulie could take me as his date and then I could, oh, make my move on Brett. That gives me just under three months to become noticeable."

"Not bad, but I'd approach this in stages. By the time you get to the party you already want him to know you're alive. So I was thinking we'd come up with some great idea for you to pitch to him regarding catalogue sales. It's the use-what-you've-got method. You're a catalogue girl. He has to approve ideas. See?"

"A special promotion. An insert. Wow. I better make it fast. Maybe something we're overstocked on. Not bad, Pinky, my friend. You are really smarter than I always knew you were."

"That's because I'm a year older than you and

almost married Bernie Mayo. I would have been Pinky McGee-Mayo. Pinky Mayo-McGee. Pinky Mayo." Pinky rolled herself backward in a fake tragic flop, her hand on her forehead.

"Yuk. But Bernie was booted out, so you were saved."

"He didn't like my cooking."

"What's not to like? Six minutes in a microwave, and magic." Patricia pulled the scarf through her fingers like a magician.

"Let's go poke around the sales floor and see what's overstocked. I'll tell them to put me on beeper if any alteration emergencies come up.

"I have to finish these."

"Oh, for heaven's sake. Here, hand me a stack and I'll staple scarf bags onto orders."

"Fine, these are all scarf-only orders. Don't staple through the plastic bag and snag the silk."

"Duh, hand over the stapler and no one gets hurt."

Patricia was always amazed at the efficiency and speed Pinky could manage when pressed. Her twenty orders were processed and ready to go to shipping in mere minutes. The alterations department was alerted and Pinky turned on her beeper.

They dropped off the scarves in shipping, then took a walking tour of the sales floors, department by department. Pinky took notes and they chatted with the chatty sales girls.

"They all look like clones sometimes, don't they? You don't think that section of the basement we can't ever get to is really a cloning lab, do you?" Pinky whispered.

"That's the security office."

"And so many blondes. You'd think they'd vary the mold once in a while."

"We live in an area dominated by Scandinavians."

"Oh, have some imagination." Pinky made a face at her.

"Second floor north, men's apparel, men's shoes." Pinky imitated an elevator attendant, who they'd done away with years ago. "They keep the men really far away from everything don't they? No wonder we never meet any. What's that all about?" They crossed a wide expanse of gray and black vinyl floor and climbed a few stairs to the carpeted men's section.

"Pinky, you think too much. Look here, wow,

there are just piles of these things. NFL neckties. Why aren't they all sold out? Football season has begun, yes?"

"It's in full swing. They are rather off the beaten path. We may have something here. Timely, overstocked, macho, preholiday, the wives could order one in time for the holidays knowing there is nothing they can buy their husbands that they'll like anyway. It fills a need."

"I'll take some samples. We'll finish and see if we find anything better." Patricia held up four ties to the floor manager and nodded. He waved at her and she and Pinky hit the escalator trail. No doubt they'd have to go to lingerie. Maybe Lizbeth would be at lunch.

"Better hit the ladies' room. My gallon of water has topped the tank," Patricia said.

"Do you think Mrs. B.N. can talk like that? The correct phrase would be, *I need to powder my nose.*"

"No one actually powders their nose anymore. That's silly."

"A society matron cannot sniff at convention. Let's go powder our noses." Pinky walked with the strangely accurate air of a "Sadie Married Lady," as they called it.

"You're good, you know? You should be on the stage."

"All the world's a stage, and all the men and women merely players; they have their exits and their entrances, and one man in his time plays many parts." Pinky held her hand aloft and delivered her Shakespearean speech.

"Come on Shakespeare, let's pee."

Morning came softly as a kitty's tail swishing against her nose. Or rather Asta, the fat cat, tickling her with his long feathery tail. Patricia groaned and pushed him away. The clock radio clicked on. Asta always beat the clock. An upbeat pop song bounced out of the radio. Ugh, she was still so tired.

The week had droned on like a television devoid of anything interesting, left to blather in the corner of the room, unchecked.

But it was Saturday! And Paulie had promised to make eggplant Parmesan now that he was dateless again. He'd sworn it could be done in a more or less low-fat manner.

Okay, when you wake up thinking about food, you know the diet has kicked in, Patricia thought.

She stumbled up and ran to do all the appropriate things before she subjected herself to the daily humiliation of the scales. Scales must only be approached before any food or beverage is consumed, with an empty bladder, and completely naked. Scales will then be in a better mood.

She slid through the pocket door of the bathroom she and Pinky shared, shivering in the October morning chill despite her flannel pajamas. Paulie's socks helped, at least. A quick toilet stop, then Patricia headed for the sink and her toothbrush just so she'd be fresh and minty before she got the bad news. Although a few pounds had slid their way off of her body, it was no doubt due to the mass amounts of water she'd had to swallow to get the strange pills down her throat.

Her scalp felt all tingly as she bent to smear baking soda toothpaste on her Sparkle Plenty toothbrush. She scratched at the top of her head and raised up to check her teeth in the mirror as she brushed. Two days ago she'd noticed they were a bit yellow. She'd have to get some funky strips to whiten them if she kept up this self-improvement gig.

Her eyes still foggy, she felt like she was looking at a negative of herself in the mirror. Whoa. She put down the toothbrush, spit, and splashed water in her eyes and mouth. She rose up again. Surely the ghost of herself had vanished from the mirror and her newly slim face would stare back at her.

She gasped.

She stared.

She screamed.

She raked her hands through her hair.

She screamed again. Little odd multiple screams.

Pinky slid her side of the bathroom door open.

She stood there for a moment, then her mouth just dropped open. She raised her arm and pointed, but no words came out. Then she moved toward Patricia until she stood behind her. Her fingers slowly combed through Patricia's hair, feeling it and looking at it. Pinky stared over her shoulder into the mirror.

"Wh-what have you done?" she stammered.

"*Nothing!* I woke up and there it was," Patricia answered.

"Meow." Asta sat on the old-fashioned bathroom tile and stared up at them. He didn't care that Patricia's hair had turned stark raving platinum blonde. He just wanted canned chicken livers with a side of kibble.

"It must be the drug." Pinky held up Patricia's hair like a deranged hairdresser, checking the roots for signs of reversal. Patricia did the same thing from the front.

"It must be."

"Has to be. We're both seeing this, right?" Pinky asked. "You see blonde. Snowflake blonde. Blonde as Jean Harlow. Blonde as Dagwood's Blondie. Oh my God, you are Kim Novak in *Vertigo.* We have to get you the gray suit and the black cocktail dress and take you up to the tower."

"No tower!" Patricia shrieked.

"Look! Look at your eyebrows. They match." Pinky came around to her side and pointed at her eyebrows.

No wonder she thought she'd seen a negative in the mirror. She *was* a negative. Patricia had a very, very strange thought. "Oh my God." She threw off her flannel granny nightgown like it was on fire, then stared down between her naked legs.

They both screamed.

Complete blondeness.

"How much weight did you lose?" Pinky asked, still staring at Pat's bottom half.

"Four pounds."

"Get on the scale, you look thinner."

Patricia obediently shuffled to the scale and stripped off Paulie's thick white socks. She climbed on and watched the red LCD numbers search for a total. Always a chilling moment.

"Ohmigod, I've dropped ten pounds! Ten pounds in one week." She put her fists to her mouth and squealed like a guinea pig.

"What's all the screaming?" Paul came thumping down the stairs, ran straight to the open bathroom door, and stared. He'd gone through all the possibilities as he dashed down the hallway: spider, mouse, maybe a live bird that Asta brought in for a visit.

Instead he saw a strange woman standing naked in the bathroom with Pinky. She turned slowly toward him, almost like slow motion.

Paul took in her body from one tip to the other, like any startled healthy male would do. Her breasts were full and shapely, and her nipples were hard from the cold morning air. Her legs were long, her waist curved in like a smooth, beautiful sculpture. Her hair was that baby blonde color—like sunlight had haloed her head.

He gathered all of this in, his breathing on hold. He looked into her cat's-eye amber eyes. He sucked in his breath quickly—so quickly his head snapped backward and hit the doorframe. He'd know those eyes anywhere. It was Patricia.

She looked as surprised as he felt. They both froze. Well, she froze. He rubbed the back of his head where he'd hit it. Pinky grabbed something off the floor and threw it to Patricia. Paul watched as she gracefully raised her arms and slid her nightgown over her head. Rose floral flannel covered everything.

Then he felt something he'd never felt in regard to Patricia. He felt a pure heated rush of arousal. He was completely absorbed in the vision before him.

"She's blonde. All over," he said.

Pinky walked right into him and shoved him through the doorway into her own bedroom, sliding the pocket door closed behind them. Pinky also noticed his boxer shorts.

"Cool it, tiger. We're in crisis mode here. I'll explain later. Go take a cold shower."

"Cold shower," Paul repeated. "She's beautiful."

"Men," Pinky huffed. She left him there and slipped back through the bathroom door.

"She's blonde," Paul repeated to himself as he walked back up to his own room. "Blonde."

Chapter Four

So quick bright things
come to confusion.
Shakespeare

Paul was playing opera on the Bose stereo. That was always a sign he was upset about something. Puccini rattled the windows of their house. Puccini was the worst sign of all.

But Patricia had bigger problems than *Madama Butterfly* this morning.

"I can't go to *work* like this," Patricia wailed. She lay prone on her bed. Pinky perched on the edge of a chair, staring at her like she was an albino monkey at the zoo.

"First, it's Saturday. But when Monday rolls around you can't *not* go to work. Paychecks trump all personal hair color problems," Pinky reminded her. "Although your hair is truly the strangest thing I've ever seen. Are you feeling okay otherwise?"

"Fine, really, my scalp tingles a little." She sniffled.

"When you signed your life away to these quacks, did they mention this side effect?"

"Not really. The papers just said there might be certain reactions they weren't aware of."

Pinky snorted. "Certain reactions. Good one."

"They scratched me with all sorts of needles to check for allergies. I looked like I'd tried to give Asta a bath."

"Well, get up, girl. You can't lie around crying in your soup all day. Paul put on Puccini and he's cooking some huge breakfast. You'll probably gain back those ten pounds in one sitting."

Patricia grumbled, pulled herself up, and caught sight of her reflection in the dressing table mirror. "Oh *God,* what have I done?" she squealed.

"You *are* thinner. Pull something out of your thin clothes pile and get dressed. I want to see you in the light of day." Pinky patted her leg. "We'll figure out what do to with you." Pinky rose up and left Patricia to her own thoughts.

Good old Pinky. She was so practical. No matter what bad thing befell them, she'd make the best of it. When Patricia had to pay some overpriced dentist to fix her cracked tooth and she ended up short on rent, Pinky sold some of her vintage clothes collection and filled the gap. When they started having trouble with the water pipes, Pinky dated a plumber for three whole months. Talk about sacrificing yourself for the cause. Of course, that plumber was pretty cute.

Patricia got out of bed, slipped on her glasses, and sat in front of her vintage dressing table. The aging mirror cast strange spots over her reflection, but she could clearly see how shockingly different she looked.

She rearranged her hair into different styles and tipped her head from side to side. Maybe if she washed the hell out of it her own color would come back. Ha. Maybe it would all fall out and she'd be bald and thin. That would be more her luck.

It didn't look so bad, though, being blonde. She had a little Marilyn Monroe moment in front of the mirror, puckering her lips, twisting herself fashion-model-style. Her usually round cheeks looked slightly more angular. She almost felt . . . pretty. She looked a little like her younger sister Heather, the pretty one, with the reddish hair and the constant parade of boyfriends.

Patricia ran to the closet and dug around for a sweater she hadn't worn in years. A black beaded vintage thing she'd "grown out of," so to speak. She slipped it on and added a bias-cut knit black skirt from the far back of the closet where clothes she used to fit into dwelled in the darkness so they couldn't torture her with their taunts—*You used to fit into me, fatso!*

She'd need a better bra, but she looked pretty damned good. Patricia had a moment. A tingling goose-bump moment, which was different from the Marilyn moment. A rush of excitement zinged over her. She felt a strange, uninhibited freedom slide into her mind.

She was no longer the unnoticeable little brown bird. She was an exotic creature. She was beyond her sister Heather or even her sister Carol. She was beyond Myrna Loy. She was a blonde bombshell.

* * *

Paul slathered butter in the hot skillet and rolled it around till it melted and coated the pan. He threw in the chopped leftover corned beef and mixed it up with cooked potatoes, onion, and beaten eggs. He felt like his ordinary Saturday morning corned beef feast was slightly off-kilter.

Or was that just him? An image of Patricia, naked and blonde, flashed through him faster than butter melting in a searing skillet. Puccini swelled in the background.

He sucked his breath in and felt heat course through his body. The curve of her hip, the way she stood there without covering herself, her full, round breasts, and that blonde, blonde hair filled his thoughts. He flashed on what it would be like to have her beautiful nakedness next to him. To run his mouth over that curve of her hip and . . .

"Yum, looks fabulous as usual, Paulie. Smells fabulous, too, but I think it's burning, buddy." Pinky put her hands on Paul's shoulders.

Paul jumped awake, scraped his turner against the skillet, and saved the hash from burning. "You scared me," he said.

"It's a scary morning. Pretty soon it will be Halloween," Pinky said. She nabbed a stray piece of corned beef and stood next to him, nibbling, eyeing him as if she had a preview screen into his recent fantasy.

He didn't look at her. "Looks like Halloween started early in this house. What the hell happened to Patricia?" Paul stirred his corned beef and sipped coffee at the same time.

Pinky went to pour herself coffee. "Shall I make toast?" She was stalling. He knew these women so well.

"Why don't you ask *me*?" Patricia's voice came from behind him.

"I'd be glad to. And I'm sorry about the naked thing. I didn't think." Paul answered without looking at her. He needed to not look at her until he regained his reality base.

"Hey, we covered that in our rental agreement, remember? The 'See You Naked' clause? We all agreed to just move on back to normalville if it ever occurred. Naked happens."

"I remember." Paul also remembered the other things they'd written. No sexual adventures on site without prearrangement, no getting involved with the housemates on pain of eviction. But today he realized they'd left out a few things. Like realizing the woman who's been living in your daylight basement is actually a sexy, desirable creature.

"Wow." Pinky uttered but one word.

He heard Patricia pour herself coffee. He heard the spoon tinkling against the sides of the cup. He kept his eyes on his corned beef.

"Make toast, Pinky," he commanded her.

"Yes, sir."

He caught a whiff of some kind of citrus scent and followed it with his nose. He couldn't not look. He had to look. He twisted off the burner knob and moved the skillet off the heat.

"Wow." He repeated Pinky's word. Patricia leaned against the counter and sipped her coffee as if she didn't look stunning in that black beaded sweater and clingy skirt. As if her new blonde hair didn't swoop like Veronica Lake hair across her cheek and curl up in a sexy wave against her shoulders. He drank her in like fine red wine. "Rye or wheat?" he asked oddly.

"Paulie, it's the same me, I'm just suffering a very odd side effect from an experimental drug I took, being of less than sound mind."

"You took an experimental drug? Why? Are you sick?"

"No, I'm just fat. Or I was, anyway. Or am,

sort of. I still need to take a good ten pounds off, but this is a good start."

"That's just crazy. You were fine before. I liked you before."

"Yeah, but you didn't get a hard-on every time you looked at her before," Pinky blurted out.

Paul looked at her with all the insane I'm-going-to-kill-you-now emotion he could gather into his face and send her way. Death by non-verbal glare.

Pinky laughed at him. Patricia sputtered in her coffee. Both women laughed openly. In his kitchen. Why should he make these women meals? He should just send them to their rooms and make them eat Pop-Tarts from their own kitchen.

"Breakfast, anyone?" He straightened his glasses and grinned with his teeth gritted.

"I made sourdough toast. Let's plate it up, people." Pinky pulled Paul's fat white restaurant china out of a drawer and handed out a plate to each person. "Get it while it's *hot*," she joked.

"How can a man keep his dignity with you two?" Paul piled his plate with hash, turned around for Pinky's toast, and grabbed silverware for all of them out of the drawer.

"Dignity is overrated," Pinky answered. She went over to his Bose stereo and turned Puccini down to a dull roar.

The three of them sat around the vintage Stickley table they'd scored at an early morning garage sale, eating and talking about movies, trying to remember any movie they'd seen that had been made in the last five years. Of course, the whole Middle Earth deal, the Harry Potter deal, and the Matrix series descending into horrid visions of earth in the future, but that hardly counted, being of the epic variety and required for everyone to see.

For some reason Patricia's mind kept wandering to that morning they'd found the table, painted white, dirty, covered with dust and mason jars. She and Paul had declared it too ugly to live.

Pinky, their resident antique expert, had freaked out, handed Patricia her paper Starbucks cup, thrown herself under the table where the wood hadn't been painted, crawled back out covered with dirt and cobwebs, and told them to keep their mouths very shut for a few minutes, but not to leave that table for anything.

She and Paul had obediently sipped coffee and stared at Mason jars as if they were Roseville originals. They'd been caught in the excitement of Pinky's treasure hunt. Pinky had come back with a huge grin on her face. She'd ordered them to unload the mason jars and hustled Paul through loading the thing into the trunk of his Volvo sedan, secured by bungee cords.

Once they were all safely in the car, she'd squealed and ranted about the Gustav Stickley mark on the table.

She showed them books with pictures of similar tables back home, and after Paul had stripped and sanded and stained the beautiful grained oak, it was a piece to behold. Pinky would often flip up the homespun linen runner they kept on it and show people the joinery and construction.

This table was their most excellent find of all times at a steal of a price. A beauty hiding beneath ugly paint and dirt. Maybe that was *her* as well.

"Patti, are you there? I hope that stuff hasn't affected your brain." Pinky poked her arm.

Paul finally stopped talking about Stephen King's *The Shining* and blurted out what he was undoubtedly thinking but hadn't said out loud.

"How could you do such a thing? It could damage you."

"No animals were harmed in the testing of this drug. They just got skinny enough to slip through the bars and escape," Patricia joked.

"I want you to stop taking this stuff." He pounded his fist on the table. "And I want to know everything there is about it. I have a right to know what you've done to yourself!"

Now, Paul had never done such a thing before. Patricia and Pinky stared at him. Sure, he'd had animated moments during the last election and some table-pounding had occurred, but since they were all in agreement on their social philosophies, it was more punctuation than demando commando.

"Dude," Pinky said.

"Patricia, I mean it." he stood, pushed his glasses up, grabbed his empty plate and coffee cup, and stomped into the kitchen. After a few moments of clanging dishware, he stomped right outta there and headed for the master suite—his "fortress of solitude" room, as they called it.

"The master has spoken." Pinky looked at her

with big, surprised eyes behind her big round black-rimmed glassed.

"Geez, what's with him? I only have a few weeks to go. It's a three-week trial."

"Hey, I actually agree with him. What if you get other weird symptoms? What if you lose too much weight?"

"I could lose thirty pounds and still be considered normal-sized. I don't want ribs showing or anything, I just want to be able to wear Ann Taylor and have Brett Nordquist stop in his tracks when he sees me." Patricia raised her hands to the sky in a dramatic gesture. "This is *every* woman's dream. Just look at the new Ann Taylor ad in the October *Martha Stewart*. It's Brett and me and our dog and two lovely daughters, and I am wearing Ann Taylor, damn it!"

"Honey, put down your hands, because I think you accomplished stop-in-his-tracks already. You look stunning. Do you think the hair will change back when you stop taking the drugs?"

"It could, but this stuff is some new DNA-altering deal where your genetic tendency to pile on the pounds might actually be, um . . . erased?"

This time Pinky threw her arms up. "You took a DNA-altering substance? I want you to give me all the paperwork and let me read it, too, as long as Paul is insisting. Also, I am personally escorting you to that lab for a little checkup Monday morning. Let's see what they have to say about the alterations of your pigments." Pinky sat back and gave Patricia the once-over slowly. She sipped her coffee and looked thoughtful.

"What, did my eyes change to blue, too?"

"No, but your hazel eyes look green today. The blonde really makes them stand out. I was thinking . . ." She took a great pause, which made Patricia slightly nuts, so she fidgeted with her napkin.

"Stop fidgeting. Now, listen. Even though you might turn green next, or lose your entire head of hair, we have this small window of opportunity. We've got the tie promotion, we've got the striking new you, let's make this count. We'll redo your wardrobe, get some contacts, because damn, girl you look like a librarian in those glasses."

"Marilyn Monroe wore glasses in *How to Marry a Millionaire,* and she was quite a strudel in them." Patricia rearranged her silverware on her plate.

"You are not Marilyn Monroe. But you are quite a strudel now. I'm going to have to alter some of my vintage dresses and get you fixed up. So we'll see how early that lab can take you, then make a late afternoon appointment with Brett to talk about the NFL tie promotion. Pattikins, what man can resist talking about football with a gorgeous blonde?"

"Am I gorgeous?"

"Almost. Need makeup. Need new eyes, need new clothes. You've got to class your act up."

"For crying out loud, do I need new boobs?" Patricia asked.

"No, you've got plenty there, but we'll have to lift and separate them."

"I always wondered why that sounded appealing to women."

"You do realize we'll have to hit the lingerie department and face Lizbeth for that one."

"Yuk. That will take all the wind out of my sails."

"Let's see if she even recognizes you. This will be great." Pinky actually rubbed her hands together and looked like a mad scientist.

She leapt up and cleared the rest of the table.

"Come on, you know how this goes, we clean if he cooks, and we have to get altering. I have to drag my sewing machine out of the closet and set up shop. As a matter of fact, you're on K.P." Pinky clattered the dishes into the kitchen and took off.

Patricia set herself to work on the kitchen cleanup and stared at the beautiful dining room table across the room. Okay, she just needed a strip job, sanding and refinishing and a coat of wax. *Then* she'd be fabulous.

Then Brett would fall madly in love with her. Then Paul could be best man at their wedding, and her sisters could be bridesmaids. She'd beat them *both* to the altar. Ha. Too bad she'd have to talk to her parents again when she got engaged.

Oh yes, her parents, who disapproved of everything she even *thought* of. But how could they disapprove of her marrying a high-powered guy like Brett, with old family money and good looks and the whole package? They couldn't even say their favorite phrase—*Why can't you be more like your sister?*

Which sister had become irrelevant. Carol the

Perfect, the dental hygienist engaged to a handsome dentist, or Heather the Cute One, still in college, still cheerleading, majoring in Husband Hunting.

Oh sure, they'd disapproved of her literature degree and told her she needed library science or a teaching degree, which she didn't do, which earned her the *We told you so* when she couldn't get a job after college. And of course they announced they wouldn't pay for grad school since she hadn't listened to them so she better save up for it herself. *That* was going extremely badly; she probably had a total of two hundred bucks in her savings after five years.

Patricia slammed the dishwasher door closed. Thank God for Nordquist's and her stupid job that got her out of their Mercer Island house of Total Control Freakiness.

And thank God for Pinky, who spotted a kindred soul across the lunchroom table, and for Paul, who had already found fellow New Yorker Pinky, although she was a Brooklyn girl and he was a Bronx boy. And for how he took them both in as downstairs housemates five years ago. Gosh, five years went fast.

So here they were, the Three Musketeers, years later, and this was the first time Paul had looked at her with lust and hunger in his eyes.

What was it with being blonde anyway?

Paul took off his apron, wadded it up, and threw it in his bathroom hamper. He stalked over to the bedroom stereo, put vintage Dylan in the CD player, and moved the track list to "Tangled Up in Blue."

These women today, they were out of hand. Patricia should listen to him. Patricia needed to embrace the wisdom of a man and stop making crazy decisions.

Why, if it weren't for him, they'd be eating frozen lasagna out of their microwave instead of his homemade spinach ricotta and portobello mushroom lasagna. If it weren't for him, they wouldn't know eggplant from okra.

He was just getting no respect in his own home.

Back in New York men were multitalented. They cooked big Italian meals and were known for their kitchen skills. Back East being a handbag buyer was a respectable profession. Men understood leather and the entire garment world permeated large portions of Manhattan. Which didn't keep his brothers from giving him shit, of course, but they were obligated by virtue of him being the oldest, he figured. Revenge of the younger brothers.

At least they had respect for him, anyhow, even if his mother always mentioned what a good husband he'd be, and how he should settle down and get married to a nice girl hopefully of the Catholic persuasion, and that she should live to see grandchildren by these boys of hers, shouldn't she? They all looked up to him as the oldest male.

And even though his mother ran her family with an iron Italian hand, keeping her three sons and husband on track, his father would occasionally lay down the law. No matter what, that was it. Mom would busy herself with something in the kitchen and he and his younger brothers would know there was not a chance in hell she would stand up for them or cross their father.

But Patricia, she was out of hand.

Man, life was going to get weird, he just knew it. His buddy Patricia had just morphed into a butterfly—the kind that you can't stop thinking about because they flutter through your head all the time.

If he wasn't careful, he was going to get all tangled up in blonde.

Chapter Five

The fool doth think he wise, but the wise man knows himself to be a fool.

Shakespeare

"Well, hush my mouth and call me a ringtailed skunk." Pinky elbowed Patricia in the ribs. The minute they'd entered the lab waiting room, the jig was up. A strange assortment of people sat reading year-old copies of *Better Homes and Gardens* or *Smithsonian* magazine. All four of them had blonde hair. Not just your average coincidental Summer Blonde, Born Blonde, Golden Blonde, but Drug X Blonde, which was a particularly interesting shade of wipe-out-your-old-color-and-start-over.

"You, too?" An older woman, who definitely must have been a brunette before, spoke to her.

"Yes, apparently." Patricia was shocked and hardly knew what to say. Several people started talking. *"One week?" "But lost weight"*—little phrases caught her.

The receptionist, even though her midriff was covered this time, started to look worried. She pushed some panic button and tried to look calm, but her gum-chewing became faster. Dr. Bender himself came out quite quickly.

"Hey, Doc, what's the deal? Are we going to lose our hair?" one person called out.

"Now, folks, we don't want you contaminating the study by talking to each other. Let's get all of you into rooms and I'll talk to each and every one of you individually. Don't worry, everything is going to be fine."

Pinky whispered to her. "Boy, this guy is tap-dancing as fast as he can, isn't he?"

"Shhh. Let's see what he has to say." Patricia followed him, Pinky in tow, to a sort of locker room, same as last time. She got undressed in one of the small dressing rooms and changed into a gown, then made her way to the numbered room he'd assigned her. Pinky followed like a guard dog.

Time passed. Much time. Pinky was getting antsy.

"La, la, la, I've read every stupid magazine in here, now. I can tell you how to slim down your thighs in a week and cook drek food for five in thirty minutes. Remind me not to have children, because damn, what a pain in the ass they are. See here, Barbara Jean Wolinksi is writing in asking how to keep her five-year-old from torturing her three-year-old. What ever happened to the good old spanking? The thing that worked with our parents is that once in your life they whacked your butt for a very good reason and for the rest of your childhood they just threatened to repeat the original spanking, which worked because you still remembered that handprint on your ass."

"Pinky, I believe they have found some alternatives now."

"Parenting is useless without the fear factor."

"Just wait till your little cherub looks up at you with big brown eyes."

"Since it will be immaculate conception, that

will be the Second Coming and I figure he'll need a strong hand."

Pinky stared at a picture in a magazine of a happy couple. She'd like to meet someone, she would. She should have paid more attention to the guys in college and nabbed herself a nice accountant major or something. But somehow she'd just known she wasn't ready, and whoever Mr. Right was, she hadn't met him yet.

Besides, who says a woman has to be married and all that to be happy? She could launch her own line of apparel and revel in the life of a businesswoman instead.

But deep in her Irish Catholic roots she felt the longing for a husband and children. Like Jo in *Little Women,* finally finding the professor. It must be some subliminal programming her parents had slipped in there.

And she wanted that for her friend, too. She looked up at Blondie and smiled. Patricia wanted it even more than she did. Their biological clocks were no doubt kicking in. And the ticking was getting very loud.

Dr. Bender finally opened the door and Pinky sized him up for husband material. Oh man, she was slipping into that whole mating game mind-set. She put down the magazine and looked him in the eye.

"So, Doctor, exactly what have you done to my friend here?"

"Well, from what we can figure the drug kicks in some dormant albinism gene in a certain type of person, and wow, weren't we surprised."

Dr. Bender went on to delivered a long-winded explanation that included the fact that they had high hopes for reversal of pigmentation after the final week when the drug departed her system, but maybe it altered more than the fat gene so I hope you like your new look because you might be stuck that way, and my, how nice blue looks on you now and don't forget you signed that paper and can't sue us.

"Are my eyes going to turn pink?"

"Highly unlikely. It seems to be limited to hair follicles, but please report anything unusual such as, um . . . mood changes or behavior changes, besides just the physical stuff."

"More unusual than my hair turning platinum blonde?"

"Sorry about that, it didn't show up in pre-trials at all. But as long as your physical statistics stay stable, I'd say it's a temporary anomaly."

"You mean I'll wake up brunette again just as quickly?"

"Oh no, I can almost guarantee it will be gradual. This is similar to a medical condition called alopecia areata. Although how we managed to duplicate that condition is still a mystery. But fear not, we'll keep a close eye on you. I want to see you twice a week for the rest of your trial."

Dr. Bender had been tapping his cheek with the non-ink end of his pen the whole time he was talking, with thoughtful looks and carefully chosen words.

"Thank you, Dr. Bender. I'll try and keep all this in mind," Patricia said.

Dr. Bender patted her hand. "You are filling out all your journal entries, right? The initial weight loss is the highest as far as we've seen. It should be more gradual after that."

Patricia nodded, and after a few vital statistics were taken, like her blood pressure and other odd samples, including one of her hair, Pinky stood up to say goodbye to Dr. Feelgood.

"It's nice she has a good friend keeping track of her like you, Miss . . .?" Dr. Bender asked.

"McGee." Pinky smiled and stuck out her

hand, shifting her red Kate Spade bag to her other arm, hating herself for doing the flirt thing. The *flirt* thing. She needed lunch.

"Nice handbag."

"Our landlord is a handbag buyer." She blushed. "We get samples."

"Well, tell her she has good taste." Dr. Bender let go of her hand and nodded—with a smile.

Pinky didn't bother to go into the whole handbag he/she explanation, but smiled back.

As soon as he was gone, she turned to Patricia and blurted out her thoughts. "He's cute, isn't he? In a kind of nanotechnology mad science way, I mean."

"What's this? You like the white-coated type? I'm shocked, Pinky. I thought you were holding out for an Irish nobleman."

"They're too moody." Pinky shrugged. She snapped open her handbag and slipped Dr. Bender's card from the desk display into her wallet. Just in case she wanted to lose twenty pounds and have her hair turn platinum blonde. Yeah, that was it.

"Okay, next stop, One Hour Contacts, or wherever we can find you some quick new eyes." Pinky grabbed Patricia's arm and headed her for the locker room. A nice blue would go with that blonde.

Patricia stood alone in the waiting room of Brett Nordquist's fancy seventh-floor executive office. She'd been too nervous to eat lunch, so her stomach was growling. Great. Her arm was draped with NFL ties. Pinky had stayed up late and altered a vintage slate blue dress with a sweetheart neckline and draped accents off the hip insets. It was very forties. Blue dress, blonde hair, new blue eyes, she was ready—on the outside anyway.

She'd glanced at herself in the large mirror so many times her neck was starting to get a kink in it. Also her new contacts were sort of not exactly right, so she kept trying to adjust her eyesight before she ran into a wall.

Patricia saw the secretary smirk at her from her big mahogany desk. She was going to glare back at her, but the intercom buzzed and Patricia was escorted in. She felt like Dorothy going to see the Wizard. The great and powerful Brett.

Brett was talking into his headset and absentmindedly waved at her to sit.

"How about Friday, then? That's an entire

week. Isn't that enough for you?" He sounded slightly whiny.

Strange, thought Patricia.

His eyes grazed her direction and stopped. He looked at her carefully. Patricia sat up a little straighter and smiled a big smile.

"Look, we'll continue this talk later. I have company," Brett said. He removed the headset and set it aside.

Patricia could swear she heard a female voice screeching through the microphone until Brett cut the phone with a swift punch of a button.

"Hello, Mr. Nordquist, I'm Patricia Stillwell. I work in the catalogue department. You asked to see me regarding the memo I sent regarding the tie promotion?" Patricia realized she'd overdone "regarding," but it was too late. She stuck out a tie.

Brett had been staring at her as she stumbled along, his chin resting on his hand, his elbow on his desk in a thoughtful pose of examination. She felt like a bug pinned to a microscope slide.

"I don't remember seeing you before. How long have you worked here?"

"Almost five years," Patricia answered, leaving out the whole I-used-to-be-a-fatter-brunette deal.

"And to think I didn't notice you before. I must have been blind." He finally detached from his pose and took the tie she offered. "I liked your idea. Great Christmas gift. We'll have to move fast." He got up and came around to her side of the desk. "Of course, we'll have to have a few meetings about this. You and I, that is. Such as lunch? Have you had lunch?"

Her traitorous stomach growled loudly. "No, I guess I haven't had lunch," she answered, rolling her eyes.

Brett laughed. He laughed a sort of executive laugh. Patricia tried not to think about the fact he was laughing at her stomach.

"Well, neither have I. Let's go. We'll call this a working lunch. Do you mind if we eat downstairs at Via's?"

"That would be lovely," Patricia answered. She felt like she was in a robotlike shock. Thirty seconds and Brett had danced around the desk, asked her to lunch, and removed all the ties from her arms. He took her hand and sort of pulled her out of the chair. They were out the door before she could think, which was probably good.

"Dianne, I'll be out to lunch for an hour. Downstairs at Via's."

"No problem. Shall I let that be known, or keep that quiet?"

What an odd question, Patricia thought.

"Let it be known." Brett flashed her a smile and took her elbow. Patricia felt slightly naked without her NFL ties, her Zucchino Chocolate Fendi handbag (one of Paulie's best samples,) or any little thing to cling to. Brett stared at her. She gave him another smile with her Angelina Jolie lips done in burgundy red by Pinky this afternoon.

Out of the corner of her eye she caught sight of Pinky, spying. Patricia cocked her head and behind Brett's back made the hysterical female face at Pinky. The face that said, *Save me but not really!* They both knew it well.

Pinky was lurking about, talking to one of the secretaries, probably waiting for her. She was far from her main department, the men's floor, with the many inseams and cuffs that needed altering for all the various men with short arms or long legs or vice versa that made up her days. She looked out of place.

They got on the elevator; Patricia waved a tiny wave to Pinky.

"Friend of yours?" Brett asked.

"Yes."

"She's kind of an odd duck, isn't she? I've had her do some alterations on my suits."

"Odd but lovable. She's my roommate," Patricia replied. She wasn't going to sell out her pal in the first five minutes of her sorority rush with Brett.

"Ah," was all Brett said. "Well, now, tell me all about yourself."

Patricia figured anytime a guy wanted to know all about you he really just wanted to tell you all about himself.

"Oh, I'm just an average gal. I grew up around here, just like you. I went to the U. How about you?"

"I went to Stanford. I wanted to go to the U, but my parents preferred to spend their college money elsewhere, so where their money went, so did I." Brett laughed.

"Makes perfect sense to me," Patricia replied.

She glanced at Brett and thought how young he was, really. He couldn't be more than one or two years older than her, maybe early thirties. And here he was, manager of the flagship store of the West Coast chain of Nordquist stores.

The elevator dinged and they stepped out onto the sixth floor. Sixth floor: china, housewares, customer service, Java Jive Coffee Shop, Via Restaurant—Patricia did Pinky's elevator operator imitation in her head to distract her from thinking about beautiful Brett. He had on an interesting dark blue serge suit, which blended nicely with her dress.

As she walked slightly behind him, letting him lead the way, she pretended they were shopping for housewares. She pretended they were filling out their wedding registry in her head. *Oh Brett, how about the Portmeirion? Too flowery? The Dansk would work for everyday, wouldn't it? Oh, I prefer sterling myself, darling, and yes, you are right, the Royal Doulton has more class. Did you even know Donna Karan had a line of tableware? Oh yes, I adore the Flora Danica, dear, but it's just too expensive. What? Oh, you are the most generous fiancé I've ever had.*

Patricia rattled on in her head as they passed

the various china patterns. She paused on the Flora Danica and feasted her eyes on the beautiful pattern. For some reason, expensive china gave her a pang of longing unlike anything else. This one was way out of her ever-lovin' reach, even with her employee discount. A cup and saucer went for five hundred bucks. Patricia sighed.

"Window-shopping?" Brett asked.

Sheesh, she didn't think it was that obvious. But, of course, what she was really shopping for was . . . him. She put on her new, more deceptive face and smiled. "Pretty china always calls to me."

Brett actually paused and looked at the Royal Copenhagen display behind the glass case. "Quite lovely, isn't it?"

"Divine," Patricia answered, referring to both the china and the man.

"You have expensive taste."

"A girl can dream." No kidding. She caught her reflection in the glass case and still felt a zing of shock seeing her hair so very, very blonde.

Brett gestured toward the entrance of Via. "Let's dream of lunch, I'm starving."

Fairy tales can come true, she hummed to

herself. Having lunch with Brett, oh yes, she was having lunch with Brett. Maybe a buzz would go around the room. *Who is that woman having lunch with Brett? That one, the blonde?* Since no one even knew she existed before this, they would hardly know who she was.

Paul could hardly believe his eyes. He'd barely sat down and ordered and his gaze had fallen on Patricia, *his* Patricia in an intimate booth for two with Brett Nordquist. What the hell was she doing having lunch with the boss?

That snot-nosed, shifty-eyed, smarmy son of a bitch, he was leaning her way, clinking his glass against hers, probably lying his head off about something. Like Brett had even known Patricia was alive before today. What had changed?

Then it struck him again that she looked amazing in her blue dress, with her new, shockingly blonde hair.

Paul shook his head. Why, oh why did her hair color change the way he thought about her? She was the same old Patricia, quirky and full of spit and vinegar, able to quote great works of literature at the drop of a hat.

His Patricia, who always thought the best of

everyone. But sometimes Patricia was so naïve. Did she know that Brett Nordquist had been dating Lizbeth Summers for over a year now? Did she know Lizbeth had put out the ultimatum on Brett? No ring, no ding? No more private lingerie showings till he came up with a giant Nordquist-sized rock for her finger?

And did she know Brett had been bargaining for more time?

Paul thanked the waitress for her quick delivery of his lunch and tried not to look their way. After all, it was none of his business if she wanted to date the devil.

Speak of the devil . . . here came Lizbeth. Paul turned his face into the shadows and pretended to eat his seafood linguini. Oh God, he hoped Patricia remembered some of that self-defense he'd taught her.

The click click clicking sound of Lizbeth's heels was sharp against Via's parquet wood floor. Each click made Paul jump a little. He was damn glad she wasn't his girlfriend. What a temper on that woman. Paul braced himself to come to Patricia's defense.

From what he could gather without actually getting up and listening, words were being minced, diced, and handed out. Paul put his hand on Patricia's shoulder. Patricia smiled. Lizbeth cocked her pretty blonde head and removed her hands from her hips. No food was thrown, and no water splashed in anyone's face. Lizbeth, apparently satisfied, turned on her heel and departed.

Of course, she left a wake of gossip trailing her like a sexy, sleek speedboat shooting the waves across Puget Sound. One of those fiberglass jobs.

Paul poked at his linguini for an interminable amount of time, ignoring Patricia and the scumbag. He finally realized he'd lost his appetite. He signaled his waitress for a check. His waitress was very nice, and on another day he might have applied his suave Italian self to getting to know her better and perhaps scoring her phone number. Today, he just paid.

When the receipt came back it had her name and phone number and a little smiley face written on it. She winked at him and flounced away. Now, here was a girl who would take his advice. She'd shown no hints of making stupid decisions when she'd recommended the linguini. He took her number and tucked it in his suit pocket.

One more glance Patricia's direction only made him crazy again. He watched her get all flirty with Brett. Then she looked like she was crying. She dabbed at her eyes with her white linen napkin. He couldn't let idiot Brett make her cry. Paul geared up to head over there. But then she raised her head and laughed a big Patricia laugh.

Paul shook his head again. She was just laughing and flirting. *His* Patricia didn't do that stupid flirt thing. Hadn't they had long talks over a microbrew beer-tasting on the deck this summer about not putting on a false face in their never-ending search for the right mate?

After all, perfect mates had to accept you the way you were, didn't they? Paul closed his eyes and rubbed his temple. He was all mixed up. He wanted to rush over there and pull Patricia right off that slick red leather bench seat and drag her out of here, kiss her hard, and make her forget all about Brett. For a moment he pictured her captured in the executive elevator, her warm red lips giving in to him.

He closed his eyes and buried his face in his hands. All he could think about was running kisses up her neck and into that blonde fluffy hair of hers.

He had to stop. This was one of his best friends and one of his housemates. He rubbed his forehead and dismissed the runaway fantasy.

When he looked up, the cute waitress was looking at him funny. She was a redhead, a nice solid redhead. He should focus on someone like her and forget his temporary insanity with blondes. Well, one blonde in particular. The new, improved Patricia the blonde.

Chapter Six

Things are often spoke
and seldom meant.
Shakespeare

Damned contacts. Tears kept welling up and leaking down her face. Of course you can't expect to get a good set of contacts in less than an hour. That's like the fast food of contacts. They were *Want fries with that?* contacts.

Perhaps it was the garlic bread she shouldn't have eaten and the way she'd wiped her eye after eating it that resulted in a streaming, watery downpour. Some smooth date she was.

Except Brett didn't really know this was a date,

which came in handy when Lizbeth inquired about the purpose of their lunch.

Brett seemed quite pleased with himself after that, and since she'd departed he'd paid special attention to Patricia the tearful yet bold.

And Lizbeth seemed to believe the whole NFL tie promotion meeting b.s. But the truth was they hadn't talked about the ties for most of lunch.

What they'd talked about was Brett's college days at Stanford, his privileged childhood, and apparently Brett's favorite topic besides himself, Lizbeth.

Lizbeth this, Lizbeth that, Lizbeth and I are seeing other people now. Somehow that didn't quite ring true, what with her causing a minor scene in Via by stomping through the entire restaurant and burning eyeholes into Patricia's head. Wow, if looks could kill, she'd be flat on her face in her Cobb salad.

But, of course, Brett had lots to talk about regarding his own life, because it was so much more interesting than the rest of the little humdrum people around him. She could hardly blame him, and she egged him on to tell her more, more, and more. Knowledge was power when it came to man-woman relationships.

For instance, now that she knew he'd gone to Paris last spring (with Lizbeth, of course) she could try out a few French phrases on him.

But he didn't remember much of his traveler's French. Lizbeth had seen to the translating. She was better at it, apparently. Maybe when you wore the fancy French lingerie it just rubbed off on you, because she certainly couldn't have studied it.

Geez, here she was making blonde assumptions again. Just because Lizbeth was stunning and blonde didn't mean she was dumb. And when Brett dumped her for good, she'd have no trouble at all finding a new boyfriend.

Patricia smiled at Brett, who was still going on about something, and patted her eyes with her napkin again. If she took out the contacts, she'd be blind as a bat.

"That's so interesting, Mr. Nordquist," she said.

"Call me Brett. All my friends do. Patricia, right? Can I call you Patti?"

Patricia had always abhorred that particular nickname but oddly felt it suited her new look. "Sure," she said.

"Are your eyes better?"

"I'm all better now. I really must get back to work. If you want to get a tie flyer into the next billing cycle, I'll need to get this up to advertising. So have you decided to go for it?" How brave and assertive she sounded. Like she cared about the ties at all. She only cared about the door those ties opened—to Brett.

"Of course."

Patricia started for her purse, a little off-center from having a glass of wine for lunch. Good thing she was a public-transportation-to-work girl. She pulled out her debit card cleverly disguised as a credit card.

"What are you doing?" he asked.

"Paying for my lunch."

"And deprive me of a tax deduction? Please. We'll just put this right on my expense account."

"Well, thank you very much." Patricia smiled. Ah, the power of an expense account. Just think what being married to a department store mogul would be like. She faded into a shopping spree fantasy. *Oh, clerk, please put that on Brett Nordquist's expense account, and order me six more place settings.* It was better than dessert, which she had wisely declined.

Brett signed the bill the waitress brought over and rose to leave. "Shall we?"

Just that easy. Sign and leave. Patricia slid from behind the table, gathering her skirt edge as it rose up her thighs. She looked up to see Brett getting an eyeful. There *was* quite a bit of thigh there to fill his eye. That part hadn't exactly melted away.

But Brett didn't seem to mind. She smoothed herself as she rose.

"Thank you for lunch, Mr. Nordquist."

"Brett, remember?" He held out his arm for her.

"Brett." She walked beside him, giddy with herself.

"Now, you just let me handle the advertising department on this one. I'll get the whole thing set up. All you have to do is gather up those ties. I'm sure Ken in the men's department won't have any trouble with letting you steal his floor stock."

"Okay, but I'm perfectly capable of taking care of those details." Patricia was a little surprised at Brett's takeover.

"Don't you worry about all that. And we might

have to get you an assistant. How have you managed to fill all these orders by yourself?"

What was she, a delicate little flower of womanhood? "We do take on extra help during the holidays, Brett."

"Let's just put one on early this year to give you a hand. I predict this promotion could be very big."

"Thank you, I hope it will. We should talk about reorders."

"Sweetheart, I'll have it all packaged up and sent over to your office. You know, a girl as pretty as you should be working on the sales floor, not cooped up in a little office in the basement."

"It's close to shipping." Patricia must be wine-affected for letting Brett call her sweetheart. But wasn't that what she'd always wanted?

"Where would you like to work?"

Quick, who makes the most commission? she thought. It had to be either furniture or jewelry. The highest-ticket items in the store. Or maybe handbags. Those suckers were high-cost. Then again, Paulie might feel weird about her working there.

"Fine jewelry," she blurted out. "Diamonds are a girl's best friend, after all."

Brett gave her a strange, sharp look. Not the reaction she was looking for. Then he suddenly got all cozy with her as they reached the executive elevator. "I'll look into that," he murmured.

Patricia was a little confused, even without her glass of Chardonnay. She'd just brought this big promotion idea to him, and now he was talking about transferring her to another department? Gee, she kind of liked hiding out in her little catalogue office away from the madding crowd.

What now? She stayed quiet as she felt his hand on her back, guiding her into the elevator. She had a strange flash of him being the kind of guy who liked to "guide" a woman in bed. She hated that hand-on-the-back-of-your-head feeling.

In the elevator she noticed he was staring at her. He pushed B for basement. She must get a ride home out of the deal.

"You're hair is quite unusual. You must be one of those real blondes." He was staring at her.

"As real as they come," she said.

"Would you like to have dinner with me tonight?"

Oh man, Paul was making chicken cacciatore. Her third-favorite meal. A departure from meatloaf Monday.

"You're very pretty, you know?" Brett moved closer to her.

She wondered if he was going to kiss her. He bent in closer. She could smell his Eu Sauvage cologne. A shiver of mind-tingling proportions ran over her body. She leaned back against the wall and tilted her face up in his direction. A kiss on the lips by Brett Nordquist? Wow.

The elevator door opened on B. Damn fast elevators. When the doors opened all the way, there stood Paul. Brett straightened up. He gave Paul a very guy-thing look.

Paul turned a very interesting shade of red. It was hard to see under his recently acquired tan from his last buying trip to Italy, but Patricia knew it was there.

"Miss Stillwell, just the person I was looking for." Paul reached into the elevator and grabbed her by the arm. "We really must talk about that red Prada bag in the Christmas catalogue. We're having some problems with distribution." He dragged her out of the elevator.

She turned briefly and waved to Brett. "Thank

you again," she said. Paul reached in the elevator and punched seven, the executive offices. "Thanks, Brett, I'll take her from here."

The doors whooshed closed in front of Brett's surprised face.

"Geez, Paulie, boss *interruptus* there." Patricia squiggled away from his grip.

"Since you're just frittering away your extra-long lunch, we'll add a quick cup of espresso to that. You look drunk."

"One glass of wine." She shrugged.

"Didn't your mother ever tell you alcohol can impair your judgment?"

"My mother told me too many things," she snapped.

"Well, you should have listened." He took her arm again and headed her toward the stairs. She assumed he was heading them to the coffee bar situated across the walk from Via back up on six.

"You are being a twit, Patricia. Brett Nordquist is an egotistical self-involved blowhard."

"Egotistical and self-involved are the same thing." Patricia skip-walked to keep up with Paulie.

He kept a hold on her. "Did you know that

he's been dating Lizbeth Summers for over a year?"

"So what?" Patricia was being snotty now. Paul was being a big macho Italian pain in the butt.

"She wants a ring, and he won't give it to her. They're in some weird standoff right now."

"Sounds like the end is at hand. If he really loved her, he'd want to marry her."

"Oh brother. Who would have figured you for a Pollyanna?"

"That's me, sunny side up." Patricia trudged up the last stair.

"Did he ask you out on a date?" Paul asked.

Patricia was surprised he'd guessed. "None of your beeswax. What are you anyhow, my brother?"

He kept herding her toward the escalator and guided her on like a kid. She'd jerk away from him, but with the small amount of tipsy she was experiencing she'd probably take a header down the escalator, so she let him hold on to her while they switchbacked up more floors.

"I'm going to get some coffee into you and sober you up. Did you eat anything for lunch, or just make a fool of yourself instead?"

"Shut up, you big Italian sausage!"

"Great comeback, Patricia. Italian sausage." Paulie laughed at her.

They got off on the sixth floor and he steered her to the Java Jive. Paul put her in a chair and ordered two espressos and an espresso brownie for each of them.

"Damn it, Paulie, in case you hadn't noticed, I'm dieting. You put this brownie thing in front of me and I'm a weak-willed chocoholic."

"Eat up. You need sugar." He set their tiny white cups and saucers down beside the brownies, then sat across from her.

"Now, listen. Drink that, and listen. Brett is most likely just using you to make Lizbeth jealous."

"Maybe he's sick of her and wants a change." Patricia took a big bite of her brownie.

"Oh, come on, this is Lizbeth Summers we're talking about."

"Maybe she bored him to death."

"You've got brownie bits on your lip." Paul took a napkin and dabbed her lower lip. He stared into her eyes. Then he got all flustered and moved to drink his espresso.

Patricia stirred two teaspoons of sugar into hers. It always tasted like medicine to her, but she loved the buzz. And a teaspoon of sugar helped the medicine go down. Two did an even better job. She sipped some of it and shuddered. "Whoa. Strong today."

Paul had gotten very quiet and just sort of glared at her while he drank his espresso.

When the caffeine hit her system, she started to feel sympathy for Paul and his supposed mission. "Paulie, I'm sorry, I know you're just trying to protect me. But I'm a big girl. I can take care of myself. And I hate to tell you this and break all your illusions about me, but *I actually have a thing for Brett.*" She whispered that last part because they weren't completely alone, and after all, he was their boss.

Paul groaned and rubbed his forehead.

"Not only that, I don't care if he's using me to make Lizbeth jealous. It might be my only chance with him. Up until this blonde point in time Brett didn't know I existed." Patricia sat back and picked up the rest of her brownie. She hoped Paul understood her. "And by the way, I won't be home for dinner. I have a date with Brett."

Patricia remembered she hadn't answered Brett's question, being sucked out of the elevator by a rampaging Italian. She'd have to call him and accept.

His head was pounding and he wanted to strangle her. Either that or he wanted to kiss her. What the hell was he going to do now? She refused to see reason, and he was getting more confused by the moment.

He ate his brownie in three bites and tossed back the last dregs of his espresso. Then he sat back and watched her taking little pinches of her brownie as if that would give it less calories. He'd seen her do that before—pinch at desserts and eat them with her fingers, slowly.

He'd talk to Pinky. That's what he'd do. Pinky could fix anything. He'd tell her to stop altering vintage dresses and making her look so delicious. No more helping with the makeup and giving her those luscious lips. And were her eyes blue now? Dinner with Brett. That was tragic.

"Chicken cacciatore," he said. "Your third-favorite?"

"Sorry," she said.

He shook his head. Would this all wear off when her hair changed back to its normal color?

Would she stop throwing herself at Brett then? He just wanted things to get back to the way they used to be. Just the Three Musketeers and their cat facing the world each day. He wanted to wind the clock back on Patricia—to her pre-blonde self.

Paul heaved a sigh. "I'll save you some left-overs," he said.

Chapter Seven

Love looks not with the eyes, but with the mind; and therefore is winged Cupid painted blind.

Shakespeare

Patricia caught her reflection in the mirror behind the bar and jumped. Who was she? Well, whoever she was, she was out to dinner with Brett Nordquist, swigging down Sazeracs two at a time. They were so small and fruity and delicious. She gazed over at Brett through a haze of Sazerac sweetness. Bring on the free-range chicken, mister, she thought, I need to soak up some rum.

That reminded her of the old Andrews Sisters

song which she began to hum under her breath "Rum and Coca-cola."

"Hey, I know that song." Brett was holding his liquor better than she was. "My grandmother used to sing it."

"Mushical family?" That didn't come out quite right, but it was close.

"Not really, just crazy Grandma and her sisters. They used to make us all have a talent show for the Thanksgiving holiday reunions. I think that was just so they could do their Andrews Sisters imitation, because the rest of us were pathetic. I played "Louie Louie" on the trumpet every year until I wasn't in band anymore. Then I hid."

Patricia laughed. "Your family is just as strange as the rest of us." That also didn't come out right, but also close.

"Everyone thinks just because we're rich we have a perfect life."

"*Pffftt*. I should have this problem." Patricia realized she'd made a *pfftt* sound and spit on Brett. Also she sounded a whole lot like Pinky and her Brooklynese. Or was it Paul's Bronx accent? It was also possible she'd just been a little rude.

Brett wiped his eye and smiled. "You don't drink very often, do you." It wasn't a question.

"Nope. But it's sort of fun, isn't it?"

"Speaking as one who overindulged his way through college and hasn't stopped yet, yes."

"So, Brett, have you seen any movies later?"

"Lately, I think you mean. Why, yes, Miss Stillwell, I have." Brett looked amused. "I saw the remake of *War of the Worlds*. Great special effects."

"I'm into remakes. I like to go back and watch the old ones first. Have you ever seen the *Thin Man* movies?"

"I can't say I have."

"Myrna Loy is brilliant. Not that William Powell is any slouch, but she is the perfect foil."

Free-range chicken appeared before her, thank God. Patricia knew she was babbling. What should she say to Brett? How did a girl talk to a man and get him to fall madly in love with her?

She politely waited until Brett's grilled salmon was in front of him and proceeded to dive into her chicken. It had a mushroom risotto side dish. Now, it wasn't as good as Paulie's risotto, but it was damn good. Paulie only made risotto on special occasions, since it was so tedious.

Both she and Pinky had been put on stirring duty many times.

"This is delicious. Do you like to cook, Brett?"

"No. We have a cook. He's great."

Oooh, a cook. They had a cook. She had a cook, too, but it was Paul.

"I hear you. My housemate Paul does all the cooking."

"You live with Paul Costello?

"And a girl, too."

"Any funny business going on there?"

"No."

"So you and your girlfriend live with this guy, and no one has, like, snuck into anyone's room at night?"

"God, no!" Patricia let out a hearty laugh. "We're all just friends and he lives upstairs and we live downstairs, except for meals, because he is the best cook. He's taught us all about Italian food. His family is New York Italian, but they moved here about six years ago. You know Paul? He's the assistant handbag buyer."

"The guy who grabbed you out of the elevator today. Sure, I know all the buyers."

"Hey, he speaks Italian, and they needed someone to go with Henri to the shows in Milan and all that. So he took the job. He's really talented in many ways. He has a degree in English, did you know that? He's actually a writer. And by the way, back in New York being a handbag buyer is a perfectly respectable job that doesn't reflect on your sexual preference one way or the other. As Paul says, leather is a guy thing."

Brett stared at her blankly, then took a bite of salmon. "Sounds like a great guy," he said.

Okay, Patricia had just violated some date rule for sure. She stared at her beet salad and tried to figure out how to save the conversation. Sheesh, going on about Paul like that probably wasn't her wisest move.

"So," she asked, "what do you do for fun, Paul?"

"Brett," he corrected her with a smirk.

She died, then smacked herself on the forehead. "Brett, I'm sorry. Too much rum."

"I ski, I play tennis, I chase women,"

"You devil," Patricia said. She tried to be flirty. "What else?"

"Okay, I like to travel. My father and I just got

back from a trip to Japan. Is there something in your eye again?"

She dabbed her napkin to her eye. Damned contacts. This time she didn't get garlic in there, so things cleared up quickly. "No, I'm fine. New contacts. Steamy chicken. How was Japan?"

"Everyone was very short."

An entire country summed up in one phrase. Apparently Brett was a man of few words. Patricia gazed upon Brett, the man of her dreams. She imagined the two of them in their wingback chairs in front of a roaring fire in the ol' Nordquist mansion. She'd be reading a Jean-Paul Sartre novel. And Brett, he'd be snort-laughing over the newspaper funnies. It was beautiful. She giggled.

She needed to be better at this. She needed to get in touch with her inner blonde.

"So, Brett, that must be very exciting, traveling the world."

"I do like to get away from the store as much as possible. I used to be the road representative. I liked that so much better than managing the store, but Dad said I should learn from the ground up if I'm going to take over the company someday."

Patricia made mental notes about Brett's future career with Daddy Nordquist. Brett must be the chosen son. She knew there was a younger brother in there somewhere. "Road representative? What's that?" she asked.

"I traveled the West Coast and visited all the stores as the family representative. It was great when we were opening a new one. I'd get to stay in that town for a month or so. It was exciting to watch a new store go up. Dad would come along on those trips, but he'd be busy with the details and I'd be having a great time. Just great."

Patricia imagined Brett partying with the local girls in his fancy hotel. How old was he now?

"How old are you now, Brett?"

"Twenty-nine. The old three-oh is looming. That's why Dad says I should learn the grind. You know, settle down."

"Get married?"

"That's the idea." Brett looked up at her as if he'd let a secret slip. "In theory anyhow. Generally, you know, settle down, quit partying, and get to work."

"Your life is so interesting, Brett." She batted her eyes at him. That made the left one water again. Note to self: No eye-batting. She dabbed.

"Thanks." He sat back and drank his white wine. Wine he'd ordered, sniffed, tasted, and all that jazz. Paulie could do that, too, but he usually just picked a good bottle and swigged it down with her and Pinky. Her life was interesting, too. Mostly because she had Paul and Pinky in it.

"You're very pretty. I can't believe I didn't notice you before."

"You've been busy with Lizbeth." Oops, a little more daring than she had planned on. But she listened for his reply.

"Damn. That woman is so stubborn. I can't figure women out sometimes." He lounged in his chair, sipping wine, but seemed slightly agitated at the same time.

"We're really simple creatures with simple needs. I'm sorry things didn't work out with you two." She smiled coyly.

Brett pulled at his collar nervously, even though he'd loosened the tie and left it half cocked since his third Sazerac. "She just wanted more than I could give."

The waiter came and whisked away their dinners. Dessert and coffee were ordered, even though Patricia knew she was living on the edge. Eating flan with a caramel drizzle and taking experimental diet drugs didn't go hand in hand. Also, hadn't she made some vow to try and keep her diet reasonable? Dr. Bender wouldn't approve.

As to Lizbeth and Brett, obviously, if she'd been the right woman, Brett wouldn't have had any problem making a commitment to her. Patricia tugged at the waist of her red cashmere sweater, a vintage number from Pinky's collection with elbow-length sleeves and a V-neck that showed off her cleavage.

She reached in her beautiful red Bottega Veneta woven leather handbag—last season, but still fabulous, thank you, Paulie—and pulled out her vintage black and gold compact. She checked her face and it was still intact, red lips and all. This stuff really did stay on forever.

God, she was being so girly. But the reapplication of her lipstick and the sexiness of that would have to wait until after flan. After flan. She giggled again. Sounded like some kind of postsexual moment.

"You seem to be enjoying yourself, that's good."

"I am. I'm having a very pleasant evening, Brett. Thank you for taking me out on the town."

"Would you like to go dancing?"

Dancing was not something Patricia specialized in, except on rare occasions when she and Pinky got into a boogaloo frame of mind. She, frankly, sucked at it. But hey, she was a new woman tonight. She was wild, she was free, she was not herself. She felt like her old inhibitions were a fuzzy memory.

"I'd love to," she blurted out in a spontaneous moment of blondeheadedness.

"Look what the cat dragged in." Pinky held the door open for her. Pinky had on her Nick & Nora flannel pajamas with garden gnomes. Her straight brown hair was a tangled mess of bedhead.

The pattern of Pinky's pajamas made Patricia a little dizzy. She was damp from a drizzling rain and fairly drunk, and waved Pinky off. "Can't find my key," she mumbled.

"Good grief, girl, you changed purses and left it in the old one. Are you okay? Brett didn't take advantage of your secret desire to be his wife, did he?"

"Shhhhh. you'll wake up Paulie. You'll wake up *me*. Shhhh." Patricia put her finger to her mouth and peeled off her wet coat, dropping it and everything else in a puddle in the hallway.

Pinky closed the door behind her. "We have to get up in four hours anyway. And so do you. Real people don't party on weeknights."

"It *was* a little empty out there on the town. We went dancing at some club. But they threw us out at two o'clock."

"That's fairly normal. Now come with me. You just need some sleep." Pinky took Patricia by the hand and led her down the hall toward her downstairs bedroom.

On the way they saw Paul in his boxer shorts with his arms crossed over his naked chest. Gosh, he still had his great tan all over from Italy and from his kayaking adventures. Paul had taken to zipping around the lake in his kayak like a harbor seal. Patricia smiled. Paul was actually extremely sexy. His wavy dark hair and dark brown eyes were very handsome. And his muscles had definitely moved to the buff side from all that rowing.

What was she thinking? He was just a fun guy. Maybe he and Pinky should get together for more than corned beef hash. Paul and Pinky sitting in a tree. What a great idea. If she wasn't all focused on her Brett project, she might think differently about ol' Paulie after all these years. Sometimes something was right under your nose and you didn't see it. Her thoughts got all jumbled at this point.

Once in her room, Pinky helped her get undressed. She fell into bed naked. Her face hit the pillow and she stuck there. Pinky pulled the covers up around Patricia.

"He kissed me," she muffled through the pillow.

"Was it star-studded?"

"It was okay. He went for a grope, but I told him you wouldn't approve, and that I wasn't that kind of girl yet."

"Good for you. Now go to sleep and dream whatever dreams may come now that you are blonde."

Pinky tucked her friend in under her pink floral duvet and trudged back to her own room, scuffing her Sylvester slippers across the dark wood floors. The yellow glow of their hallway nightlight guided her along.

Patricia Stillwell had gone crazy. Why she'd

agreed to help her win Brett Nordquist was, at this moment, a complete and stupid mystery. Brett was ill suited to Patricia. He was probably just toying with her. He certainly wasn't up for a commitment.

Pinky had hoped a date with Brett would turn on the lightbulb for Patricia. But apparently she had her heart set on Brett and his old-money life and his old-money mansion. That was understandable, in a sort of *Tammy and the Bachelor* kind of way.

Asta growled at Pinky when she reasserted herself under the covers. Asta believed any bed was his bed and the humans were just taking up too much space.

Maybe Patricia and Brett would find some common interests. Maybe it wasn't wrong of Patricia to pursue being the new socially responsible maven of the Nordquist family fortune for years to come.

Maybe it was seeing someone else's dreams come true that tempted Pinky into accepting these sorts of things.

Maybe they'd both watched too many old movies.

But she'd never seen Patricia use such radically unwise judgment in her life. Maybe that drug was changing more than her hair.

Three o'clock in the morning. It was three o'clock. What the hell was Patricia thinking, dragging in here at this hour, ringing the damn doorbell, waking everyone up? She'd never come in this late in the entire five years he'd known her.

Paul lay flat on his back in his dark room with his eyes wide open, arms crossed behind his head. Light off the water of Lake Union shimmered like a ghost against his terra-cotta-colored walls, dancing and rippling.

She'd been drinking, too. Good thing he always had the girls carry cab fare. No doubt Brett Nordquist had been drinking even more. Brett was a party boy. A rich, spoiled party boy. And here he was at twenty-nine sitting pretty in Daddy's company.

Paul thought of his own father and how his peculiar talent for creating accounting software had changed their lives. Before they'd moved to the Seattle area and his dad had started working for Microsoft, he'd been an accountant doing books for a dozen small businesses. Businesses like dry cleaners and florists that barely made ends meet. They'd lived a fine life before and after the move. Even with lots more money, they'd stayed grounded. Paul admired that in his dad. His family had a solid, positive foundation.

It wasn't so much rich or poor, it was the foundation. And Patricia's family hadn't given her that foundation, for some reason. Maybe that's why a big powerful family like the Nordquists attracted her.

What was she thinking anyway, that she'd nab Brett on the rebound from Lizbeth? She'd sure decked herself out for the kill tonight.

She'd looked very pretty in her red sweater with that new wavy blonde hair of hers. That sweater showed off her figure very nicely. He was going to kill her. She was all screwed up. That diet drug must have affected her brain. What had happened to his sensible, creative, cautious friend?

Paul couldn't stop thinking about Patricia in her red sweater. He closed his eyes and right away the sensation of running his hands over that cashmere flashed over him. Her breasts would be so soft and sexy underneath. Imagine touching her for the first time and having her respond to him.

Imagine her letting him pull her close and work that sweater right off of her. To taste her lips and watch her eyes as he made her all hot. She had on a satin bra under there. He could tell by the way the sweater moved. Satin to put his mouth against and make her nipples hard with his touch.

Her red lips looked so full and inviting. And her hair, her crazy hair would feel like silk between his fingers. He imagined her crawling into bed with him all naked and pale and blonde, her red-painted fingernails scratching his back as he entered her. He'd be gentle and amazing and make sure she was ready for him. Then he'd move in her until she went crazy underneath him.

He got an enormous erection. Paul thumped his fist against his head. Why was he torturing himself like this? He flung off the covers and stalked down the hall, then down the stairs. He heard Pinky snoring.

He twisted the knob of Patricia's room and walked over beside her bed. She was quiet as silk under her puff of a quilt. He watched her sleeping. He felt himself longing to slide under those covers with her. He ached for her. He ached to kiss her over and over again and make love to her until she slept in his arms.

Why hadn't he figured this out sooner? Why was he suddenly interested in her after all this time? Maybe it had to do with the fact she'd never really had a serious relationship until now. She'd had a few random dates, but basically he and Pinky were her life outside of work. Maybe he was seeing something he should have seen a whole lot sooner. That he didn't want Patricia to be with anyone else but him.

And what was he going to do about it *now*?

He leaned over her bed and tucked the duvet up around her bare shoulder. Then he kissed her forehead softly. "Goodnight," he whispered. He felt drawn to her in the strongest way possible.

She startled him as she caught his arm and turned herself toward him.

"Paul?" she whispered. Her voice was wispy and sexy.

He couldn't help himself. He leaned in and found her sweet, full lips. As he kissed her he felt the heat rush over his body.

Patricia surprised him and pulled him closer. Somewhere in his mind he had a brief thought this might not be the best idea, but it ended so very quickly when she moved her hands all over him and he realized she was completely naked.

It happened so fast from that moment on. It was like a dream. From the moment he slid under the duvet and her bare skin met his, he lost that thinking ability and could only feel her touch. Everything after that went in slow motion, with nothing but sensation and emotion.

He gathered her in his arms and kissed her deeply, with all the pent-up passion he had within him. Her lips burned with his kisses. She twisted her arms around him and pulled him closer against her. Her leg slid over his and when he ran his mouth down her neck and slowly kissed his way to her breast she arched against him so perfectly he let out a groan of pure pleasure.

He could feel himself throbbing between her legs, still encased in his pajama bottoms.

She moved again when he touched her nipple with his tongue, then slid his hand around and cupped her breast into his mouth. A beautiful sound came out of her lips that he'd never heard before from Patricia. A slow moan of lust that made her open her body to him like a ripe pink rose opening to the morning light.

He needed to hear that again. His hand moved down her side and slid into the dark, sweet excitement of her body, and as he touched her he felt her already throbbing with arousal. She was wet and ready and felt so sweet he closed his eyes and let the sensation of making love to her roll over him like the waves of smooth water he rowed across. She was liquid pleasure.

It was odd how much control he felt in the middle of losing control. He felt her mouth search his out again as he slowly brought her to a climax. She screamed a quiet scream into his kiss and arched even harder against him as he felt her throbbing turn wild and hard.

He pulled her close and made her pant with unending rushes of her own pleasure. She wrapped herself completely around him and then he felt her hands untie his pajama bottoms. Now, this was a seriously dangerous thing, and before he could even complete that thought he felt her slide the clothing off his body and turn like a slippery sea creature under him till she was on top.

He tried to speak, but she covered his mouth

with her hand. He watched her beautiful breasts and her hips poised above him and then he lost all of his sense and let her move herself onto him. Slowly she slid him deeply into her. *So* slowly she began to move against him and he felt her climax again, the tiny hot button of flesh throbbing and burning like a match lit between them as she moved herself in small, gentle circles over him.

He cried out her name and pulled her down onto him. Then he touched her cheeks and kissed her so deeply she made that sweet, amazing sound again. He felt addicted to that sound.

It made his arousal even harder and that made her cry out her sound even more, and in the smoothest, slowest possible way they swayed together over and over again like a dance they'd just learned, until finally he felt the heat white-flash over him and he held her hips and arched hard against her and let himself go. *Oh* God, she felt so, so good, and she collapsed against him and moaned for her own sweet, throbbing climax.

And then
his brain
came back.

He didn't want to move, because if he moved he would break the spell of magic that had held them captive for the last hour. If he moved, he'd have to realize what he'd done.

She fell asleep entwined with him and at last he moved her gently to her side and even then she kissed him in her sleep with her arms still around his neck.

He ran his hand down the length of her body, over her smooth round hip, and up the soft sweetness of her breast and her neck and into her beautiful waves of blonde hair. Then he touched her across her cheek and lightly skimmed the swollen fullness of her lips.

Those lips. She had kissed him with the deepest, most passionate mouth he'd ever known in his entire life. Her whole being went into those kisses. He felt scarred for life by her kiss.

Chapter Eight

The course of true love
never did run smooth.
Shakespeare

Whenever Pinky McGee needed order in her life, she did one of two things. She either started a thousand-piece jigsaw puzzle like a Currier and Ives or a Charles Wysocki where the houses grew piece by piece and the sky and sea reflected each other like a blue-green mirror; or she started a sewing project.

This time it looked like she had decided to make a Hollywood glamour girl dress for her newly blonde friend Patricia.

Sometimes Pinky reminded him of the spunky girl mice in Cinderella—the ones that knew better than the boy mice how to revamp an old gown into a fashion statement. But hey, boy mice knew how to get a cat tied up in knots.

She had dragged her dress dummy out into *his* living room and surrounded herself with bolts of fabric, pins, measuring tapes, patterns, and odd items only seamstresses understood—like pressing hams. They'd had a few discussions in the past about this—turning his spaces into workrooms—but he hadn't won any of those sparring rounds. She claimed the light was better up here. Besides, he liked to watch her create things. He admired creativity.

So he had surrendered, knowing it kept Pinky sane. And they needed Pinky sane because she was the glue that held their little jigsaw-puzzle life together.

But *this* morning the puzzle pieces were completely unglued and scattered to the four winds.

"What's all this? Paul asked. "Don't you have to work today?" He stood in the kitchen, itchy in his go-to-meeting suit, haunted by his night with Patricia.

And work was beating in his head. Today the open-to-buy approvals were being handed out and a "Spring Trend" meeting with all the buyers was set for ten A.M.

It seemed like he'd just finished holiday in August, and here he had to start planning his flight to New York in November for the spring market. Things were always hoppin' in handbags. He snort-laughed his coffee, nervous and off-kilter about everything. He wondered if it showed all over him. He wondered what every moment would be like from now on.

Pinky looked up at him from her pins and needles with an odd look on her face. Could she see it in his eyes?

"Handbag humor," he explained.

"Only in your own head, Mr. Costello." Pinky grinned at him with her mouth full of pins. "I took a random day off."

Her pins always freaked him out. He felt shaky. He tried to make conversation, but all that was on his mind was Patricia. "So, Pinking Shears, what are we going to do about our Patricia?"

"Let her experience nature's consequences, I guess." Pinky shrugged.

Nature had certainly made an entrance last night.

Paul came over and sat down next to Pinky. He drank his coffee carefully, treading on thin ice. "Nature can be harsh," he said quietly.

"Who knows, maybe she'll fit into the Nordquist family jungle. Otherwise, let's hope the learning curve is swift and painless."

"I doubt that," Paul said.

Pinky looked at him with a raised eyebrow. "Which, that she'll fit in, or that the curve will be swift and painless?"

"Both. Why are you helping with this Brett thing?"

"I guess I like to see fairy tales come true," Pinky answered.

"Fairy tales. Bullshit. Brett is all wrong for her." Paul got up from his chair and went to the kitchen. He clunked his coffee cup on the counter. "Here's a fairy tale for you. It's Tuesday. I didn't make meatloaf yesterday and now we have no leftovers for meatloaf sandwiches. There's a ton of chicken cacciatore, though. So eat."

"God, Paul, you don't have to get so animated about it." Pinky looked at him funny.

"Where is Princess Patricia?" Paul asked. He

was incredibly tense about seeing her face to face this morning.

"Last I heard she was experiencing nature's consequences in the bathroom this morning. I have a feeling she's going to be calling in sick today."

Paul shook his head. "She can't handle her liquor. She never could." He realized at that moment the gravity of what he'd done. He'd let himself seduce Patricia while she was under the effects of alcohol. Or did she seduce him? Either way, it was nothing but trouble.

Except when his mind slipped back there it was so amazing that shock waves of memory moved over him.

"Go to work. I'm here. I'll dunk her head in the toilet and make her see the error of her ways." Pinky waved him off.

"You do that. I'll see you for dinner, I hope."

"I'll be here."

"You know I have to leave for New York at the end of the month. Can we get things back to normal by then so I don't have to worry the whole time I'm there?"

"The question is, what is normal?"

"Damn it, just . . . the way it was before, you know?" He felt the untruthfulness of that statement all the way to his bones. Nothing would ever be the same after last night.

"Things change, Paulie."

"Well, make it stop. I'll make some risotto to go with the chicken tonight and we'll all play Scrabble and turn in early." And he'd have a talk with Patricia when she felt better about what happened. They could be sensible and return to their old life, right? They could just chalk it up to nature's consequences and too many cosmopolitans, if that was what he tasted on her lips, that sweet cherry flavor. He lost his thought in a rush of guilt.

He had to leave before Patricia appeared. Paul filled his travel mug with coffee and headed out. He stopped to grab his leather briefcase and overcoat out of the closet.

"Have a nice day, dear," Pinky called after him.

Paul came over and gave Pinky a peck on the cheek. "Fix it, Pinky. Fix this stupid thing with Brett. Make her see the light."

"Are you taking the car?"

"No, I hate parking. The bus is fine."

"You rich buyers are supposed to travel in style."

Paul smiled. "I must have missed that memo."

They were eye to eye. Pinky's dark brown unblinking eyes were scaring him. He saw things there. *She* saw things back.

"Uhhh. Need coffee." Paul heard a ragged voice from the hallway and turned to see Patricia wrapped in his old terrycloth bathrobe. They all called it the "sick robe." It was a sign, for sure. Their eyes met and a very odd moment passed between them.

"She'll need a fresh pot." Paul looked at his watch nervously.

"Go, I'll do it. You'll be late." Pinky waved him off. "You need to get to work so Patti the Party Pooper and I can have the best spring samples from New York this year. So tell them you need more money to spend so those reps will shower you with gifts. I want one of those hobo bags for my new spring look."

He could tell Pinky was rambling him out the door. She also put her hands behind him and shoved him on his way. No subtlety there. He wondered how much the amazing Pinky had figured out. He wondered how he was going to live with himself today.

As Paul went out the door, Patricia flung herself on the sofa and curled her legs up under the robe. "Shoot me now, Pinky, make the pounding stop. Just one quick shot to the head."

"Looks like you already did." Pinky went to make a fresh pot of coffee. "And how are we doing?"

"I called in sick. You'd think yakking your guts up would make you lose a few pounds. Apparently not."

"You're still taking the wonder drug, aren't you?" Pinky asked.

"Yes, but I have to be able to keep it down." She moaned and held her head. Talking hurt. The faint taste of sweetness from six Sazeracs made her feel nauseated all over again. "Tell that coffee to hurry. It's an emergency."

"Coffee isn't your friend. Drink this first, then eat this." Pinky brought a cup of hot tea and a piece of toast over to her and set them on the coffee table. "Herb tea. They actually make one for hangovers."

"And we happen to have it?"

"There was that Christmas eggnog moment we all had last year, remember?"

"Oh yes. Who knew that eggnog could pack such a wallop?" Patricia accepted Pinky's gifts and sipped the tea. It wasn't half bad with honey in it.

Pinky sat down on the other end of the sofa.

"Ouch." Patricia had to hold her temple for a moment.

"You've been bad."

"Am I grounded?" Patricia grimaced.

"According to Paul you are."

A faint memory mingled with an overall body tingle awoke from the dark recesses of Patricia's mind. She must have dreamed about Paul. That couldn't have actually happened.

She talked, pretending she hadn't just remembered what she thought she did. "What's with him lately anyway? Mr. Grumpy. I don't think he likes Brett. That's terrible, because when we're married I want you two to come over all the time. And he has to be my best man at the wedding."

"I think Brett gets to pick the best man."

"Okay, Paul can give me away."

"I don't think Paul wants to give you away." Pinky gave her a look.

"Oh fine, be difficult."

"No, I mean, *I don't think Paul wants to give you away*. Do you understand?"

"No, I don't understand," Patricia snapped, but she did, and it was scaring the crap out of her. "Call me stupid."

Pinky rolled her eyes. "Okay, stupid, I think Paulie might be having feelings about you."

Patricia looked sharply at her friend. Should she tell her? Should she confess? Was it all a dream? She drank more tea. "We're all just friends," she said firmly. "That's not going to change. We have housemates rules, and, well, Paul is just attracted to blondes."

Patricia thought hard for a minute. Her head throbbed. Should she tell her best friend what happened?

"Although . . ." she said slowly.

"Although *what*?" Pinky leaned closer.

"I have something to tell you." Patricia paused. Maybe she'd try the grandma's-on-the-roof method. "Paul kissed me last night."

"He came to your room?"

"I think he was just checking on me." She set her tea down carefully and eyed her friend.

Pinky sat back with a smug look on her face. She crossed her arms. "You are the worst liar in the entire world, Patricia Stillwell. Don't even try."

Patricia swooned against the couch cushions like a true drama queen. "Oh holy shit, Pinky, unless I was having the hottest dream of my life, Paul and I made love last night."

"You *what*?"

"You heard what I said, don't make me say it again."

"Oh my God. I mean, I knew he had feelings for you, and I knew he was going crazy with you chasing Brett and all, but how did you . . . how did he? What were you thinking?" Pinky had her hands on her cheeks like the screaming man in the art museum.

Patricia was shaking. Her hands were trembling. "Look. We just had a moment. We reached out in the darkness and there was the other one, and it was just so amazing that we didn't stop."

"Did you use any birth control?"

Patricia didn't answer, she just covered her face with her hands.

"Right under my nose." Pinky shook her head.

"It's a little complicated, but I'm sure we are both adults and we can just talk it over and it will be fine."

Pinky leaned over to her friend and put her hand on her knee. She talked very quietly and had a slow smile on her face.

"Was it incredible?"

"I woke up and I couldn't remember whether I'd had the best dream of my entire life or the best sex ever," Patricia answered, sliding her hands off her face.

"So you think you can just, oh, shake it off and get back to normal?" Pinky shrugged.

"Hell, I don't know. I'm not his type in real life. He was probably just starved for sexual attention."

"What type, intelligent, funny, and talented?"

"Blonde and bouncy."

"Have you looked in the mirror lately?"

"Oh shit." Patricia had forgotten she was now blonde and bouncy. Whenever she woke up, she had to relearn her whole face and hair and all other parts that used to be brown and familiar. "You don't suppose he's fallen in love with me now that I'm blonde? That's kind of twisted."

"I'm starting to wonder."

Patricia waved her off. "I can't even deal with Paul. I have Brett to figure out."

"You can't be serious. You aren't going to go ahead and keep dating Brett after last night, are you?"

"Well, why not? It was just a momentary, crazy thing. We both probably regret it and, well, lots of women have taken a step backward before they took the big step into marriage. I can't lose sight of my goals just because Paul climbed into my bed last night. Or I pulled him into it or whatever happened."

"You might have to pace yourself, from what I'm seeing."

"I just need to get my sea legs." Patricia smiled. She sipped her tea, which had turned rather nasty the farther down the cup she got.

"Girl overboard." Pinky got up and went for a coffee refill. "Eat all that and I'll give you coffee."

"What are you making?" Patricia grasped at a subject change and pointed at Pinky's sewing project.

"I'm not sure. I thought I'd make you a dress just in case you got asked to go somewhere fancy."

"You're so sweet, Pinky. Don't forget to charge me for the fabric."

"Oh, I will."

"I did get an invitation of sorts."

"You did?"

"Brett asked if I'd like to be his date at the big Halloween party his parents throw every year. Gosh, these people throw parties for everything. I thought I'd aim for the Christmas party, but I didn't figure on this invitation."

"Halloween. That's not far away. I guess this means we won't be having our annual open house that weekend?"

"Why not? You and Paulie can do it."

"It's not the same without the three of us. But hey, how can you pass up a big to-do at the Nordquist mansion? After all, you'll need to scope the place out and decide how you're going to redecorate it after old Lars Nordquist kicks the bucket and you and Brett move in." Pinky had a decidedly sarcastic tone to her voice.

"Of course, there is his brother Eric, but he's younger."

"I bet there are enough rooms for the entire clan."

"Yes. I'll just be gracious and invite him to live with us. Then his wife and I can run the entire estate and keep things shipshape." Patricia lapsed into a full-blown fantasy of Christmas day at the mansion. "We'll put a fifteen-foot tree in the entry rotunda so when you come in it's the first thing you see."

"Only fifteen-foot?"

"Any more would be ostentatious."

"Of course. Silly me."

"The family tree can go in the center parlor so the children can just run down the stairs and see what Santa left them."

"The little darlings."

"We'll have dinner set in the dining room on the big table and, you know, all those sugar-glazed fruits dripping off pedestal arrangements and those Italian wedding cakes encased in spun sugar—like that one Paulie made for Christmas one time?"

"Visions of sugarplums danced in their heads."

"And I'll have all the girls dressed in red velvet

with a matching gown for me. You'll have to make those for us."

"No problem."

"With a vest for Brett and the boys."

"How many children? Maybe I better get started on those."

"Five. Three girls, two boys."

"Five little Nordquists all in a row."

"Oh, Pinky." Patricia lifted her head off the sofa pillow and sighed a huge I-want-*that* sigh.

"You're awfully good at this."

"I've had lots of practice."

"And will Paul be the new gardener and sneak into your room when Brett's away and give you the best sex you've ever had in your life?"

All Patricia could do was groan.

"So what shall we make you into for the big Halloween ball?" The ever-practical Pinky thumped them back to earth. But right now, earth was still three feet off the ground.

She'd had two dates with Brett. Well, lunch was sort of work, but dinner was a date, and she'd just had sex with her housemate of five years. A more sophisticated woman would be able to sort all that out and neatly get on with her life. It wasn't like Paul had asked her to marry him or anything. She'd just keep dating Brett and sort the Paul thing out as she went. "I was thinking Jean Harlow."

"Slinky white satin. Diamonds. Your new pale hair. I can see it. A halter dress draped across here." Pinky made air-dress movements.

Patricia might be the queen of domestic fantasies, but Pinky was a woman of pure vision when it came to the creation and design of clothing.

"When I'm rich I'll back you in your own fashion business," Patricia announced.

"Thank you, my benefactress. I am eternally grateful. Now chew down that toast and for God's sake take a shower and get into some clean clothes. We have to start this project rolling."

"I'm impaired."

"Tough. Jean Harlow didn't bat an eye over a late night and a roll in the hay with her landlord."

"Tough girls finish first." Patricia raised her fist in the air lamely.

"Right."

"Get me some Advil, okay?"

"Get it yourself, tough girl."

Patricia wasn't feeling like a tough girl today. She had feelings she'd never had in her life. Something kept compelling her to play out this crazy scenario with Brett.

Her insides were churning with confusion and feelings she'd never felt before. She thought of Paul's kiss. She thought of Brett's kiss. She thought of Paul's loving touch. She thumped her head against the pillow and felt a searing pain shoot through her temples. It was no less than she deserved. She was a mess.

Paul's meeting went long and he wondered why Henri wasn't there. Lately, Henri had increasingly left things in his hands. He worried about the old guy. He worried about a lot of things these days.

Brett had arrived late to the meeting and looked hung over. As they broke and started filtering out the door, Paul went up to talk to him, the prick, keeping Patricia out that late.

"Brett."

"Paul, right?" Brett sucked down coffee and rubbed his eyes.

"You're dating my housemate."

"Shit, keep your voice down, buddy. Lizbeth has spies everywhere."

"I thought that was the general idea." Paul cut right to the chase.

"Oh, I guess you're right. I'm just a little out of it this morning. Hey, you know how it is."

"No, how is it?" Paul leaned against the wall with his arms crossed, looking down on Brett still in his chair.

"Women. Lizbeth is just being stubborn. Patricia is very beautiful. I like to be surrounded with beautiful things."

"Watch yourself. Brett, things could get complicated."

Brett always talked like everything was a joke. "I made it clear to Patricia I'm just out for some fun. She seems to be enjoying herself. Why, do you two have a thing going? Not that I mind sharing," he said in his joking manner.

Paul fought back the urge to punch Brett in his Nordic nose and watch it bleed. "If I did have claims on her, I would mind." Paul clenched his teeth. "But if Patricia is fine with your arrangement, there's not much I can say until she gets smart and dumps you."

"She's a pretty little thing. You let that one get

by ya, buddy." Brett got up and gave Paul a punch in the arm.

"I guess I did." Paul punched him back. Harder.

"Ow. Watch it, pal, I'm still your boss," Brett joked.

"I'll remember that." Paul took the opportunity to get out of the room before he did something he'd regret. Something that might cost him his job. He sure as hell didn't know what to think about Patricia this morning. He was completely undone by their encounter last night. This whole thing was crazy.

On the way down the hall he thought about his job. He loved going to Milan, and New York was always great, what with seeing his grandparents twice a year.

He'd even gone to Offenbach, Germany, last spring for the big International Leather Goods Fair. Henri had been training him well. But did he want to be Henri's replacement?

What happened to his high and lofty goals of writing a novel someday? He was going to teach Italian and literature and be one of those guys in the tweed jacket with leather patches on the elbows that made young minds expand with cultural and intellectual knowledge and then write a great historical novel of staggering genius on the side.

Okay, he'd seriously watched *Dead Poets Society* too many times when he was young. Now here he was, up to his eyeballs in handbags, and no book on the back burner.

Paul decided to head down to the basement and see if his shipment from Spain had arrived. Last time they'd had to get rid of a few strange bugs that hitchhiked along in the packing material. His department manager, Mrs. Hanagan, had begged him to check on incoming crates after a spider crawled up her hand and she'd practically fainted. Poor pale, redheaded Mrs. Peggy Hanagan. But she was a whiz at display and they got along pretty darn well.

Peggy had a family and liked to keep her hours sane. They always worked out a way to give the weekend hours to the young hungry girls who liked their commissions to be fat.

When he got to the basement, of course, he passed by Patricia's catalogue office. She still hadn't come in and it was almost noon. He'd thought maybe she'd straighten up and get herself in after all. She and Pinky probably decided to have a girls' day together.

He and Patricia had to talk as soon as possible.

As he walked past the door he noticed a dark-haired young woman in the office. It was getting close to holiday; maybe they'd brought in a temp.

"Hey." He poked his head in. "I'm Paul Costello, assistant handbag buyer."

"Hey back, I'm Terri Barnes. I'm the new catalogue gal." She was somewhat plain and wearing a button-down-collar floral print shirt and gray slacks. She reminded him of Patricia from earlier times.

Paul stood in the doorway. What the hell? "What's going on?" he asked. He started looking around the room and saw an empty box with Patricia's "desk monkey" in it. He'd given her this fuzzy orangutan for her birthday to drape over her lamp.

"I guess Patricia Stillwell is moving to another department." Terri shrugged. "I was just told to come in and start. But I think she was supposed to be here to go over things with me.

I'm not sure what happened, so I figured I'd just go over the catalogue orders and try and familiarize myself with her system."

"I'm a friend of hers. I'll check up on her and get her in here for you. I'm sure she'll want to help set you up properly. She's actually a nice person."

"Thanks, Mr. Costello. I appreciate that," Terri said. Paul nodded and as he walked away, he pulled out his cell phone. The cell reception in the basement left him without a signal. He wanted to be sure Patricia heard every word of this.

He abandoned his incoming handbag check and headed for the elevator. What the hell had Brett done? Or maybe it was Patricia herself. Paul headed for his second-floor office and kept checking his cell phone on the way. Finally he saw some action.

"Pinky?" He had autodialed home and she picked up quickly.

"Paul, what's up?"

"Let me talk to Patricia." He had to face her sometime and now he had two things to talk to her about.

"She's pinned into a paper dress. Can I have her call you back?"

"No. Give her the phone. This can't wait." He sat down behind his desk and picked up a pen. He was a sketcher. When he talked on the phone he drew geometric shapes. This time he drew spirals.

"I'm here," Patricia said.

"Well, you should be *here,* because you don't work in catalogue anymore. Did you arrange that, or is it as much of a surprise to you as it was to me? A Miss Barnes is in your office putting your monkey in a box." That sounded a little weird, but he was free-falling.

Basic dead silence came from the other end of the phone.

"Patricia?"

"W-wow. That was fast. I didn't think it would be that fast," Patricia stammered.

"So you did know or didn't know?"

"I sort of did and sort of didn't."

"You should get in here."

"I will. I'll come right away."

"Eat lunch first. There's leftover chicken in the fridge," he said.

The dead weight of their not discussing what happened last night practically pinned him to the ground with its hugeness. He rubbed his forehead.

"I have to get unpinned. Stop being so bossy."

"Obviously you need someone looking out after you."

"Apparently we both do," she said sharply. "Thanks for calling, I appreciate the heads-up." Patricia hung up.

He hung up the dead phone and put his pen down. God, that went so very badly he couldn't even imagine it having gone worse. He had to talk to her face to face and get this whole thing out in the open.

So she knew about her job, sort of? Paul wondered where she was transferring to and smacked himself for forgetting to ask. Probably to be Brett's personal assistant—he thumped his fist on the desk hard.

He was going nuts. He had violated their sacred housemate law. God only knew what the cost would be.

At least he would have the memory of making love to Patricia to keep him warm at night. The thing was that it only made him want her more.

* * *

Pinky stuck her three times before she was free of the paper pattern dress she'd fitted to her. It hadn't even registered except for a quick ouch. She felt completely numb today except for a strange tingling in her lips and an odd hum that rumbled through her body every time she thought about Paul and last night.

She had to think about something else. And she had plenty to think about, really. "Pinky, I think Brett transferred me to fine jewelry. He asked me at lunch yesterday where I'd like to work."

"Brett is nothing if not a fast worker," Pinky said.

"He could have told me, or warned me, or *something*. Men never think ahead," Patricia said.

"Or maybe you're fired for not putting out on the first date."

"Ha ha." Patricia stuck her tongue out at Pinky. "How do you know I didn't?"

"You told me last night. You said he kissed you and went in for the grope but you put on the brakes. Thank God, because that would make you a genuine slut, sleeping with two men on the same night."

"Aurghhhh, Pinky, don't even say that. Even the thought of it makes me ill." Patricia pulled on the bottom of her new push-up bra. "This thing is torture."

"But look, it lifts and separates." Pinky made motions emphasizing her figure and talked like a wispy advertising announcer.

"You are *so* funny. Paul said I had to get my butt down to work because this girl is packing up my stuff. He said my monkey was in a box." Patricia laughed.

"Honey, your monkey *is* in a box. Go put on that black dress. Fine jewelry ho's always wear black."

"Fine jewelry *ho's*?"

"You'll find out," Pinky said.

"I'm not going to turn cheap and slutty just because I'm a blonde, you know. I'm retaining my inner brunette." Patricia gave Pinky a dirty look and stomped off.

"Hold that thought," Pinky called after her. When Patricia left the room, Pinky thumped herself down on a chair and had herself a think. She thought about cats and how they can't be forced into anything. How they'll do the naughtiest things like jump up and eat the butter on the counter and look you in the eye when you catch them. And if you aren't looking, they'll do it again, because they just love the butter.

Maybe nature's consequences would turn out differently than she figured. Maybe last night would unravel her friend's blonde breakdown. It sure was going to unravel something.

Chapter Nine

She is mine own,
And I as rich in having such a jewel . . .
Shakespeare

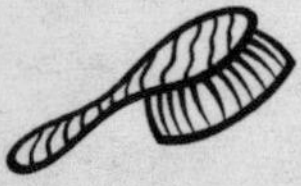

Paul was right, her monkey was in a box. And so were her framed photos, her matching vintage deco desk set, and anything remotely personal. She'd clobber the girl, but most likely Terri Barnes was just following orders.

It fascinated her to see Terri, a reflection of her former self. Patricia even had a blouse just like Terri's. It was a Dockers blouse with a little stretch in it to make it more comfortable around the extra pounds in the middle.

"Wow," Terri said as they shook hands. "No wonder you've been moved. You're beautiful. They shouldn't hide you away in the basement."

"Thanks, Terri. I've never thought of myself that way. I have to say, the basement has been cozy. I hope you like it as much as I did." Patricia looked around her little nest and felt a serious twinge of regret and panic all at once.

Had she hidden herself away down here? And what, just because she lost some weight and her hair went platinum, now she was to be displayed? That was just very scary and sort of Stepford.

She and Terri sat down to work and it was surprising to her how simple her job really was. In a few short hours she had Terri completely trained and ready to take over everything, including the NFL tie promotion. Of course, she'd get some holiday help in pretty soon and they'd keep her company down here.

It had always been great when they opened up her oddly impermanent wall, enlarged her space, and joined two more desks into the mix. There'd been some very fun people over the years.

Patricia still felt like the bottom of a shoe and it didn't help getting all . . . nostalgic.

When it came time to pack up her stuff, it all

fit in one box and one grocery bag. That was kind of pathetic. "Terri, I'm leaving you my miniature fake Christmas tree. It's a tradition down here during the holiday rush."

"Thanks, Patricia." Terri patted her arm.

The phone rang and Patti automatically picked it up. "Catalogue," she answered. Then she looked at Terri, who smiled at her with sympathy.

"Hey, Patti, it's Brett."

Brett had taken to calling her Patti. It was sort of cute. Sort of. "Hi, Brett." Patricia noticed her heart still revved up with the sound of Brett's voice.

"Great time last night, *r-i-g-h-t*?" He actually drawled *right* out kind of long like a bad comedian. He was so cute. Sort of.

"Great time, Brett." Patti had guilt. It hit her like a slap in the face. Big fat guilt. But she and Brett had hardly made any commitments to each other, so why did she feel guilt? Probably because she just wasn't the kind of girl to have sex with one man when she was engaged in a sort of serious manhunt for the other. Guilt meant she still had a conscience. That was a good thing.

"I've moved you upstairs. You're moving on up to the big time Patti! Fine jewelry!"

To a de-luxe apartment in the sky, she thought. "Thanks, Brett, that was a big surprise."

"I know. I love surprises, don't you?"

"When do I report to the sales floor?"

"Just go on up there now and introduce yourself. The sales manager will tell you your new schedule. Even better, I'll meet you there and impress them all. See you down there—or up there, in your case—in a few." Brett hung up.

Patricia was thinking that Brett introducing her might not be the best idea. Women got their noses out of joint for less than thinking you were sleeping with the boss. Five years in the backside of retail had taught her a whole lot more about women than she'd ever wanted to know.

She was stuck now. "Well, Terri, I'm just upstairs on the first floor if you need anything." Patricia put on her coat, hefted her box into her arms, slid her purse straps up her shoulder, and grabbed the shopping bag by its paper handles.

"Good luck, make lots of big fat commissions!" Terri opened the door wider for Patricia.

There was that. Sweeter than a bonus, the trickling commission wagon. She'd be making more money. As she walked to the elevator, Patricia kept going through the positives of her change in location. She'd get the selling-floor discount. That was a big one. The automatic twenty-five percent. Paulie got the big buyer's discount of thirty-three percent, but they kept a close eye on his purchases—except during the holidays.

She and Pinky would always stock up on wardrobe basics using Paulie's discount right after Christmas when everything was marked down. It seemed like the company turned a blind eye from December until about February. Then they had to behave.

She struggled to keep her box held up, resting it against the elevator railing.

After the ding and door opening, Patricia stepped out into the bright lights of the main sales floor. Although the fall decorations were still up, there were hints of holiday creeping in column by column. A huge red candle here, a giant golden holiday ball with striped red and gold ribbon there, display people scurrying around like elves. She knew the signs. It was starting to look a lot like Christmas—in October.

The first floor had ladies' shoes, scarves, handbags, accessories, and the nasty cosmetics girls who would spray you in the eye with J. Lo's new fragrance if you distracted one of their customer potentials. Speaking of Stepford, those girls were just scary.

The junk jewelry, as they all called it, took up a center counter, but the fine jewelry was in its own little special corner. Mostly so they could stick extra cameras and security all over the place and keep a tight eye on the goods.

Patricia made it past the center escalators and almost to the carpeted edge of fine jewelry when her paper bag handles gave way. She grabbed at the handles, which only caused it to rip completely open.

The contents of her paper bag exploded like a Fourth of July sparkle fountain and clattered to the hard linoleum floor.

As she scrambled to grab her bobble-head Disney character collection like a juggling clown, she went down on one knee. Then the ever-familiar feel of her stocking running in a large zipping rush ran down her leg. She could feel her cheeks burning.

A quick glance up made her feel slightly ill again. Brett was standing with the formidable Madam Gaffer, who reminded Patricia of the Wicked Witch of the West, but prettier. Madam Gaffer was a German woman who knew her diamonds and everything else, or so Pinky had told her.

Pinky knew everything about everyone at Nordquist's. She said alterations people are invisible to salespeople, so they hear twice as much dirt as anyone else.

Well, here was one for Pinky's logbook, Brett and Madam Gaffer staring at her as she tried to shove Bobble-Head Dopey into her over-stuffed box.

Finally, Brett came over to her—she could see his expensive Italian shoes and his legs from her kneeling position. "Gosh, that's a mess," he said. "Listen, I've got to run. Madam Gaffer is waiting for you. Chin up, cutie."

And with that, Brett vanished.

Her eyes teared up. It wasn't the contacts this time, it was Brett being too busy to pause and help her. But before she could burst out crying and curl up in a fetal position on the floor of Nordquist's, a pair of male hands lifted her to her feet.

"I'll take care of this. You go meet the madam." Paul smoothed his hand across hers in a gesture that was so comforting it made her want to cry for other reasons. "We'll talk about last night later."

"God bless you, Paulie," she said. Patricia straightened her black dress and adjusted her pearls, which were really Pinky's pearls from her confirmation day a million years ago, she'd said. She had the best friends in the whole world.

And Paul had set her mind at ease with just a touch. He was speaking to her, he was ready to talk, and surely they'd be a sensible pair and not let last night come between their friendship.

Paul picked up Patricia's treasures and loaded them into a plastic shopping bag he'd grabbed on his way to her. He borrowed some tissue paper from the scarf salesgirl and wrapped each bobble-head carefully. After all, these were collected on their two trips to Disneyland.

As he wrapped and packed, Paul remembered

being dragged into the Tiki Room for the fourth time so the girls could sing "Let's All Sing Like the Birdies Sing" until his ears rang.

He watched her go up to Madam Gaffer, who looked damned scary to him, with her tightly pulled-back slate gray hair and severe black dress, but then Paul saw the older woman put her arm around Patricia's shoulder and lead her into the inner sanctum of fine jewelry.

So it was true. She'd been transferred to fine jewelry in one quick day. Paul wondered how Patricia felt about the change. She wasn't one to move quickly into a decision.

For the past few days he'd been thinking about taking Patricia and Pinky to New York with him on his next trip. The holiday decorations would be up, they could catch some shows, and he could take them to a musical. Pinky had family there, and his grandparents still lived in the old neighborhood. They could take a few weeks of vacation time. Although he didn't know if either of them had time coming, and Patricia starting in a new department might be difficult.

Tonight at dinner he was going to ask the girls about New York and bring up the whole subject of their lives. A nice risotto would make that conversation go down better. A nice risotto would mend the tear in the fabric of their sanity that last night had caused.

He had to make a stop at Delaurenti's to pick up his supplies for tonight. Maybe some crusty bread, balsamic vinegar, and olive oil on the side, too, and a nice Shiraz.

Cooking was the thing that helped him create order in his life. Just like Pinky and her dress dummy, he had his pots and pans and his family recipes. Cooking would help.

It occurred to Patricia that aside from 14K gold and sterling silver, she knew absolutely *nothing* about fine jewelry. What she thought she knew about pearls just went out the window as Madam Gaffer showed her the incredible variety of pearls the world had to offer. There were dozens of shapes: baroques and seed pearls and pearls that were green- or rose-colored or almost black. There were pearls from Australian, Tahiti, Japan, and the South Sea Islands.

This was not a good day for a hangover.

Finally, probably sensing her brain freeze,

Madam Gaffer put her to work at a back desk scribing tiny golden tickets with codes and prices. But she was going to have to abandon the blue contacts and put her reading glasses back on from now on. Tomorrow.

She had to admit after being introduced to the fine jewelry inventory, it was true. Diamonds were a girl's best friend.

From her perch slightly above the selling floor, she heard the voice of Lizbeth Summers. Mandy, the other fine jewelry associate, was waiting on her. They seemed to be old friends.

Patricia heard whispers, then Lizbeth asked Mandy to show her a jade pendant. Not your average jade, either, the really expensive stuff called apple jade. She remembered seeing it in the case. It was shaped in a perfect circle and threaded through a gold chain and it was a cool three hundred ninety-five dollars for this thing that was the size of a quarter.

"Oh, it's beautiful on you," Mandy exclaimed. "But when are you and Brett going to get serious and buy that marquise diamond?"

"That's up to him. He just needs to grow up a little and get all his foolishness behind him," Lizbeth answered.

"Yeah, him and every other guy. Isn't he dating someone?"

"I wouldn't call it dating, I'd call it slumming."

The two girls tittered with laughter. Patricia considered pushing the plant perched on the edge of the upper wall down on Mandy's head but decided it would not be a good career move. That bitch. As if she didn't know Patricia was behind that wall within clear earshot. Both of them could just go to hell.

And Brett would be lucky to get away from Lizbeth. If he wanted to *slum,* Patricia was more than willing to be the distraction that kept him from deciding to marry Lizbeth.

When the little dear had purchased her jade piece, Mandy took the three-step climb to the loft where Patricia sat.

Patricia raised her head from her work and gave Mandy a big, nasty smile. Mandy tried to return some kind of look, but it seemed like Patricia had preempted her and Mandy went to her corner, somewhat speechless.

So here she was with Mandy, who somehow managed to either play into Lizbeth's little scheme or had plotted to make sure Patricia knew good and well that Lizbeth knew she was dating Brett.

She knew that he knew that they all knew. It was one of those nasty little circles that can go nowhere good.

Patricia focused on her scribing and ignored Mandy to death.

Madam Gaffer called her name and startled Patricia out of her deeply meditative state. She straightened up and got herself down on the selling floor.

A handsome well-dressed older man stood behind the glass case pointing at a few items.

"Watch now, Patricia," Madam said softly. She took out a black velvet board and pulled the diamond tennis bracelet out of the display case. "Mr. Martin is a good customer. He won't mind if I teach you a few things. Notice how I never turn around after I've put the item out for display. Of course, Mr. Martin would never run off with our diamond bracelet, but someone else might. If he decides to look at another item, we would put the bracelet away *first* and then move to the other area, see?"

"Yes, I see." Patricia stood with her hands linked behind her and listened carefully.

"It's nice to meet you, Patricia." Mr. Martin smiled at her in a way she'd seen before. His temples were graying, but the tiger was obviously still in the tank.

"Thank you, Mr. Martin," Patricia replied.

"I think this will do nicely. Can you gift-wrap that for me, Patricia?" Mr. Martin asked.

Madam handed her the bracelet. "You'll find the boxes and supplies on a table upstairs next to where you were sitting." She turned back to Mr. Martin. "Thank you, George, we appreciate your business."

He handed her his credit card and winked. Patricia noticed that wink as she glanced back once more before ascending the stairs.

As Mr. Martin finished his transaction, she wrapped the pretty bracelet in their special red box with a white ribbon and delivered it to Madam for inspection.

"Very nice, Patricia. Now keep your eyes open and your mouth closed." Madam put her finger to her lips.

The next customer was a beautiful blonde

woman dressed in a designer camel-hair coat and tasteful jewelry and accessories. She was rich, no doubt about it. Her hair was smoothed into an elegant sweep. Patricia studied her closely.

"Good afternoon, madam," the beautiful blonde said. She had a tense quality to her voice and a sad, bitter look around the eyes. "So what have we bought today?" The woman put a gloved hand on the top of the counter and Madam patted it softly.

Madam Gaffer then brought out a tennis bracelet identical to the one she'd sold Mr. Martin.

"Oh, I see. Well, let's have this one instead—a bit bigger, with the sapphires and diamonds. I fancy myself in a blue dress for the symphony fund-raiser next month. And the matching earrings as well."

"They will look stunning on you, Laura; the blue against your hair and your blue eyes." Madam called the woman by her first name. So far she hadn't heard that happen much today. Madam put the diamond bracelet away and took out a fabulous combination diamond and sapphire bracelet with matching earrings that clustered like wisteria blossoms. Many, many little sparkling gems.

In a few minutes the items were put in velvet boxes, no gift-wrapping, and the mysterious Laura was gone.

Patricia had straightened gold chains and looked busy while she'd watched.

Madam Gaffer came over close to her. "So, you understand?"

"I'm not sure. You have special customers?"

Madam tsked at her. "That was Mrs. Martin. Laura Martin."

"She wanted to know what her husband bought for her?"

"No, my goodness, did you just arrive off a turnip truck? George Martin has a mistress. After Mrs. Martin had lunch with him he made his usual once-a-month stop into our department. He's been at this for years. Every time he buys jewelry for the mistress, Mrs. Martin buys herself a nice gift. She calls it her special reward for putting up with him."

Patricia stared at Madam Gaffer. "How in the world do you know all this?"

"Keen observation," she replied in a slight

German accent. "Besides, once on a very bad day Mrs. Martin confessed all to me. Now we have an understanding."

"What a dog."

"George Martin? He is merely an egotistical aging gentleman who thinks he is so clever as to get away with his illicit affairs." Madam waved her hand in the air.

Then she looked Patricia in the eye with a hard glint. "But more importantly, Patricia, he is our good customer. There is much to the art of fine jewelry, and being discreet is part of the job. George Martin spends thousands of dollars a year with us, whether it's by his own hand or at the hand of his unfortunate wife. Therefore, we will keep his secrets that he thinks are so secret, and we will keep Mrs. Martin's secrets as if we were priests in the confessional. Now do you understand?"

"I do," Patricia answered.

"Good, now get back to work and you can have the next sale that comes in. I'll watch you."

Patricia felt rather sick thinking of the unfortunate Laura Martin and how sad and bitter she'd looked. So this was what Pinky meant about the fine jewelry ho's. Or was it Mandy and her claws, or just the whole eat-what-you-kill commission jungle laws? A fine confusion set itself in her head and she decided just to separate gold ropes from snakes and not try to sort out anything more than chains.

At the end of the day they pulled all the display pieces into the back room for lockup and Mandy kept her distance. Patricia hadn't made any sales, but she'd talked to a few people just to get the hang of showing pieces.

"Patricia." Madam stopped her as she was sliding her coat on and handed her a card. "Here is your schedule. Your black dress is lovely, but tomorrow if you have something cut a bit lower, I'd advise you wear it. Not too much, just enough. Your hair is also lovely. You will be our most elegant girl. Think of yourself as elegant. Maybe sweep the hair up off the face and a bit more makeup. You look pale." Madam turned and left her there holding her card, trying to get her coat on.

Think of herself as elegant. Show some cleavage. Tart up a bit. Patricia sighed. She could feel her flannel pajamas calling her. She closed her eyes and thought of Paul's chicken cacciatore and his risotto and, last of all, her lovely bed.

The bed that she and Paul had made love in. But tonight that bed was hers alone.

"Ready for dinner, sweet thing?" Brett strolled into the fine jewelry department jolly as you please. He looked very boyish and like he'd been up to no good.

Patricia felt a very small groan escape her lips. Farewell to flannel. How could she pass up a date with Brett?"

"What a surprise, Brett." She smiled.

"I figured we'd celebrate your new job. First day and all that."

Patricia felt the eyes of Mandy burning down on them. How sweet of Brett. She was hungry. Maybe she'd get home early enough to get a taste of the risotto, too.

"Sounds heavenly," she said.

"You should put your hair up in one of those sweeps. I just saw the most elegant blonde over by the Estée Lauder counter."

Patricia smiled. Up-do's, elegance, cleavage; there was more to being a blonde than she'd thought.

For just the most fleeting moment, as she looked over at Brett with his ruggedly Nordic good looks, she saw George Martin's face instead, superimposed over Brett's.

"Good grief," she said out loud.

"I know just what will fix that. You need the hair of the dog that bit you. We'll go to Wild Ginger for ice-cold sake. I love it that way. I bet you will, too."

Ice cold sake. Wild Ginger. Gee, that sounded elegant, didn't it?

Chapter Ten

Much that we call evil is really
good in disguises.
Shakespeare

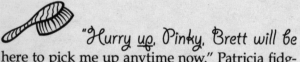

"*Hurry up, Pinky, Brett will be* here to pick me up anytime now." Patricia fidgeted. "I have to be Halloween party ready!"

"Hold still and take it like a woman." Pinky smacked Patricia on the bare arm. She'd had it up to her eyeballs with the new Patricia, and she was going to get sewn into this dress if it killed her.

"Ouch, you are such a bitch!" Patricia smacked her back.

"If you'd been home for more than five minutes for some fittings, we wouldn't be here now."

"I'm sorry. Brett apparently wanted to spend a whole lot of time with me."

Pinky sniffed. More like Brett wanted to parade Patricia through a series of highly visible hot spots and make sure Mandy reported all to Lizbeth over the last few weeks. Patricia was being such a *fesso.* And here it was October, the big night of the Halloween party, and she was being so difficult. Maybe she'd sew this dress a little tighter and make *breathing* difficult. Pinky snickered to herself.

"You look fabulous, Patricia, so just behave. Now, Jean Harlow's hair was shorter than yours, but just about the same color. It's probably what made her kidneys fail at twenty-six. Peroxide poisoning."

Pinky removed a handful of pins from her mouth to be sure Patricia heard her on the early demise of Jean Harlow. She could take a clue from Jean. In the five years she'd known Patricia, she never imagined her dragging in at all hours with the faint odor of tequila on her breath.

Patricia twisted herself around. "You shouldn't say things like that. I'm only taking my experimental drugs for the recommended course."

"I wonder if you will revert to being a brunette after you stop taking the stuff. Maybe then you'll regain some of your common sense." Pinky stuck her with a pin on purpose.

"*Ow,* you did that on purpose."

"Did not."

"Well, look at me, at least I'm dropping weight."

"I'll say. Although whether it was the drug or the late nights and not eating properly, it's hard to say."

Patricia put her hands on her hips. "Pinky McGee, you are just jealous. You're jealous because I haven't been spending time with you."

"This is the part where your best friend talks some sense into you regarding your recent behavior and choice of companions. But I tried that last weekend."

"I'm sure things will slow down. They better, because I slowed him down plenty last weekend."

"He's trying to score a touchdown?"

"Just because he got a first down he thought he could go for the goal line."

"You are terrible at football analogies." Paul's deep male voice boomed from the kitchen. He must have overheard. That made Pinky uneasy.

Paul went on. "How's this one? He's first and ten with pretty good field position but still well out of field goal range. Or maybe you mean this. He only got that first down on a defensive holding penalty and he's still having trouble moving the ball. He'll need to show something positive on offense if he hopes to score on this drive, otherwise he'll have to punt." Paul had a terrible sarcastic tone.

Pinky stood up, facing Patricia. She watched the embarrassment creep into Patricia's cheeks.

"Look at you, Paul the swashbuckling dashing pirate. I could have made that for you easily, you know," Pinky distracted everyone from the discussion of Brett's passes on or off the field.

"Pinky, my dear, I didn't want to add any more stress to your life."

"That's very gallant of you, sir. Well, here you two are, off to the Halloween ball. I'll just stay here and huddle by the fire."

"I told you four times you're welcome to come along with me," Paul said.

"Oh, *pu-lease,*" Pinky groaned. "Okay Pattirella, you're ready to roll. Here's your feather-trimmed wrap and opera gloves, Miss Harlow. Remember you turn into an ugly orange pumpkin at midnight. Or in your case, a brunette."

"*So* funny." Patricia pulled her gloves on and draped the boa-trimmed wrap around her shoulders.

There was a knock on the door and Paul strode over to answer it, his cape billowing.

"That's *Captain* Costello." Pinky did her Johnny Depp imitation.

Patricia smiled at her. She looked so elegant and vintage Hollywood in her costume. But Patricia's late nights were reflected in dark circles under her eyes. They'd spent a sizeable amount of time concealing them with makeup.

Some strange muffled conversation went on between Paul and most likely Brett, a decidedly naughty-type trick-or-treater. Then the two men emerged from the entryway. Paul and Brett. Two identical pirates. Same exact costume. Pinky tried to keep from laughing.

"Oh my," Patricia said.

"Looks like great minds think alike," Brett said.

"Or the costume rental store has a limited selection," Paul said flatly.

"Patti, my little pumpkin, you look delicious enough to eat." Brett came over to her and took her by the hand. "Are you ready to roll? The limo is full of my old school friends, but there's room for one more."

"I'm *ready*, Brett."

"Oh, I love the sound of *that*," Brett growled, and nuzzled her neck. Then he ran his hands down the length of her satin Jean Harlow gown. He made another animal sound.

Pinky thought she might yak up. Patricia seemed dazzled by Brett's gesture. "Brett, you are so funny." Patricia grabbed the pretty beaded handbag Paul had hunted up especially for this occasion. A vintage bag they sometimes used for display in the handbag department. Pinky thought that was more gallant than Brett's pawing and growling. Pinky also didn't like the sound of that *I'm ready* comment Patricia had made.

They swept out the door with Brett whooping and making pirate dialogue. Pinky and Paul stood in the quiet for a minute.

"Jesus, Pinky, this is just too much." Paul strode around the sofa and flung himself in their leather chair. The long white ostrich feather that adorned his black pirate's hat quivered with anger. "I assumed that Brett would be done with her sooner than this. I can't believe he's still parading her in front of Lizbeth's nose. Something is just so wrong about all this. If I were half the pirate I should be I'd run him through with my trusty sword."

Pinky sat across from him on the sofa of many colors and let out a long breath that she'd been holding in. "It's just disgusting, isn't it? I could seriously vomit watching them together. You're going to have to keep an eye on her tonight. There is no other way to keep her from doing something extremely stupid. She cannot give her womanhood to Brett Nordquist. She's resisted so far."

"That's going to be rather difficult, seeing as I'm supposed to meet Dani at this party."

"Dani? Ditzy Dani? I thought you were through with her."

"I had a moment of pity when she begged me to be her date."

"A girl like that couldn't get a date?"

"She thinks there is something between us and probably kept waiting for me to ask her, but

I never did. Then she waited too long and was dateless."

"Did she get that assistant shoe buyer's job?"

"Yes."

"So what does she need you for?"

"Don't know. All I know is I sense disaster in the air. You have to come with me. I'm just a guy. I can't handle all this intrigue."

"You can't ask a seamstress to go to a costume party an hour before it starts. That's cruel."

"I bet you've got something in your closet. Go look."

Pinky scowled at him, but she knew he was right. Their buddy Patricia was about to fall into the unscrupulous hands of Brett Nordquist and his school chums. They had to save her.

As Pinky went to scrounge up a costume, Paul thunked his head back against the chair, which pushed his pirate hat forward. He flung the damn thing off onto the floor. The distasteful, enraging sensation of seeing Brett put his lips on Patricia hung with him like bad wine; that bad, bitter taste in your mouth that lasts for days. Even knowing she hadn't slept with him didn't help.

At this very moment, he hated Brett Nordquist.

He and Patricia had finally gotten their own crazy night straightened out and, despite the amazing flashbacks of their lovemaking that haunted his every sleepless night, they'd done a good job of setting it aside for the sake of their friendship.

Paul heard a shriek of laughter from the downstairs vicinity of Pinky's room and jumped up to see what new disaster awaited him. At least Pinky was still a brunette two minutes ago.

"Oh my God."

"Shut up and zip it." Pinky turned around.

Paul bent down to Pinky's level and found the zipper pull. He slowly stuffed her into the felt-and-foam-and-feather creation. "Now turn around and let me see."

She was a flamingo. Pinky the pink flamingo.

"Where the hell did you get this?"

"Remember that swimwear show we did last May with kids and all the cute dancing critters?"

"I only remember the women earlier in the show."

Pinky thwapped him with her wing. "Dog."

"Can you get around in that thing?"

Pinky waddled around. "Sure. The car might be a problem, but we've got your Volvo and that's got a sunroof."

"Okay, we'll just stick your flamingo head out the sunroof and go rescue our friend."

"I better pee first. It won't be easy after this. Unzip me again."

Paul sighed. He'd been such a brother to these girls. Until he and Patricia had changed all that. Things *needed* to change, though. And most of all with Patricia. He unzipped Pinky, who stepped out of her costume and stood there with pink tights and a tank top.

"Okay, give me five minutes. It's not like my face is that noticeable through pink netting, but I'd like to at least look presentable in case I meet a nice boy flamingo."

"Meet me in the living room." Paul wanted nothing more than to go break up Brett's plans. Or Brett's legs, maybe. To think he'd sleep with Patricia in the middle of using her to make Lizbeth jealous made him want to hurt the guy.

But why should he be surprised about Brett wanting her? Patricia was beautiful. She'd been an angel in that white satin dress. It had hugged her curves in all the right places. He hadn't been able to take his eyes off her. He had to admit to himself he had serious feelings about Patricia—or some kind of feelings beyond the most-tender-and-amazing-sex-ever kind of feelings. Maybe he was just as bad as Brett.

When the Nordquists threw a party, they didn't pinch pennies. Patricia stepped out of the limo with Brett and his old high school buddies and a few of their dates into a regular high-end harvest fair with some hauntedness on the side. This must be the work of professionals, she thought.

Patricia wondered what it would be like to be mistress of the manor, hiring party planners. She trailed past a dazzling entrance display of flowers, pumpkins, gourds, and vine maple lit with tiny sparkling lights.

Brett was still messing around with his jerky friends, so she stepped inside as the butler, or in this case Lurch the Butler from the Addams Family, opened the door for her. He was green and very tall.

"Good evening," he said in the perfect Lurch voice.

"Good evening to you, too."

"May I announce you?"

"Jean Harlow," she answered.

"As I suspected," he replied with his long drawn-out fake accent.

Patricia stepped in behind Lurch, temporarily forgetting about Brett.

"Miss Jean Harlow," he bellowed.

She floated in, knowing there was hardly a soul here she knew. What the hell, that almost helped her feel less tense.

"Hello, Miss Harlow, I'm Mrs. Nordquist." A pale creature resplendent in the beauty that money can buy, decked out in a Marie Antoinette costume, stood before her.

"Why, hello, you must be Brett's mother. I'm his date, Patricia Stillwell." Patricia held out her hand.

Mrs. N. looked a bit confused, but covered it up with a wave of her fan and a roll of her eyes.

"Brett's getting his friends out of the limo. Not an easy feat." Patricia laughed. My, she'd been bold to just introduce herself to her future mother-in-law like that.

Brett's mother gave a dry laugh. "Ah, yes. You look charming, my dear. Do come in."

Other people were starting to arrive, so Patricia moved to the side to wait for Brett. She waited, and waited. She leaned on the marble entry table. She gazed into the mirror hanging above the table and was still startled to see herself as a blonde. Her Jean Harlowness made her all the more pale and ghostly, in her opinion.

In a moment of realization as she looked in the mirror Patricia realized how out of place she was. She'd grown up in a lower-end suburban neighborhood. The people were great, but the concept of opulence was far, far away. This was the big leagues. She shivered.

She tired of waiting for Brett and wandered down the smooth stone stairs to where the noise was. There was quite the crowd already.

She and Brett and his crew were late arriving because, of course, on the way here Brett and his buddies had to stop at the Metropolitan for a drink. Oh, they'd made quite the buzz in the crowded Metropolitan Grill with their costumes and all. She'd been elbowed and pinched a few too many times as they'd all crowded into that bar.

She rubbed her hip where one particular gentleman had taken a pinch of her flesh. But then she'd managed to elbow him in the gut pretty nicely.

So here she was. Alone. Brett still playing with his boys. A waiter dressed as a mime came by and handed Patricia a champagne cocktail. She took a sip and the bubbles tickled her nose. It was delicious.

Not that she needed another one without any food in her. She'd already had a Cosmopolitan at the bar. She nabbed another waiter who had a tray full of appetizers. Cheese, it's what's for dinner.

A sense of loneliness came over her. She drifted through the gypsies and ghouls, looking for someone with an original costume. A potato walked by and she followed him into a large room with a grand piano in the corner. Someone was playing the Alfred Hitchcock theme, and quite nicely, too.

The potato stopped to talk to a flamingo. Now that was more like it. As she came closer, something about that flamingo looked familiar. She was a short thing, but for her long neck and head swaying above. Her legs were pink and graceful, with little fake bird feet over her shoes.

A mad scientist had his back to her and was chatting with the flamingo, too. His hair was sticking straight up and died with a green tinge.

Wait, that flamingo was *Pinky.*

"Pinky, is that you? Thank *God.*"

"Jean Harlow, my most elegant creation, I'm sure you know Dr. Bender." Pinky gave her a veiled grin through the thin pink net that covered her face.

The mad scientist turned around and looked Patricia over carefully. "My heavens, it's quite striking, isn't it?"

"Dr. Bender, what are you doing here?" Patricia was stunned to see him out of context in his white coat and green hair.

"Dr. Bender went to college at Stanford with Brett, did you know? He's actually a friend of the family." Pinky patted Dr. Bender's shoulder with her wing.

Patricia got an odd chill. Hopefully, Dr. Bender would keep her secrets.

He must have seen the concern wave over her. "No worries, we have that doctor-client confidentiality going, Patricia. I'm just here to relax."

"James is a film buff, Patti, can you imagine?"

Pinky seemed pink with delight. "That's so great Dr. Bender. Pinky and I go to the Grand Illusion at least twice a month." Patricia smiled and watched Pinky with Bender. It was cute, particularly in a flamingo costume. The potato was talking to a pirate and a flapper. The Flapper was old Oreo teeth herself, so the Pirate must be . . . "Paul?"

He turned around. "Oh, Patricia, you remember Dani, don't you?"

"Charmed, I'm sure." Dani did a little flapper move. She looked snockered. At that moment the waiter showed up and handed them all fresh champagne flutes with strawberries floating in them. Dani squealed and tossed hers back rather quickly.

Patricia raised her eyebrow to Paul. Paul shrugged. "Let's find the buffet table and soak up some of this champagne, shall we?" he suggested.

"We'll catch up." Pinky waved.

Paul put his arm around Dani, then around Patricia's shoulders, which felt oddly comforting. His blousy pirate shirt showed off his great chest. It continued to amaze her how Paul's physique was so attractive. She could feel the strong muscles of his arms as they walked together.

Patricia got the oddest flash of wanting Dani to flapper herself off into a nice corner for a nap. She gave herself a mental boot in the head. She and Paul had resolved this thing. Bringing up the deliciousness of their lovemaking would only make her crazy. Besides, she had other plans.

The buffet table was resplendent with food and whimsical displays, including carved pumpkins that had smoke curling out of their mouths. She swigged down the rest of her champagne and took up a plate.

As they moved down the line, Dani in front, her in the middle, and Paul behind, he whispered in her ear. "Where's Brett?"

"We arrived in the limo and he just sort of vanished. I guess he had to show his high school friends a car or something. They yammered about cars the entire time at the Met and on the drive."

"You stopped at the Met Grill?"

Patricia leaned his way and spoke quietly. "I was just an accessory to the fact."

"Patricia, you've got to stop this drinking binge you've been on."

She turned to face him and showed him how extremely displeased she was that he was ordering her around. "Shut up, Paulie, you aren't my keeper."

He glared back at her. "Well, someone better start, because you are out of control."

She was so mad she couldn't think of any nasty thing to say back. She slapped a big piece of roast beef on her plate.

Dani looked at them and smiled, her little feathered headband bobbing to the music. She obviously didn't hear their conversation.

"Didn't you get partying out of your system in college?" His voice sounded quite harsh.

"No, I studied for four years. And I don't want to talk about it anymore. You're spoiling my fun."

"Grow up, Patricia. Brett is a class A party boy. He's only dating you to make Lizbeth jealous. He only wants to toy with you until she caves in and takes him back. He has no intentions toward you that don't involve a roll in the sack."

This he decided to tell her in the buffet line? Patricia felt the anger well up in her. "I'm in love with him," she hissed.

"Then you are a foolish girl, Patricia Stillwell."

His words stung. She knew it was all true about Brett and Lizbeth, but she didn't want to hear it at this particular moment. She'd wanted to keep her illusion in place for this night of fantasy. Patricia put her plate down on the long table between the ranch dip and the crudités. "I thought you were my friend." She swung around and stalked away from him.

"I am," he called after her. "Friends tell each other the truth."

"Geez, Paulie, that was harsh." Dani hiccupped.

"Don't call me *Paulie,*" he snarled.

"Sorry, sweetie, it just rubbed off." She laughed and threw her body at him as best as she could with both of them holding buffet plates. "Rubbed off, see?" She shimmied and her fringed dress shimmied with her.

Paul gave her a gentle push away. "Let's get you some food, shall we?" He loaded a few things on her plate while she wasn't looking.

"Oh, screw you. You're just no fun tonight. I'm going to find a new playmate. I saw a very cute prince over by the fireplace. Ta-ta, grouchy." She flitted off toward the large black marble fireplace that could be seen from the open French doors of the dining room.

He was just glad he'd put some protein on that plate. There would be one less completely blotted girl to worry about. She'd sure gotten a head start on the champagne before he'd arrived. He watched her fringe sway as she walked. Damn, she was a fine woman. Too bad he wasn't the slightest bit interested in her.

That prince was Eric Nordquist. That should be interesting. The younger brother of Brett was holding court. Paul noticed Lizbeth in a Cleopatra costume. She had a dark brunette wig on, but it was her, all right. Great makeup. Very thin fabric. She was a regular jewel of the Nile. Lizbeth looked pretty chummy with Eric. Wow, maybe she'd changed brothers. Eric looked at Lizbeth with a very hungry, adoring look.

"Oh God," Paul said out loud. He watched through the doorway as strange things began to unfold like a bad Greek play. Brett came in holding his bourbon, or actually *not* holding it well—it sloshed while he walked. It looked like he just slowly, casually crossed the room to his brother, but as he approached, the volume of their conversation got very animated and loud.

Then he saw Patricia follow him over. This couldn't go well. Paul left his plate on an end table and got his pirate self ready for a fight.

"You son of a bitch, you think you can move in on her?" Brett slurred his speech and got right up close to his brother Eric. His pirate hat hit Eric's crown.

Eric pushed him backward. Brett stumbled.

"Oh, shut up, Brett. You certainly made it clear you weren't interested in a commitment. That means I'm free to date *whomever* I *like*." Lizbeth sounded very loud and bawdy, particularly on the last few words.

It was very obvious to Paul that of all the tipsy blondes in the vicinity, Lizbeth was the absolute tipsiest. She was three-sheets-to-the-wind drunk and still swilling champagne cocktails.

"Not my own brother, honey. This isn't a family deal."

"Screw you, Brett. You're an ass. She can do whatever she wants." Eric had wisely set his drink down.

"Brett, don't." Patricia had come up behind Brett and taken his arm. "She's not worth it."

Paul's adrenaline shot up. That probably wasn't the best thing to say on Patricia's part. He kept walking toward the trouble. She may be mad at him, but he couldn't let her get hurt.

Brett shook her off his arm. She stumbled backward. Cleopatra-Lizbeth took one step toward Jean-Harlow-Patricia and slapped her in the face. Patricia regained her footing despite the slap, and gave one directly back to Lizbeth. A very loud, smacking comeback slap. Jean Harlow would have been proud.

Brett the pirate grabbed his brother the prince by the fancy collar and dragged him a few steps away from the fireplace. Prince Eric punched Captain Brett in the stomach. Brothers always knew the best place to hit the other brother. Brett started to collapse. His pirate hat fell off. Lizbeth forgot to hit Patricia back and leaned to Brett, who was doubled over. Good thing that sword was fake.

Paul took this opportunity to get Patricia the hell out of there. He grabbed her arm and pulled her toward him. Brett regained himself and took Patricia's other arm. Lizbeth grabbed Brett.

The two pirates were locked in a tug-of-war for Patricia, so of course Paul did what any man would do—he gave Brett a good punch in the nose. Blood gushed. Brett let go of Patricia.

Paul held on to Patricia, who started to struggle against him. He swung her around and threw her fireman-style over his shoulder. She was so surprised she couldn't even start beating him on the back with her fists for at least a full thirty seconds.

Paul bounded up the sweeping staircase with her on his shoulder. Her weight loss was quite evident at that moment—he'd picked her up a few times in the past. She was a light package tonight.

"Put me down!" she screamed.

Paul heard laughter from the main floor as he ascended the stairs with Patricia. He'd been to this house before, at another party. There was a main landing almost like a reception room that opened out onto the second-story balcony. Some fresh air would do her good. The French doors were open and he walked out into the darkness with her, then set her down.

As soon as her feet hit the floor, she slapped him in the face. *"Bastard!"* she screamed.

Paul felt his face where her dainty little hand had left a burn. My, wasn't she the slapping little wench tonight. It made him smile. She raised her hand, to repeat the slap, he assumed.

He grabbed her and pulled her close, crushing his lips to hers. Her sweet, rose-petal lips tasted like champagne and honey and he devoured them. He devoured her like he had the night they'd made love, but with even more passion. Because now he knew he was in love with her.

She fought him for a moment, but he held her tight. Then she softened, and melted into his kiss. He ran his hands over her silky satin bare back, and pulled her into him even deeper.

He slid one hand up the side of her hip and across the slippery white satin dress, then brushed against her breast gently. She gasped. He wove his fingers into her blonde hair and kissed her again, his deep desire for her crushing into her mouth, exploring and tasting her.

He had wanted this again for so long it made him ache. The darkness surrounded them and for just a moment there was nothing in the entire world except her. She made that sound he loved and for one tender moment she touched his face gently as he kissed her.

"I love you, Patricia," he whispered in her ear. His heart ached as he said the words.

Then he felt her stop, then push him away. He took a step backward and saw her eyes glittering with tears.

As all things that happen without warning,

what happened next was so shocking it surpassed all the sensations Paul was already engulfed in and changed their entire experience in a blinding flash of fateful insanity.

A strange flock of people descended upon them in that very dark, secluded corner of the Nordquist house. People who were running, yelling, punching, and shoving; Egyptian girls and pirates and princes and flappers and a very familiar flamingo. Paul even thought he heard a dog barking somewhere in the mix.

And in that little slice of darkness, in the middle of complete chaos and drunken drama, his moment of confession and passion was lost to the sound of one lone descending scream going over the stone railing of the second-story balcony.

Chapter Eleven

O mischief, thou art swift to enter in the thoughts of desperate men!

Shakespeare

Amid the screams and darkness and horrible rushing of people, Patricia was haunted by two things: one was the sound of someone's body hitting the ground below, the other was Paul's words, which still stung her heart with emotion.

The only thing she could actually think clearly about was the overriding question: Who fell? Her eyes had grown accustom to the dim light and from the glow of the landscape accents below she could see the back of someone laying face-first on the lawn. A black cape had settled over the person's head, so she couldn't be sure which pirate it was.

Pirate! Not *Paul*. It couldn't be Paul. He had been kissing her. He had been whispering in her ear. But it could be, because he'd let go and then all the people had rushed in and someone had been fighting and screaming and, oh my God, *it could be Paul*. She turned to run downstairs and smacked head-on into Pinky in her flamingo suit.

Pinky grabbed her. "It's not Paul," she said.

"Thank God." Patricia leaned against her friend. Then it slowly crept over her that if it wasn't Paul, it was Brett.

"Brett?"

"I think so," Pinky answered.

Patricia looked around her at the people still standing on the balcony. Lizbeth was crying hysterically, clutching the doorframe dramatically. Dani was looking over the edge of the balcony, hand to her lips, trembling with shock.

"Come on." Patricia took Pinky's hand. They made their way down the stairs and through the crowd. She got as close as she could to Brett's impact site. She could hear him moan. The position of his body was not anywhere near normal.

Wait, he *moaned*! He wasn't dead . . . yet.

By now the sound of an ambulance siren could be heard in the distance.

Dr. Bender was talking to Brett, close to him on the ground. He used his mad-scientist stethoscope several times, pressing it gently to Brett's back.

Next to them, on his knees, was Brett's brother Eric. "I'm so sorry, so sorry, Brett? Brett?" Brett's mother and father were standing there, the father holding the mother away. She was crying.

Paul appeared at last, along with the emergency personnel, who ran across the outside lawn guided by Lurch the butler. They went to work on Brett immediately. Paul helped clear everyone away. He looked into Patricia's eyes with a haunting intensity. He didn't ask her to move.

Patricia turned away while they put all the collars and straps and boards together. Then came the sound of Brett being moved, which was the most awful sound she'd ever heard, even worse than the sound of him hitting the ground.

Once he was on the board, they carried him to the ambulance. He had all sorts of head stabilizers and neck braces on, but Patricia ran next to them all the way to the driveway. She leaned toward him just as they were about to lift him into the ambulance.

"I love you, Brett. You're going to be okay," she called. What a lame thing to say. It was obvious from what she saw that he had at least a broken leg.

In the aftermath of the ambulance screaming away, she felt completely numb. Pinky found her and led her to where the Volvo was parked. Paul was already in the driver's seat.

They exchange no look, no words. Patricia climbed in the back seat with Pinky, whose flamingo head stuck out the top of the sunroof. Pinky put her feathered wing around Patricia. They drove down the long paved driveway of the Nordquist estate, stately rhododendrons on either side of the road creating dark green shadows.

"Take me to the hospital," she demanded.

Without a word, Paul turned the car toward the entrance to the highway that would take them to Bellevue General Hospital.

Hard as had been to leave Patricia at the hospital alone, Pinky had to get out of her flamingo costume. Paul had made sure Patricia had cab fare. Their exchange had been awkward. He'd wanted her to come back with him, but knew she wouldn't. He also made sure she had her cell phone tucked in that tiny beaded purse. He made her understand he would be calling if he didn't hear from her by ten-thirty.

Back at the house, he and Pinky were nervous as skittish cats. "Unzip me, please." Pinky held up her wings and turned her back to Paul. "What a hell of a party."

"Why were you with all those people, Pinky? What happened anyway?"

"Honestly, I'd seen you take Patricia upstairs and when Brett and his brother went in for round two Lizbeth went completely nuts. She went from calling Brett names to throwing her arms around Eric, then Brett, then she swore she was going to yank all of Patricia's hair out. When she headed up the stairs at a full run, Brett went after her, then Eric after Brett. I followed to try and warn Patricia."

"What a scene." Paul helped Pinky climb out of her costume.

Pinky left the room to get to the bathroom after being trapped in her pink prison. Paul made two cups of tea from the hot water he'd turned on when they'd returned. It was an old habit of his, coming home and turning on the kettle for tea for his girls.

He brought Pinky a smooth, fat white cup of steaming green tea with ginger. They sat across from each other, holding the hot cups in their cold hands.

"What happened out there on the balcony, Paul?" Pinky looked him straight in the eye.

"Are you sitting here asking me if I pushed Brett off the balcony? As much as I despise the guy, it wasn't me. I thought maybe it was you."

"Attempted murder is best *not* attempted in a flamingo costume." She smiled weakly and took a sip of her tea.

"Maybe it was just an accident," Paul said.

"Maybe not. Whatever it was, it was done in a moment of temporary insanity and alcohol-induced stupidness. I guess that's why these rich boys have limos—so they don't have to concern themselves with driving anywhere, seeing as they drink half the day away."

"It catches up with you eventually."

"Most of us learned that somewhere around eighteen, or maybe as late as twenty-one, if we were delayed in our ability to score beer."

"What does Patricia see in Brett, Pinky? I can't understand it."

"The stuff that dreams are made of," Pinky answered. "And what about you and Patricia on that balcony? That was very Rhett Butler of you, my dear, carrying her off and up the stairs like that."

Paul answered as vaguely as possible. "Whatever happened, it shifted quickly back into Brett's corner."

"Oh yeah, dropping off a balcony really trumps a kiss for attention-getting tactics."

"He didn't throw himself off there on purpose, Pinky." Paul, despite himself, laughed.

"True. I wonder if anyone helped him over. Enough people would have liked to see him out of the picture, that's for sure."

"Don't you think it was just an accident?"

"I guess. Dr. Bender said Brett probably survived because he was so drunk. The drunk, it seems, bounce better."

"And you and Dr. Bender hit it off? This is the guy who turned our Patricia into Jean Harlow?"

"He's a research scientist. He's just doing his job." Pinky smiled. "Let's stick to *your* love life. What now?"

"Things will work out however they are supposed to. You can't force love." Paul got up and untied his cape.

"This from the man who carried a girl up the stairs over his shoulder. Well, I can tell you that a wise move on your part would be to pack up some regular clothes for Patricia and drive back to the hospital."

"I'm way ahead of you on that one." Paul walked over and left his tea in the kitchen. "Help me grab some jeans and a sweater for her and I'll head out."

Pinky was very helpful and got a change of clothes together for Patricia while Paul washed up and got out of his pirate duds.

As he got in the car, he looked back at his house with the amber and green Frank Lloyd Wright–style stained-glass windows flanking the front door. The glowing porch light shone golden over the entryway and the landscaping lights added another layer of beauty to the darkness. The house was so welcoming, but partly because of who lived there.

Until now. Things were going to be very different now. It was obvious that Patricia had chosen Brett. He had to deal with that. Was he so selfish that he'd make her life miserable because she'd chosen another man?

He loved her too much for that. But standing by and watching her with Brett was going to kill him.

At the same time, she probably never needed him as much as she did now. How did life get so complicated?

Chapter Twelve

There is little choice in a barrel
of rotten apples.
Shakespeare

The only other time Patricia had been in the intensive care ward was when her grandfather had been recovering from open-heart surgery and had ended up dying in the hospital. She wasn't fond of looking through glass windows at people in pain.

Brett was trussed up like a turkey in splints and pulleys and traction devices. His parents were by his side. The nurse had kindly told her what was going on, even though she couldn't go in. Brett was under observation for twenty-four hours, being monitored for internal injuries and head trauma, but amazingly had survived his fall with only a broken leg, a broken jaw and two cracked ribs.

Patricia gazed through the glass and thought about those last minutes on the balcony before Brett had tumbled off. Paul's kiss was stuck in her mind. And his words. She was all mixed up.

"Amazing, isn't it?" Lizbeth Summers came up behind her so quietly Patricia gave a little start.

"What?" Patricia snapped.

"That he could take a fall like that and only come out with a few broken bones," Lizbeth answered.

Patricia turned to look at Lizbeth. "I'm sorry I was rude to you at the party, and I'm sorry I slapped you."

"Well, I'm sorry I slapped you first. I was stupidly drunk."

Lizbeth looked beautiful in her dark brown coat with its black fur trim. Even on a hospital visit she looked great. Lizbeth was a woman you knew would marry well. Patricia realized she still had on her Jean Harlow costume.

"I was, too. I'm not much of a drinker." Patricia returned a weak smile.

Eric Nordquist followed shortly after Lizbeth. He nodded to Patricia, and went into the room to join his parents.

Once they were alone again, Lizbeth looked at Patricia with an oddly calm gaze. "You didn't push him off the balcony, did you?"

"No. Did you?"

"Not me. I couldn't see much, but I'm sort of thinking he just tripped over the dog. They have a greyhound that raced up the stairs after us. He's such a slim sort of ghost dog, probably no one even saw him."

"I didn't notice a dog."

Lizbeth gazed through the window at Brett and his family. "Look, Patricia, let's lay our cards out on the table. Brett and I have been on and off for two years. I told him there'd be no more fun until he made a commitment and gave me an engagement ring."

"So I heard."

"Oh yeah, leave it to the great Nordquist grapevine." Lizbeth sighed.

Patricia heard a bitter edge in Lizbeth's comment. She'd never thought maybe being the great Lizbeth Summers might not be so happy. Wait a minute; this girl could have any guy she wanted. She was beautiful and . . . she was talented in something, right? "How did you end up working for Nordquist's, Lizbeth?"

"I needed a job. Clothes are the only thing I know anything about. That and parties."

"Aren't your folks rich?" Patricia blurted out. "I mean, you seem so . . ."

"Of the manor born?" Lizbeth laughed. "I won a contest that put me through modeling and finishing school. So I learned how to use the right silverware and walk and dress rich, but my parents are divorced.

"My mother couldn't afford to send me to college. I wasn't much of a student, so I've had to rely on my looks. And in case you haven't thought about it, those looks don't last forever. A girl has to get her ducks in a row before she starts to fade."

"So do you think Brett will ask you to marry him?" Patricia felt a chill run over her as she said the words.

"Either Brett or Eric. I don't much care which, although I'm starting to be partial to Eric."

"Did you start going out with Eric to make Brett jealous?"

"Sort of. We've all just known each other for the past few years and I decided to hedge my bets. I just want to marry into this family one way or the other. And honestly, I was very mad at Brett for trying to play me for a sap by, well, dating *you*."

Patricia felt a rush of heat run into her cheeks. "I guess I'm an idiot."

"Why? You stand to make out pretty well. Especially with Brett laid up like this. He'll need some comforting. I'm not very good at that sort of thing."

"You don't care?"

"If things work out for you, I'll still have Eric. If Brett has some sort of awakening, I'll get that ring. Either way, I have to look out for my future. Sounds cold, doesn't it?"

"Frankly?" Patricia looked over at Lizbeth's calm face as she looked through the glass at Brett and his family. "Yes. But I have to wonder about myself, when it comes right down to it. I completely understand your ambitions."

Lizbeth turned to look at Patricia. "He's got that whole exciting bad-boy thing going on, doesn't he? It's very attractive. Add the family money in there, and you've got quite a package. We had some fun times. Hard to tame, though," she said.

"Sounds to me like I better watch my back." Patricia stared down the hallway. She felt like crying.

"Who knows, we could end up related. So, hey, I guess we'd better not be slapping each other for a while. At least till after the weddings." Lizbeth actually gave her a pat on the shoulder.

Eric came out of the room looking very upset. "Damn," was all he said, shaking his head as he closed the door behind him.

"It wasn't your fault, sweetie. It was just an accident." Lizbeth looped her arm through Eric's and fell into step beside him as he walked away. She turned long enough to wink at Patricia. The famous Lizbeth saunter was still apparently functioning fine, even at this late hour.

Patricia looked through the glass at Brett. Despite what Lizbeth had said, she believed she was different than her. She loved Brett. She could tame him. He just needed to grow up a little.

She felt like she was in one of Paulie's operas. Everything was so convoluted and twisted.

"Patricia?"

She turned to see Paul coming down the hall toward her. He'd ditched his pirate costume. Her heart skipped a beat thinking of the kiss they'd shared. Why did he have to make everything even more complicated?

The closer he got, the worse Patricia looked. That pale blonde thing had passed over into deathly pallor. "I brought the car." He came up beside her. "And I brought you some clothes. Jeans and a sweater, and here, a coat." He slipped her pretty blue wool coat over her bare shoulders and leaned closer. "Even Jean Harlow has to warm up sometimes."

"Thanks for the coat, but I'll just change at home." Patricia rejected the bag of clothing, setting it on the floor. "Why did you kiss me tonight, Paul?"

He went dead silent. She'd hit him directly between the eyes and he hadn't seen it coming. Except for that very uncomfortable crackle in the air between them.

He took her by the shoulders and looked into her eyes. "I told you why."

She looked up at him. "We promised each other we wouldn't mess up our friendship."

"I'm sorry. Things have changed. I've changed." Paul said.

Patricia looked away awkwardly. "You really know how to make a woman weak in the knees. I bet all the girls come back for more," she said. Then she looked like she realized she'd said something stupid.

He let her go. "Some yes, some no," he said with a smile. "Come on. We'll just forget about it."

"I can't leave yet."

"Patricia, it's late. They won't let you in to see him tonight," he reasoned.

"I know. I don't know. I'm confused."

"Do I have to throw you over my shoulder again and carry you out of here?"

"Probably. Just take me home, I guess. Take me home before I change my mind."

Paul put his arm around her shoulder. "How is ol' Brett anyway?" They walked down the hall together, Paul steering her down the right corridors.

"A few broken bones, hopefully no internal

damage. Pretty miraculous. Lizbeth said he might have tripped over the family dog."

"Funny, I thought I heard a dog yelp. So he wasn't pushed?"

She glanced at him. "You'd be a suspect if they thought that. Or Eric, I guess."

"You talked to Lizbeth?"

"A very enlightening conversation. She reminds me of Carmen."

"The opera Carmen?"

"Yes, you know, how Carmen was so beautiful and all the men buzzed around her like bees to a flower?"

"Let's hope the rejected object of her affection doesn't come back to murder her later."

"It's all so *East of Eden*, you know? Her and Brett and Eric."

"That can't end well; it usually doesn't."

"Paul, life isn't an opera."

"Right." Paul punched the button on the elevator to take them to the parking level. "Life is a *soap* opera."

Pinky balanced her chin in her hands, elbows on the kitchen counter, and watched Paul dish out breakfast omelets and fried potatoes. Patricia poured coffee for three. It was a very domestic scene all around. Except for the odd silence between Paul and Patricia.

"Order up, ladies, no diet plates this morning," Paul said.

Pinky jumped down and helped gather plates. She'd already set the table for their usual Sunday brunch. "Look at my mini-pumpkins, boys and girls, aren't I the talented little centerpiece girl?"

"Lovely, Pinky. I like the leaves all over the table." Patricia set down the coffee and took her place.

"Straight from the Japanese maple in our own yard."

As Pinky watched her two friends talk about anything but the events of the previous day, she wondered how many more Sunday brunches they would have together. Paul was flying to New York tomorrow, Patricia was on some kind of crash course with destiny, and she had been toying with the idea of what it would be like to sew baby dresses for her own little brood of Benders.

James Bender had called late last night after Paul had left to pick up Patricia and asked if she was okay after the shocking balcony scene, and if they might see each other for a noncostumed date. He'd asked if she'd like to go to an afternoon matinee at the Grand Illusion. They were showing the 1946 *Abbott and Costello Meet Frankenstein,* along with the 1992 Francis Ford Coppola's *Bram Stoker's Dracula.*

She almost fell in love with him over the phone. But Pinky was torn. After all, it was Halloween for real now. They usually decorated the outside of the house all day long and got ready for the trick-or-treaters, and Paul would make up a big pot of his famous seafood gumbo. For some reason, she had his gumbo and Halloween permanently linked together.

"Brett is being released from the hospital today. I talked to him earlier. I'm going over to his house and watch videos and take his mind off his pain." Patricia poked at her potatoes and didn't look anyone in the eye.

"What he really needs is a bottle of Vicodin and an AA meeting." Paul stabbed his potatoes full-on.

"Shut up, Paulie." Patricia gave him a grit-her-teeth smile.

"Now, kids," Pinky said. "As it happens, I've been asked out on a date. I'm going to the fun and freaky movie fest at our favorite theater with Dr. James Bender."

"*My* Dr. Bender?" Patricia asked, her fork in midair.

"I prefer to think of him as *my* Dr. Bender for now."

"Wow. That's very cool, Pinky. A date. Finally."

"Shut *up*, Paulie, I'm very picky."

"I'm just kidding. Well, hey, that makes all three of us. I'm getting packed to leave for New York, Patricia's on a mission of mercy, and you're out to the movies."

"Will you make gumbo anyway?" Pinky whined.

"Already started the stock."

"Maybe Dr. B can come over after the movies and have a bowl," Pinky said absentmindedly.

"Absolutely. I'll carve up a few pumpkins and put them out on the porch. When you and the good doctor get back, we'll fend off the little angels and devils with Tootsie Rolls and Dots. Rot their little teeth out one more year."

"I'll try and come back early, too. Brett will probably need a whole lot of sleep anyway," Patricia said quietly.

Paul's "one more year" comment made Pinky choke up. "Things are changing, folks, we might not have many Halloweens left together." She put down her fork and grabbed a Kleenex out of her flannel shirt pocket. She loved the way her vintage western shirts had lots of pockets. She needed tissues on hand these days.

"Pinky, honey, we'll be okay. We will take a blood oath to always meet on Halloween, just like spooky old spirits. We can even do that when we're all dead. We'll haunt this house and scare the crap out of whoever lives here in the future." Paul reached over and put his hand on Pinky's arm.

Patricia was quiet. Pale and quiet.

"Well, are you going to haunt the place with us, Miss Blithe Spirit? Miss Charmed One?"

"I will come and haunt the house with you. I promise. Things are just so crazy right now," Patricia answered. She twisted in her chair and looked at both her friends. It had been a wonderful five-year run, but it was time for a change. She wanted that change. She loved them, but it was time to move on.

"Girls, why don't you come to New York with

me? You can fly standby and I'll get you a room. You can shop and look at those early Christmas decorations and eat great food," Paul said.

"Can't, I'm booked to go for Thanksgiving already," Pinky answered.

"You'll be working all day, Paul," Patricia said.

"True. But Patricia, you've never been to New York. It's time you went. Pinky, you'd love it, too. Go see your folks. I know it's short notice, but hey, we're young. And spontaneous. We're young and spontaneous, right?"

"I'm going to have to take a rain check, Paulie," Patricia said. She got up from the table and cleared her dishes. "Thank you for a wonderful breakfast. Your cooking has been the highlight of my life for five years."

"Well, don't act like it's the last meal you'll ever eat here," Pinky snapped.

"I didn't mean it that way."

"I just hope Jimmy Bender can cook as well as you, Paul, because I can't just hire you to be my personal chef for the rest of my life, can I?" Pinky asked.

"It sounds tempting, Pinkster, but I will have to pass."

"Paul, is the car free?" Patricia asked.

"Help yourself. You don't need it, do you, Pinky?" Paul glanced at Pinky.

"I believe my date has wheels of his own." Pinky made a grand gesture. "So have at it. Before you know it, Brett will buy you your own," Pinky said.

"Why would he do that?" Patricia turned to look at Pinky.

"Depends on how nice you are to him." Pinky smirked. "I'm sure he'd love to reward you for being a faithful girlfriend. And if you're *real* nice, it'll be an expensive car!"

"Thanks for the support, Pinky. You're a real live Halloween witch today," Patricia said.

Pinky stood up from the table. "First rule of best friends. Listen to the wisdom of those who know you well. And you are ignoring all our good advice, Patricia. You're blondeness has gone to your head. Brett is only going to hurt you. It's like a blinking neon sign that only you can't seem to see. Well, hey, Patsky, *BLINK, BLINK, BLINK!*"

"You want everything to go *your* way." Patricia gripped the back of the sofa. "Not long ago you understood my goals."

"Goals? I won't even address that. What about your self-respect?"

"Self-respect can be damn lonely. We both know that. And since I have turned into a crazy blonde, I might as well use it before I fade back into invisibility."

"Just be careful what you use it *for*, Patricia. And when you are done, I hope you have friends left to pick up the pieces when Brett kicks you in the teeth." Pinky stomped out of the room. After many stomping footsteps, her door slammed downstairs.

Patricia felt her head pounding. "I'm right, you know. Women only have a short span of years to attract the right man." What a stupid thing to say to Paul.

"There are other schools of thought on that," Paul said quietly.

"Can't one person in this house just support me in pursuing my dreams?"

"We do support you, Patricia. But sometimes we might not agree with you. I'm beginning to see something about how life gives us these paths, and if you take one and it's extremely difficult and chaos surrounds every step, then it might not be the right one. It's like a big hint.

Then you take this other one and not that it's totally easy, but things just fall into place all around you like some roadside orange-vested guide with a big wand saying, *Yes, go this way!* Do you get what I mean?"

"Oh, how very Zen. Yes, I get you, but I can't tell the difference between those two yet."

"That's the hard part."

Patricia paused and took a breath. Her voice softened. "Thank you for the offer to go to New York. I hope we all get to go there soon. Are you going to see your family while you're there?"

"I wouldn't miss one of my Nana Costello's meals for anything. And since I'm on the other side of the world now, she'll roll out the red carpet. Prodigal grandson and all that jazz."

"It's cool you have a family like that."

"I know. I don't take that for granted."

"My sisters are okay, but my parents, well, you know, I've told my sad tale. You two have been a great family to me."

"Things are coming to a crossroads, aren't they?" Paul said.

"I think so. I have to go pretty soon. Thanks for being you, Paul."

"The gumbo will be waiting for you when you get back," he said.

She got herself out of the room without any further discussion. All that talk about paths really made her think. Patricia felt like a window of opportunity had opened for her and it wouldn't remain open for long.

In the dressing table mirror her hair was still cool blonde. She'd been watching it carefully, having taken her last pills, wondering if it would suddenly turn back.

When she'd visited Dr. Bender, some of the other people had developed darker roots, but they had started their course of experimental drugs earlier than she had.

Sometimes she thought she saw a shadow of brunette in there, but then her eyes would play tricks on her and it wasn't there at all.

Everyone treated her differently now. Before, at work, only a few people in the store even knew she existed. Now the guys all eyed her and the women stared when she passed, checking out her outfit and makeup as most women do to really beautiful women.

Really *beautiful*? She wouldn't go that far, but she had changed. The whole color of her life had changed, and sometimes when she thought of things she did, she wondered why she did them. It was almost like the drug had affected her inhibitions along with her hair color. Talk about a deadly combination, the weakening of your former conservative self paired with a whole new look. Blonde and dangerous.

She brushed her hair into smooth curls. She looked good in colors she hadn't thought of before. Like pale blue and soft beige and white. Patricia applied some lipstick, wiped it off, and tried another color. She wanted to look her best for Brett. She went for a light bronze color to go with her whole pale and beige look.

Her friends were probably right. She didn't belong in Brett's world. But this would be the only time in her life to test that fact out for herself. She had to know just how far she could get before Brett found her out for the imposter she was: a quiet brunette masquerading as a daring blonde.

Chapter Thirteen

Did my heart love 'til now? Forswear it sight, for I never saw true beauty till tonight.

Shakespeare

Food tasted better in New York. Jazz sounded better in a Miles Davis New York way. Nathan's hot dogs tasted better, and best in the world came from the Coney Island stand. He and Pinky had agreed on that. Pizza was better at Frank's in the Bronx, and Manhattan had the best deli food in the universe.

He'd love to keep this job forever just so he could keep traveling back to New York and Milan and all the places he loved to go. He had to get Patricia back here and show her everything he loved about the city.

Honestly, his job was easy. He had an eye for goods and was well trained by his grandfather in the art of navigating around the Garment District.

Paul took the hot dog from the vendor and squirted a great deal of mustard down the length. He bit in and let the nostalgic taste run around his head. Sometimes the simple things stayed with you longer than the fancy ones.

He supposed it had made sense for his father to follow the career trail to Microsoft in Washington State, but how they could have ever moved away from their families and this place was hard to understand.

Maybe his father had been putting some distance between him and his own father. Paul knew Pops was pretty ticked that his only son hadn't gone into the family business manufacturing coats. But his dad had been a geeky intellectual guy and loved his computers. At least his aunts had loved the coat business, so hey. Pops got his family-footsteps moment.

And Paul knew it made Pops so happy when

he came to town, the grandson who picked up that "rag business" gene—so they said. He knew his grandparents doted on him. It was good to be the doted-on brother. Nick got that from Mom because he was a little slow and Mom tended to overprotect him as a kid. He and Mitch were equals in the eyes of the parents, so that left the grandparents to dote on him.

Nick had Jenny now and Paul knew that was a great partnership. Jenny was supportive of everything Nick did. Really, Nick was doing the best of any of them. He was a terrific builder and he was in his element in the Northwest with the construction boom still going strong.

Paul finished his hot dog and went for a walk around town. He didn't have appointments till tomorrow and he wanted to enjoy the city as much as possible while he was here. He had a few hours till dinner at Nana and Pops's house.

Nana Costello would want to know every bit of gossip about every member of the family. When's the wedding with Jenny and Nick, when is Mitchell finishing college, and of course when, oh, when was Paulie going to get married? How were Pinky and Patricia?

Paul thought about Patricia's new blonde hair. He thought about telling Nana about it, but she might not approve of the experimental drug thing. He thought about talking to Pops about why he couldn't seem to stop thinking about Patricia.

Their advice was important. And it was important that he get Nana and Pops to tell him their own history. How they'd been orphans from Florence in World War II and brought over to the United States together as children. How they'd ended up living on the same block with different adoptive parents, through the Catholic Church.

It was so amazing how they'd never forgotten each other and went through school in the same neighborhood, always watching out for each other. Childhood sweethearts of an even more touching variety than usual.

Their story pulled at him. There was something about the feel of the city and how many stories like theirs were floating in the air.

He should really get to work and write it, and soon, because they weren't getting any younger.

Every time he'd been back to New York, twice a year now at least for the last five years, he'd been more and more fascinated with the stories Nana and Pops told him. Maybe it was time to do something about it. He had writing skills; he was the logical person to do this. Then it would be there, written and in place for his children and their children. If he ever had any children.

Paul stared up at the murky sky of Manhattan. The November chill was on. He pulled his coat zipper higher. At least in the Northwest they'd figured out coats. A North Face jacket could really do a lot more for you against the Manhattan chill than his dad's old wool overcoat used to do.

Paul thought about his mother's parents, both gone now. Which just went to show how people slip away so quickly and quietly, taking their stories with them.

He looked into the warmly lit interior of a French café as he passed. There was a couple sitting next to the window having an argument. But just before Paul stepped out of their sightline, the man reached over and put his hand on the woman's. Then she looked at him and leaned over to kiss his cheek.

Paul kept walking. He needed to start making some stories of his own.

He stopped in front of an antique store window and peered in at a mint-condition Barbie lunch box. Oh my God, it was the 1962 black-vinyl-with-ponytail Barbie. Pinky had been searching for this very lunch box for the last three years, haunting eBay and some of her other lunch box sites on the Internet.

He pushed open the door and an old-fashioned shop bell tinkled to signal his entrance. A dapper-looking old gentleman with a bow tie sat behind the counter with a tray full of watches in front of him. He was tinkering with a gold pocket watch. "Hello," he said.

Paul nodded to him and tried to act cool. Pinky had taught him how to just hover around whatever it was you wanted with a calm air so they didn't mark you as a sap who would pay any price for the object of your desire.

He spent a few minutes poking around, then picked up the lunch box. Wow, a hundred forty bucks. That was steep.

"Are your prices negotiable?" he held up the lunch box for the guy to see.

"Can you imagine a child's lunch pail for all the fuss?" He had cool old Jewish accent.

"My housemate has quite the collection."

"Bring it here," he said.

Paul made his way to the man's counter spot and put the box down. He poked around, opened it up, and looked at the tag. "What'll you give me?"

"A hundred?"

"Hundred twenty."

"Hundred ten," Paul countered.

"Sold." The man slapped the counter good-naturedly.

Paul pulled out his wallet.

"So this housemate, why don't you just marry her instead of live in sin?"

Paul cracked up laughing. "She's just a pal. I actually have two women I live with."

"Oh, like that *Three's Company* show."

"Yes, just like that." Paul notice the owner talked about the old show like it was still running. Well, probably on some retro station it was still running.

"One of them must be good enough to marry, right?"

"Yes, one of them is." Paul stopped with his credit card in midair and couldn't believe what he'd just said.

"See?"

"She's seeing someone else."

"So what? You live with her. Get the upper hand. You can push this other guy right out of the picture. You gotta go for it when it's right. I'm Sid, by the way."

"Paul Costello." He shook Sid's hand, then handed him his Visa card.

"Like the Abbott and Costello fella? Are you related?"

"No, my grandfather had a coat factory. Costello Coats, remember?"

"Oh yeah, pretty big back in the old days, then they retired, yes? And the daughters took over."

"Yes. My grandparents live in the old neighborhood still."

"You tell them hello from Sid." Sid handed Paul his business card. "But you can't go home with a gift for one girl and not the other. What does she like? The one you are going to marry?"

The one he was going to marry. Very funny. Brett Nordquist seemed to be first in line for that honor. But he was right about the gift. How stupid of him. He had to bring Patricia a gift back, too. Not just handbag samples. "She likes photography, books, movies? Old things," Paul answered.

"Jewelry. All women love jewelry."

"True." Paul followed Sid to his jewelry case. His eye caught one particular piece that seemed to shout Patricia out at him. It was a vintage amber and gold necklace that would no doubt make Patricia swoon. Those where her favorite colors.

He thought of her hazel eyes. Her original eyes, before the contacts. He loved those eyes, glasses and all. The necklace would bring out her eyes. If she'd stop with the blue contacts, or at least change to clear.

Sid went to his register and rang up Paul's sale, then used the swiper to run the credit card. "I'll wrap this up nice for you. And you know what? Here's how to get that girl. Ask her to marry you. That works every time. Ask me, I know, that's how I got my wife Rose. And she's a gem. How many years you've lived with these two?"

"Five." Paul wasn't sure what made him keep telling old Sid the details of his life.

"That's longer than some marriages these days. You know her already, so what are you waiting for?" Sid waved his hand at Paul.

What *was* he waiting for? "God, I don't know. I need to think about it, I guess."

"Think? No man should think about marriage. Otherwise they always think *no,* then they end up alone in an old-folks home. My Rosie told me that."

Sid handed Paul the lunch box all wrapped in tissue, and the necklace in a pretty box, carefully placed in a paper bag with the shop's logo on it.

"Here you go. Promise you'll think about the girl. If you think too long, the other guy will get her for sure. And maybe that's not so good, right?"

"Thanks, Sid, I'll think about that."

"Don't think too long."

Sid waved him out the shop door. Paul stepped into the cold.

Shit. Some old guy in an antique store all the way across the country hit it right on the head. He knew why he kept thinking about Patricia, dreaming about Patricia, and worrying all the time—he was so in love he could hardly stand it. He wanted her to be his, just his, forever.

Paul stalked down the street, angry with himself. He'd probably loved Patricia for a long time and been too much of an idiot to see it.

It had nothing to do with her being blonde, and all this time he'd been beating himself up for having fantasies about her since she turned blonde, like he was a shallow dude who only liked her for her new look. But the truth was his feelings were already there, just lurking in the background. She'd just brought them up to the surface when she'd turned stark raving blonde and pulled him into her bed one night.

Patricia tried on the prettiest necklace she'd ever seen. It was a one-carat trillian-cut diamond pendant clad in a platinum setting that hung from a platinum chain. Diamonds really were a girl's best friend, especially if you got commission on the sale.

"That's lovely on you," the gentleman said.

"Thank you. You can see just where the pendant would hang on your . . . lady friend." Patricia phrased things carefully in fine jewelry.

"My wife." The man's eyes twinkled in amusement.

"Your wife, of course. And here are the matching earrings." She drew out a black velvet board and pulled the earring box out of the case with two very sparkly trillian diamond earrings nestled against the black velvet box. Black velvet was good for jewelry. She felt a little giddy for a moment, thinking of the amount of the sale if he took everything, pendant and earrings. A very sweet sale. She felt Madam subtly keeping an eye on her.

"A very special holiday present, isn't it?" She turned the box into the light and let the stunning stones pick up their maximum sparkle. "Would you like a closer look?" Patricia offered him a loupe to look through and magnify the stones. "These are particularly nice stones, with no visible flaws even under magnification. That's hard to find in a stone this size."

She felt him hesitate for a moment, so she leaned forward and unfastened the chain from behind her neck, then laid it out on the board for him to see. He smiled, then reached over and took the loupe to examine the entire set.

Patricia saw one of her blonde hairs on the velvet, stuck in the clasp of the chain. As she swiftly pulled it away, she thought just for a moment that the very tip of it was darker, right by the root. She felt a tingling flash of fear, then covered it up with a smile. "See how the platinum setting makes it look like no setting at all? It just looks like a floating diamond, doesn't it?"

"Very lovely," he said. His gaze rose up from his close examination of the diamonds and back to Patricia. "And she deserves it for putting up with me all of these years."

"How long have you been married?"

"Thirty years this Thanksgiving."

"That is truly an accomplishment."

"More on her part than mine, believe me." The gentleman smiled softly. "Wrap them up pretty for me, won't you?"

A soft but audible buzz went around behind her. Madam stepped up beside her and thanked the gentleman. "We'll have these done up for you in no time. Patricia can complete the details." She swept the jewelry into her hands and scurried up the stairs while Patricia took possession of the man's credit card. Now let's hope it went through, she thought. It wouldn't be the first time a shopper's desires had exceeded their credit card limit.

"Thank you, Mr. Watkins, I know your wife will be thrilled."

The card was swiped, and the approval code

flashed on the screen. Kind of like the winning lottery numbers. She wrote the code down and turned with a smile for him to sign the charge slip. She was trying not to dance a jig behind the counter. He signed it with flair, and seemingly without any regrets. By the time they'd finished their transaction, Madam returned with two beautifully gift-wrapped boxes.

"Happy Holidays, Mr. Watkins." Madam handed the boxes to Patricia, then held out their special black bag while Patricia slipped the two items in. Patricia walked out from behind the counter and handed the bag to Mr. Watkins, who then departed with a pleasant nod. Patricia went back through the swinging gate to stand next to Madam. Damn, that was one good sale.

Madam waited till he was out of sight, then clasped Patricia's hands between her own and *did* that little jig. It was so funny to see the dignified Madam with her little tiny feet tap-dancing on the carpet. Patricia noticed Madam had on little red shoes with straps, like dancing shoes.

"That's a nice bonus for you, Patricia. You've done very well, my girl. You are a quick learner." Madam seemed to recover from her gleeful moment and smoothed back her slightly loosened gray hair into behaving again. "Now go have a long lunch and enjoy yourself."

Patricia walked up to the loft to retrieve her beaded black sweater. Mandy gave her a cocky little look, but Patricia just smiled at her. She'd have to hunt down Pinky and tell her all about her great sale. She grabbed her squishy red clutch out of the lock-drawer and made tracks out of the fine jewelry department.

"Take as long as you want, dear," Madam called after her.

What a shame Paulie wasn't in town, they could all have a celebration lunch at the Cove, their favorite hole in the wall a few blocks away. She missed him.

The escalator seemed slow as molasses in January today. She passed by the snotty second-floor designer department and walked past lingerie to the other end. Out of the corner of her eye, as she tried not to look, she saw Lizbeth in a striking red sheath, showing a sexy black lace teddy to some sleazy-looking guy. Poor thing. No wonder she had ambitions of escaping her job in style.

Of course, she herself had the same ambition. But she wanted love, too. She did. She wasn't the kind of person to marry for money, was she? As she stepped onto the up escalator she glanced back at Lizbeth. Lizbeth caught her eye and gave her a little wave—a very Apple Blossom Queen wave. Her white chiffon sleeves billowed elegantly as they puffed out of the arm openings of the red sheath. It made her look like Lauren Bacall, but Lizbeth was even prettier than Lauren.

Patricia laughed at herself for always thinking in terms of old movie stars instead of modern ones. She hit second-floor men's and their little men's world, and headed toward Pinky's behind-the-scenes alteration world.

She poked her head through the door. "Pinky?"

"Miss Pinky in bridal." One of the very businesslike Korean ladies looked up at her and delivered the information. Pinky had learned to speak phrases from several different languages working in this department: Russian, Thai, Korean, and one other from a very interesting woman—Polish, maybe.

"Thank you," Patricia answered. Oh my God, bridal; the department that every girl in Nordquist's casually finds her way to after she turns twenty-five, Patricia thought. Just looking, they all say. Just hunting for Red October.

Just got my submarine periscope up in case I catch *the guy*.

Including her. Just having my little Vera Wang, Kenneth Pool moment, excuse me while I have a Priscilla of Boston breakdown. Bridal had its own special corner on the third floor along with ladies' apparel, children's apparel, and children's shoes.

They must have figured to catch the brides-to-be on the way out with the pretty pink layettes and cribs. Then they'd be mommies-to-be faster and come back to the source like salmon to the spawning grounds.

Patricia thought they should have put bridal on six with china, linens, and the restaurant for a quick drink after the fitting, and of course occasionally Santa Claus would be up there as well, but they picked three.

There it was, the rustle of billowing silk, the scent of fear, The bridal department. Patricia slowly made her way around the sample gown displays and back toward the dressing rooms. Pinky would be on her knees, no doubt, marking the hem of some eager girl's gown.

But Pinky bumped right into her. "*Patricia,* what brings you to bridal? Daydreaming?"

"I'm after *you*. "I made a big fat sale and I'm celebrating. Can I take you to lunch at the Cove?"

"Free lunch always interests me, my friend. Care to browse before we go?"

"You?" Patricia couldn't believe it.

"I'm just window-shopping." She looked sheepish, which was hard for Pinky to do.

"Oh, are we stuck on a certain scientist?"

"We are stuck. He was a champ at the movies, and we haven't stopped talking since. That doc that turned you into a Q-Tip is quite the guy," Pinky said.

"So let's find the least offensive bridesmaid dresses and decide what we'd make each other wear," Patricia whispered.

They scurried like schoolgirls to the more colorful selections.

"Oooh, pleated silk." Pinky ran her fingers along the ruffled edges. Shall I put you in ice blue? I could have a snowflake wedding with white and ice blue and fake rabbit fur, or feathers or something. Although feathers make me look like a short Vegas showgirl."

"I'm sorry we fought. I'm glad we could all sit down yesterday to a bowl of Halloween gumbo and scare all the little trick-or-treater kids without even putting a costume on." Patricia gave Pinky a hug.

"I'm sorry, too. I was mean. I want you to know if you really think Brett is the man for you, I'll be your bridesmaid." Pinky hugged her back.

"Look at this one, it's a Lazaro. Oh my God, it's like a mocha latte coffee thing with whipped cream. It has a little train, even. And look how the white lace stands out against the coffee underskirt. Yummy," Pinky swooned.

"I'm seeing a whole new side of you." Patricia looked at her friend's happy expression and smiled.

"You've seen me go crazy in a fabric store before, I just have a deep admiration for textiles. And look at this, it has a lace jacket so my Russian shot-putter arms wouldn't stick out like neon."

"Oh, we can't pick the second dress we see, that's just not right." Patricia riffled through the racks, pushing hangers back to get a full view of each dress. "Bleack, bridesmaid's hell." She pulled a particularly fluffy peach-toned southern number out and showed Pinky.

"Promise me you'll never do that to me."

"Only if you keep being my friend through thick and thin."

"I swear no matter what shape Brett's penis is, I will still be your friend,"

They busted up laughing and kept bridesmaid-gown-shopping, which, of course, led Patricia into the actual wedding gown section.

She saw something that made her heart betray her shallow bridal-lust and her insides flip-flop with desire. "Pinky, oh God, Pinky, look at this." Pinky ran over and gasped. The bodice had thick gold and bronze beading over a taupe ivory silk.

"I couldn't even knock it off properly. It's so amazing. That beading is stunning. You could do a whole red-and-gold-and-coffee-colored December wedding."

"Still stuck on that coffee gown, are we? And wow, that's so soon. This December?"

"Why not? Money can do a whole lot to make things happen fast."

"I'd need a good six months. I could be a June bride," she said. "Otherwise how would I fill out all those blanks in the wedding planner books?"

"There is that small detail of getting Brett to

ask you to marry him, too." Pinky put her finger to her cheek and made a face at Patricia.

"Oh, *that* pesky detail."

"Plus he has to get his cast off."

"He's getting much better. Yesterday he ate tomato soup through a straw, right through the wired-up jaw."

"That must be exciting to watch. Here, try this on. It's your size. The new shrunken Patricia size."

"Twenty pounds off of me looks damn good."

"Are you done swallowing horse pills?"

"My time is up. Halloween was the last day."

"Oooh, that's spooky." Pinky raised her eyebrows. "So come on, try this on. I'll tell Ginny we just want to play dress-up for a while."

Pinky disappeared while Patricia pulled the sample gown down off the rack by its padded hanger. She didn't dare look at the price tag. This was just for fun anyhow. The gown rustled as she carried it toward the dressing room.

Pinky was waiting for her in one of the large dressing rooms, holding a large crinoline petticoat. "These are better than the old ones. They're light as a feather, see?" Pinky held up the gossamer satin petticoat. "Slip this on." She held out the petticoat. "The gown is strapless, so I brought this." She handed Patricia a rather interesting strapless bra with a whole lotta push-up going on.

"Yikes." Patricia took the bra.

"Don't worry, you've got the goods for it. Speaking of goods, what did you sell today?"

"Three beautiful trillian-cut diamonds to one guy for his anniversary."

"What are we talking here?"

"Twenty-nine thousand dollars. Madam said I could have as long a lunch as I wanted."

"Good grief, I guess so. You earned your fine jewelry stripes today!" Pinky waited while Patricia stripped off her black skirt and sweater and climbed into the undergarments.

"Wow, so that's what holds these dresses up." She looked in the mirror.

"Suck your lips in—no lipstick on the samples." Pinky rolled the dress up and placed it over Patricia's head. It slid like the beautiful silk that it was, down her arms and into position. Pinky adjusted her and pulled the zipper up. They both looked in the mirror at her.

"Wow."

"I look like a princess. A real live princess. This skirt is amazing. Look at that back detail and the way it runches up around my rear." Patricia turned around on the small platform to see all sides of the dress.

"I know just the veil. I'll be right back. Then we'll go out to the big room. The light is better out there."

Pinky was gone long enough for Patricia to practically cry over herself in this beautiful gown. She closed her eyes and imagined walking down the aisle with her father, seeing her sisters and Pinky in her coffee latte dress waiting for her at the altar, and there would be the groom, waiting to take her arm.

Paul looked so handsome.

Wait, not Paul, Brett.

Pinky ran into the room, a veil flying in the wind of her speed.

"Geez, Pinks, there's no rush, I told you I can have as long as I want for lunch. And, well, we know you only work when you want to, so slow it down."

"Shhhh," Pinky shushed her. Pinky's big brown eyes were wild.

"Are we in trouble?"

"No, you just need to be quiet and listen."

Patricia rustled her princess self over to the dressing room door. Ear pressed to the thin wood, she heard voices.

"This one is pretty, but I want it fitted like a corset, just past my waist, then a big pouf of net on the bottom. Vera Wang had one in lace in her fall collection, with a dark green velvet ribbon," the familiar voice said. Patricia could hear the swish of sample dresses.

"Oh yes, but we're restocking for spring and summer at this point and I'm not sure if we can still order that model. You could buy the sample and have it fitted to you."

"That's Ginny," Pinky whispered.

"So what's the big deal?"

"Look for yourself."

Patricia opened the dressing room door just wide enough to peer out with one eye. She smoothed back her skirt so she could get closer. Standing on the raised platform with mirrors surrounding her was Lizbeth in all her glory, swathed in white lace, tall and graceful, her hair pulled up into a soft cascade of blonde curls.

"*Shit.*" Patricia shut the door. Her heart thumped. She felt sick and dizzy like she was going to faint.

"Yeah, that's what I said." Pinky sat down on the platform. "Didn't you tell me she'd take either brother?"

"I know she came to visit the Nordquists last night. I saw her pull into their driveway just as I was leaving. But I assumed it was Eric she was seeing. Mrs. Nordquist has been really nice to me lately, thanking me for cheering Brett up. I hope it hasn't been *Lizbeth* cheering him up."

"What a barracuda."

"I have no room to criticize. We want the same thing."

"Brett on a platter? You'd treat him better."

"I have to find out." Patricia took a deep breath, flung open the door, and stalked out of the dressing room. Lizbeth took a moment to recognize her, then looked like she was going to faint herself. Ginny actually stepped over and steadied her.

"So which one is it?" Patricia put her hands on her hips and looked up at Lizbeth, high on her pedestal platform.

"Eric proposed to me last night."

"Oh, thank *God.*" Patricia actually put her hand to her forehead in relief. "When's the wedding?"

"Christmas."

"So soon?"

"If I wait much longer I won't be able to fit into the dress."

Patricia took that all in. She didn't even want to ask. She didn't want to know. She felt dizzy again.

"When is *your* wedding?" Lizbeth looked practically ill.

Patricia waved her off. "I'm just playing dress-up."

Ginny gave her a look.

Lizbeth heaved a huge sigh, apparently relieved that Brett hadn't gone off and gotten engaged on her. Patricia figured that left Lizbeth in the trump position. She got her Nordquist man first, and no one could say Brett dumped her, because she dumped him first and held her ground.

She seemed to recover herself. "Get me out of this gown," she snapped at Ginny. "Well, if you play your cards right, we could have a double wedding." Lizbeth tried to act cheerful as she walked down the platform stairs.

"I'm in no rush." Patricia thought the idea of having a double wedding with Lizbeth sounded as tempting as liver and onions.

"You should be." Lizbeth looked her right in the eye. She gave a quick smile, then marched off to her dressing room with Ginny carrying the back of her train.

Patricia watched as Pinky gave Lizbeth a genuinely sympathetic look. Lizbeth huffed off.

Patricia motioned Pinky to come to her. She climbed up the platform and fluffed her skirts out in a very princesslike manner. Pinky stepped up next to her and adjusted the train to flow down nicely. Patricia gazed in the multiple mirrors, turning from side to side. The beaded bodice sparkled in the light.

"I think long gloves would look nice, don't you?"

"Did I hear what I thought I heard?" Pinky asked.

"Lizbeth Summers has gone and gotten herself preggers, Pinky. Wasn't she the resourceful girl?"

"Patricia, I hope for your sake that we either

turn a blind eye to who the coauthor of her pregnancy might be or get the facts straight and wish her well."

"Grab your cocoa mocha latte dress, Pinky, let's see what you'd look like as my maid of honor."

Chapter Fourteen

If I must die, I will encounter darkness as a bride, and hug it in mine arms.
Shakespeare

Patricia was thinking that their week-long girlfriend fest and celebration of her big Monday sale and her impending bonus was wearing thin. She had a slight buzz from the glass of Chardonnay she and Pinky had indulged in over at the Cove yet again. She giggled thinking of Pinky hemming all crooked for the rest of the day. At least it was Friday.

She hummed as she straightened chains, and Madam let her, smiling at her and nodding her head several times. Apparently, her golden status lasted at least for the week of the sale.

Patricia thought about going to Brett's after work. The drive in with Pinky had been in silence after Patricia told her she was once again going to the Nordquist house and Pinky would have to bus home—again. But then both of them had been morning-impaired and not too chatty.

She thought of the great chicken broth she'd stashed in a cooler in the car. Paul always kept stock ready to go in their freezer. She'd been spoon-feeding it to Brett all week.

It felt disloyal for her to feed Paul's broth to poor Brett, but it *was* an emergency. A guy could only eat so many things with his jaw wired shut, and since all of his party buddies had deserted him, she was the only remaining friend he had at the moment. Brett was starting to appreciate that.

Poor Lizbeth. Pregnant. Or had she planned it to trap Eric? Had Lizbeth tried it out on Brett first? Patricia hadn't had the nerve to ask Brett straight out. Truly, he'd looked miserable enough at the news that Eric was going to marry Lizbeth.

She also hadn't let her mind play with the

idea it might be Brett's baby—but on that thought her hand brushed a roll of gold bracelets. They slipped off the display and clattered against the glass shelf.

Madam looked up and gave her an eyebrow, but returned to her smile.

The person Patricia should ask was Lizbeth. Maybe she'd try to corner her on her break.

Speak of the she-devil, as Patricia raised her head from repositioning a dozen gold bracelets, Lizbeth stood right in front of her. She was dressed in pale green, which brought out her hazel green eyes and made her look even more beautiful. Although she did look a little green around the gills, as well as slightly stressed out.

"Hello, Patti."

"Lizbeth, what brings you to our little corner?" Patricia carefully replaced the last bracelet, then closed and locked the glass case.

"Is Mandy in today?"

"No, she took a three-day weekend," Patricia answered.

Lizbeth looked hesitant for a moment, as if she weren't sure of her best move.

"Congratulations on your engagement, Miss

Summers." Madam descended from the loft and leaned into the conversation.

"Thank you, Madam. News travels fast around here, doesn't it?"

"Virginia in bridal is a friend of mine. We often work closely together."

"Of course."

"Yes. Now, can I have Patricia show you that marquise diamond? I have two beautiful settings, a horseshoe shape in fourteen carat that shows it off to perfection, and another with a bit more pizzazz."

Patricia eyed Lizbeth. She saw that the temptation to look at the possibilities was overcoming her loyalty to Mandy.

"Sure. It can't hurt to look."

Madam stepped in the back room for a moment, then brought out a rolled-up cloth. Patricia had seen these before. All the loose stones were stored by size and cut in these rolls.

With a long pair of tweezers Madam plucked a beautiful and very large marquise-cut diamond out of the pile of sparkling stones. She put it on a tray with a little edge around it and let Patricia show it to Lizbeth. "I'll pull the settings and be right back."

"That is one gorgeous rock, Lizbeth." Patricia sort of slipped and got a bit too familiar. Good thing Madam didn't hear her.

Lizbeth laughed. "Diamonds are a girl's best friend, no doubt about it. And that goes double for me right now."

Patricia couldn't just lean in and ask her if it was Eric's baby, now, could she?

"Lizbeth." Patricia spoke in a low voice. "It is Eric's baby, isn't it?"

Lizbeth glanced up from her diamond loupe. She looked white as a sheet. There was a long pause. "It's definitely a Nordquist, that's for sure."

"Here we go," Madam said as she reappeared. Patricia could tell Madam sensed the electricity in the air. Madam chose to focus on the diamond ring instead.

"Patricia, let me show you something." She crowded in next to Patricia and brought out the two settings. With great skill she tweezered the diamond into place so it rested between the prongs that would eventually hold it in place.

The stone looked to be about three carats, as far as Patricia's still-untrained eye could tell. The setting was a polished gold, a very wide, modern, and striking affair. Lizbeth slipped it carefully on her finger, holding it over the velvet tray in case the stone popped out. It looked to Patricia like Lizbeth had done this before. *"Skilled with diamonds"* always looks great on a girl's résumé. Lizbeth had amazing nails. They were just the perfect length and she had a French manicure.

"Let's try it in the other one," Lizbeth said.

"You try it, Patricia." Madam handed her the tweezers.

The Chardonnay aside, Patricia felt an odd calmness come over her. She let Lizbeth take the ring off, then popped the stone out of one setting and into the other. The second setting was all glitz with a row of pavé diamonds down each side to frame the marquise in its own little nest of glittering side highlights.

Lizbeth slipped it on her finger. Her hazel green eyes glinted with delight. Patricia had to admit, it was pure Lizbeth.

"What's my girl got on now?" The male voice surprised her, and apparently Lizbeth as well, who jumped like a cat.

"Eric, you surprised me." Lizbeth got all smooth and lovey-dovey.

He came up beside her, put his arm around her, and kissed her cheek. "That was the idea. The girls upstairs in lingerie said you were jewelry-shopping."

"Ratted out by my own people," Lizbeth joked.

"How are you, Patricia?"

This was possibly the first time Eric had addressed her head-on. He didn't live at the Nordquist house like Brett did, and the party was something they all just never mentioned again. The rich were so good at that sort of thing.

"Fine, Eric, just fine. Congratulations," Patricia answered, nodding toward Lizbeth.

"I'm one lucky man." He gave her a squeeze.

Honestly, Eric seemed like a nice enough fellow. He had finer features and a slighter build than his brother, although he had given a good right punch to Brett's gut. Eric was the banker in the family, and somehow Patricia could see that it was a better match for Lizbeth, which was a very good thing.

"That's quite a ring, sweetheart." He looked at the sparkling mass of diamonds on her finger.

"It would be just this this one ring. It would

be my engagement ring and my wedding ring both." Lizbeth looked at Eric with her big green eyes.

"Well, that would be a bargain, wouldn't it?" Eric beamed. He was hook-line-and-sinkered where Lizbeth was concerned, no doubt about it, which was also a very good thing. Patricia felt a twinge of jealousy.

Lizbeth kissed Eric on the neck.

"Let's me and Madam have a little chat." Eric motioned to Madam and they went over to the pearl corner together.

Patricia was sure that Eric had some kind of God Almighty discount and was a shrewd bargainer to boot. She was left with Lizbeth, who had an excited flush on her cheeks.

"Looks like you're going to get your ring," Patricia whispered low to her.

"I could faint. Seriously. This is the most beautiful thing I've ever owned," she whispered back.

"It's a divine ring," Patricia agreed.

"It could support me for a year if he ever dumps me."

Patricia gave her an eyebrow. "Don't think like that. You and Eric are going to be fine."

Lizbeth looked at Patricia with an expression somewhere between pity and solidarity. "Listen to me, Patricia. Brett and Eric are grossly competitive. Brett is the worst. This is your perfect opportunity to play that card. Brett would do anything to steal his brother's spotlight. Even get married sooner.

"S-sooner than Christmas? That's, like—less than two months," Patricia stammered.

"Do you want to marry Brett?"

Patricia hesitated. "I just didn't picture myself as in a hurry, no offense."

"I'm just saying, there are windows of opportunity that speed things up for us women. It's up to us to recognize them. Either that or wait for years for them to make up their tiny little male minds. Neither of us is getting any younger. Aren't you almost thirty?"

Patricia was speechless. Lizbeth was obviously much more skilled at recognizing and *creating* these windows of opportunity than she was.

Eric and Madam finished wheeling and dealing and returned to them, breaking up their blonde-to-blonde moment.

Patricia had never felt so blonde in her entire

life. She looked into the oval countertop mirror and stared into the face of blondeness.

"The ring is yours, my dear." Madam patted her hand. "I can have the stone set by tomorrow afternoon. I'm so sorry, but you must part with it for just a day."

Lizbeth slipped the ring off her finger and carefully placed it in the velvet tray. Then she turned to Eric and gave him a big, wet, full-body kiss. The kind that melts a guys eyebrows and makes him say yes to anything. The kind of kiss only a blonde could dish out.

"Fasten your seat belts, we're in for a bumpy ride." The funny stewardess was doing her Bette Davis imitation. Paul immediately thought of his girls and their movie obsessions. *All About Eve* was one of their favorites. He leaned back and thought about some of their weekend film festivals held in the living room via the local Blockbuster video store. The Hitchcock festival had been his favorite.

"Can I get you a cocktail before we have to lash everything down?" A very pretty flight attendant leaned over his seat. She was flirting, for sure. Her sleek blonde hair was pulled into a ponytail that reminded him of a palomino horse.

"No, thanks, just ginger ale."

She smiled and shrugged. He'd have to get used to saying "No, thanks" to pretty women.

He patted his jacket pocket to be sure the ring was still in place. The security people had given him minor crap about it, but then thought it was quite funny and had a good laugh.

All it took was him having a moment of confession with his grandparents to realize he was ready to ask Patricia to marry him. He'd probably been ready for a long time, but it took the whole blonde bombshell and the Brett fiasco to bring it to the surface. How well he'd deluded himself up to this point!

But now, with his grandmother's engagement ring in the original white satin box, safely in his pocket, he was more than ready to pop the question.

Just how he was going to do that was a serious dilemma. He felt surprisingly nervous about the whole thing.

Paul looked out into the dark night aglow with the lights of the city. As they traveled east, the lights faded and stars became visible. He imagined a life with Patricia. He imagined intimate dinners at Carmine's downtown and great film festivals in their own living room, the two of them cozy on the sofa, and holidays, and taking her back to New York to meet his grandparents.

Then he imagined waking up beside her and taking her in his arms and making love to her. He could not imagine that picture with anyone else he'd ever known.

Blonde or brunette, Patricia was the one. Paul was absolutely sure of that.

Brett was holding court in the upstairs TV room of the Nordquist mansion surrounded by remotes and beer bottles. Football blared on the surround sound and Patricia offered him another spoonful of broth.

He was terribly distracted; there was no doubt about that. She could tell because he didn't even move his head to catch a big touchdown between the Washington State Cougars and the UW Huskies. He just stared at her with his Nordic blue eyes.

Those eyes looked both scared to death and angry at the same time. Something she would imagine his eyes might have looked like during his trip from the balcony to the lawn. This amused her. Marriage was just as scary to Brett as a fall off a twenty-five-foot balcony.

She was perched on the edge of a brown leather ottoman with her tray of soup next to her. Her less-fat self looked pretty good in the low-cut snug red sweater she'd changed into, and her slimmer hips had fit into a very cute black skirt with a flounce at the bottom. She'd put on red lipstick and was feeling very good about how she looked.

Her black shoes had the new pointed toes, and even though they pinched they looked extremely high-style on her feet. She thought she fit in pretty well at the mansion, for a change. Even Mrs. Nordquist had made a comment and had thanked her for taking care of her son.

His mother apparently had no personal inclination to attend to Brett's needs and had hired a full-time nurse to take care of him during the day. The nurse always looked like she wanted to hug Patricia when she got there.

The nurse told Patricia to buzz her in the kitchen if Brett needed any medication, and not to let him medicate himself because he was a bad judge of his dosage. She was also supposed to try and limit his beer intake, but not to call if he had silly whims because she was playing poker with the kitchen staff.

Patricia blotted Brett's chin with a napkin. Poor baby.

Brett grabbed the remote and put the taped football game on pause. Then he pulled her close. She let the spoon clatter into the soup bowl. "Oh, *Brett*, you'll hurt yourself."

He gave her a hungry kiss, which was a little difficult with his jaw wired shut. Patricia sat up and noticed the red lipstick smeared on his face.

"Look at you, you're all marked up." She tried to get some of it off with the napkin.

He made some comment, but not much came out from between the wires and the teeth.

"What is it, Brett? Do you need something?"

He motioned for her to bring him paper and pencil, which she found close by. He had already written "beer" several times and "need pain drugs" once.

He scribbled one word: "sex."

Patricia read the notepad. Then she smiled and shook her head. "So sorry, but no sex for you, your ribs wouldn't set properly. You're supposed to hold still." She pointed to his well-placed pillows. "No moving around."

As if she'd let their first time be with him in a cast with his body taped and wired together. She had a different idea of that, and it involved a hotel in the Bahamas on a honeymoon. She hadn't held out this long for no reason.

Brett grinned and shrugged. He motioned for the pad.

"I'll take a rain check," he wrote, then held it where she could see.

Gee, that was decent of him. "Thanks." She smiled.

His awkward request gave her some boldness. "Have you've heard whether Lizbeth and Eric have set a date for the wedding yet?"

Brett flopped back against his pillows slightly and a pain crossed his face. She couldn't tell if it was his ribs or his distress about his brother getting Lizbeth on the rebound. He nodded his head yes.

The rebound. That phrase sort of echoed in her head.

"They seem well suited to each other, Brett, and I'm sure things will smooth out between all of you eventually. After all, she's going to be in the family now."

She didn't say in the family *way* now. A little smile crossed Patricia's lips. It didn't seem as if Brett knew about that whole pregnancy part of the deal. But she wasn't too sure. She *was* sure that Lizbeth and Brett were just not right for each other. Because she would take such better care of Brett than Lizbeth would have. You can't have two spoiled needy people marry each other. One of them has to be a giver if one is a taker.

Once she and Brett were married she'd teach him what a joy it was to give to someone else. He'd just never been taught properly.

Brett looked like he was in some mild sort of agony.

"Do you need your medication, Brett?" she asked. She pressed her hand on his forehead.

He pulled her over to him so she lay on the sofa beside him. It was a wide sofa, and, her being less wide these days, she didn't feel like she was going to fall off the edge.

"Ill ooo airy ee?" he squeezed syllables through his tightly wired-together teeth.

Patricia had her arm delicately around the front of his waist a bit lower than the offending cracked rib. She looked up at him and stared into his painfully blue eyes.

"Did you just ask me to marry you, Brett? Because that's sort of what it sounded like. Either that or you're ill and need air," she joked.

"Yeth," he managed to say.

She could go on with it, asking him—*Yes, you're ill, or yes, you're asking me?* but she couldn't stand it anymore. She snuggled up close to him. As close as she could without hurting him. His broken leg was against the sofa back, so she had his good side to her.

"Yes, I will marry you, Brett," she sighed. This was her moment. Her dream come true. Her sun-rises-over-the-mountain glowing victory moment. She lay there next to him and reveled in every little sensation.

He held her with his good arm and she kissed him on the cheek. He heaved a great rattling sigh under her ear, which she felt shudder through his entire body. There was probably no physical pain that could top a dedicated playboy bachelor surrendering to marriage.

She'd just have to keep him alive long enough to get him down the aisle. Well, she meant longer than that, of course.

More like for a lifetime of happiness with him and the family—sort of a Kennedy clan thing, with Brett playing football on the expansive lawn of the estate with his three towheaded children, or should they have four?

"Would you like three children or four?" she asked.

He laughed a short laugh. That obviously hurt, which made his eyes water, so he was laughing with tears streaming down his cheeks into the pillows.

"Okay, four it is. Two girls, two boys."

Brett looked more like he was crying at this point. A great groan came out of him.

Patricia decided to get the nurse and give him his nine o'clock dose of Vicodin early.

Paul heaved his heavy suitcase up on his bedroom chair and zipped it open. The girls were going to love their spring handbag samples, most particularly two slightly flawed Birken bags he'd scored from his pal at the Hermes showroom. All those years of buying the snotty French sales rep dinner in New York after the show closed finally paid off.

Paul took the new handbags—the two Birkens,

two wild-looking Spencer & Rutherford leather, silk and canvas bags, then four of the less expensive jelly bags in great spring colors by Helen Welsh—and sat them in a row on his bed.

He couldn't decide whether the dove gray suited Patricia or Pinky better and which one would like the red Birken bag. Oh well, it didn't matter. Usually, the girls happily shared anyway.

The house was so quiet without either of them. He'd limo'd home from the airport and come home to a dark and quiet place.

Asta, of course, was all over him. He purred and tried to climb into the suitcase. Paul removed him twice.

Pinky must be out with Dr. Bender. But who knew where Patricia was? He didn't want to think about it. All her wandering ways would end soon when she saw his grandmother's ring and heard his proposal.

He imagined slipping it on her finger. She might be so surprised she'd faint. He better propose sitting on the sofa of many colors just in case.

Paul thought about the kiss they'd shared on the balcony. That split second of her surrender had been so exciting, so full of their continued passion. So reminiscent of their night together. That was a night neither of them would ever forget, as much as they'd tried to pretend it didn't happen.

He couldn't wait to take her in his arms tonight and erase all thoughts of Brett from her pretty blonde head.

Chapter Fifteen

I have full cause of weeping, but this heart shall break into a hundred thousand flaws or ere I'll weep.

Shakespeare

Pinky never pictured herself as a prude, but she was really enjoying this long, lingering pre-sex dance she and James Bender were doing. In her entire life she'd never driven a man so crazy. He'd kissed her goodnight madly and passionately at the front door and then she'd demurely slipped away from him, knowing he was enjoying this just as much as she was and that he'd be calling her on the phone the minute he got back to his house.

Not that she'd ever been considered shy. She

wasn't exactly a virgin after her college days, but this was just delicious. She'd never been a girl men pursued much. Most of her boyfriends had been like Morris Klein, a man with similar passions. They'd met at a Sierra Club meeting and Morris had won her virginity along with the environmental prize for best mass transit concept.

Pinky hung up her brown plaid wool jacket and threw her gloves in the wicker basket in the closet. She walked toward her downstairs bedroom thinking about Dr. Jimmy.

She was surprised to hear the sound of the shower in Paul's bathroom. Paul was back!

It was always Christmas when Paul came home. She could hardly stand the suspense. She couldn't. She opened his door a crack and heard him singing gospel music in the shower, his deep bass voice booming "Swing Low, Sweet Chariot."

She felt like a kid peeking at her presents before Santa got them under the tree.

On his bed sat a virtual rainbow of new handbags. She squealed, then pressed her fist over her mouth to quiet herself. The scarlet Birken bag was to *die for.* And the silky fabric bags looked like art. She was a sucker for textiles. She sneaked over quietly and picked up the pink floral back, snapping it open to see the lining. Inside rested a little white satin box. Did this come with the bag?

She set down the bag and opened the little box. Inside was a beautiful art-deco-style diamond ring. Pinky took in a quick gasping breath and shut the box with a snap. She hurried to replace it back into the purse, then got herself out of the room fast.

Holy Saint Patrick, was Paul going to propose to that Dani woman on the rebound? Not the Oreo-teeth girl. It couldn't be. With the way he felt about Patricia? No, it had to be Patricia.

She steadied herself against the olive green stenciled arts and crafts designs of their hallway. Pinky got a really, really bad feeling in the depths of her Irish soul.

Paul didn't know about Lizbeth and Eric yet, and Pinky was seriously worried about the potential boomerang results the whole fiasco might have regarding Brett and Patricia's relationship.

Although, from what she'd seen of Brett, he'd rather die than marry at his tender age of twenty-nine. Unless he thought he could one-up his brother. Her Dr. James called it a classic case of unresolved sibling rivalry.

Oh, man alive. Pinky went into her own room. Asta followed her, and when she flopped backward on the bed, Asta jumped up to purr all over her and snuggle in a neat pile of fur next to Pinky's waist. Maybe it was time to tell Patricia what an idiot she was letting a man like Paul slip away.

It was strange how perfect they were for each other. Memories came like snapshots to Pinky—like the Scrabble tournament when she finally called "uncle" and went for more popcorn in the kitchen while those two went head to head and started using obscure words she'd never heard of.

They were hilariously funny, and she remembered just sitting by the kitchen counter watching them slap little letters on the board like maniacs. Or last Christmas when Paul had struggled to get the tree into the stand while Patricia was holding it up and Patricia'd had some fleeting thought and had run for an ornament or their stockings or something and the damn tree had fallen over on him. Instead of being mad he'd laughed at her when she came back in the room and realized the error of her ways.

Pinky remembered the stockings they'd hung by the chimney with care, how they'd done all those rituals they'd all loved as kids, and how everyone had pretended to be Santa and stuffed the stockings full of really stupidly cute things—windup toys and miniature plastic animals.

Paul had set up a train around the tree just for fun, and they'd sat on the sofa in their pajamas drinking hot buttered rum in the dark, watching the lights twinkle, snuggling like kids.

She and Patricia had curled up on either side of Paul in his fuzzy polar fleece robe and moose slippers. How come neither one of them—neither Paul nor Patricia—could feel the love growing between them?

Probably because they were such creatures of habit and didn't want to change the great feelings they had together. Romance would have messed it all up.

But now it needed messing up—in the worst way. And she'd just have to be the person to start the mess rolling.

The screams of Patricia coming in the door shook Pinky out of her thoughts. Little screams.

Eek Eek Eek. Not screams of seeing some dead mouse Asta had left for them, but odd rapid-fire screams.

Pinky jumped off the bed and ran to see what the hell was going on.

"What in the name of heaven are you screaming like that for?" Pinky asked.

"Look at you in your cute brown skirt and browner sweater and that great scarf, you look so autumn," Patricia said with excitement, which was strange.

"You haven't been drinking, have you? Because I will kill you myself if you have been drinking and driving. I will take the car keys away from you forever and you'll be grounded, do you hear me, young lady?" Pinky stood with her hands on her hips.

"Oh, Pinks, you are so funny. Look at you. You're going to make such a great mother. I'm so glad you found Dr. James to play with before you hit the big three-oh. You know we don't have our looks for long, so it's a brief window of opportunity."

"You *sound* like you've been drinking," she said suspiciously.

"Not a drop. You know me better than that.

I would never do such a thing. I'm just deliriously giddy, my dear. Tomorrow at lunch we are going to put money down on your loco cocoa mocha dress and you are going to put brown velvet ribbons in your brown hair and we are going to have a Thanksgiving wedding.

"Funny how the colors will be great for a brunette. I would have much preferred a summer color scheme, what with my new look and all, but we can put vine maple in the flowers and use all sorts of candles and *oh my God* wait, look, look at this!" She held out her hand and, honestly, Pinky thought she had a miniature light rigged up to a battery for Halloween or something. A beam of light from the kitchen hit whatever was on her hand and made it glint. But it wasn't a trick, it was a big fat diamond engagement ring.

"It was his mother's. She gave it to him to give to me *tonight*. Brett asked me to marry him and she must have been passing in the hallway while I yammered about dates and all that and she was so thrilled she gave me this ring.

"You said yes to Brett?"

"You are looking at the future Mrs. Brett Nordquist."

Pinky heard the smallest sound behind her

and turned just in time to see Paul standing in the hallway in nothing but his drawstring pajama bottoms.

She just wished she could cram a sock in Patricia's mouth.

"Paul, Paul, I'm engaged!"

Paul did not answer. Paul didn't say one word. He just stepped back into his room. The door shut hard behind him and echoed in the empty hall.

Now what was she going to do, tell Patricia that Paul was going to ask her to marry him? She wasn't actually dead certain about that, and it could be a disaster if it weren't true, but judging from his reaction, it probably was. Maybe the vintage deco ring was for some other purpose.

As if.

"Well, look at you. All your dreams are coming true. And so soon, too. Thanksgiving? Remember I was going to fly home to see my parents?"

"We'll buy you a new ticket to go for Christmas. Won't you change it to be in my wedding? Please?"

"I'll think about it."

"You have to. You *are* my best friend. I can't get married without you."

Pinky thought that might be a great idea. She'd just run away to New Jersey for a year or so and stop Patricia from getting married by being permanently out of town.

"Why is Paul is upset?" Patricia asked.

Pinky just stared at her, unable to believe Patricia could be so blind. Blonde and blind.

"He can't be. I need him to be there and give me his support and love, just like I need you. You two are my family." Patricia finally moved from her spot of announcement to the sofa and sat down next to Asta, who had followed Pinky out to see what was happening.

She stroked the cat's striped fur and scratched him under his chin on his white ruff. "You still love me, don't you, cat of many colors?" She sniffed like she was going to cry and her lower lip quivered.

Pinky sat down next to her and pulled tissues out of her skirt pocket. "Why do you want to get married so fast? You and Lizbeth don't have anything more in common than a Nordquist brother fettish, do you?"

"Not hardly. I've held Brett back with a bulldozer as far as sex goes. Of course, it made it easier after he dropped off the balcony and busted himself up."

Patricia hadn't exactly worked herself up into a full crying jag, so Pinky put the tissues back in her pocket.

"Pinky, Pinky, look at it." Patricia held her hand up to the light again. "As a newly educated fine jewelry ho, I can tell you it is a beauty of a ring; four whole carats and a very high clarity rating. Not to mention the sentimental value to the Nordquist family. Mrs. N said something about me taking Brett off her hands and I deserved it. Wasn't that funny?" Patricia laughed

Pinky contemplated whether to slap her friend right now or just let her enjoy the moment of victory she thought she'd won. The prize, of course, being Brett. And a big fat diamond ring to go with him.

"Lizbeth was right."

"What was Lizbeth right about?" Pinky asked.

"This was my window of opportunity." Patricia stopped gazing at the huge round diamond on her finger and looked right at Pinky. "You know, Brett just needs a good woman to make him settle down. That tumble off the balcony must have made him rethink his life."

"Patricia, look at me." Pinky turned her friend by the shoulders and looked her in the eye. "Brett only asked you to marry him because he's on the rebound from Lizbeth, and because he wants to get even with his brother and steal the show. He wants to be even more outrageous, which is what he likes to do. Do you really want to marry him knowing all that?"

Patricia took a deep breath and looked like she was actually thinking about everything Pinky had just said. She gazed down at her ring. That wasn't a good sign. Maybe she should just shake her till her teeth rattled or lock her in the attic like in *Jane Eyre*.

"I know this all seems crazy, Pinky, but I can't seem to help myself. I've gone from a drab nobody to Brett Nordquist's fiancée in one month. How can I just walk away from all that? I've been given a total life makeover. And I would be good for Brett. I'm a steady, sensible girl underneath all this blonde hair."

"But will *Brett* be good for *you*?"

"I'll make it work."

Pinky flopped back on the sofa and groaned.

She just couldn't find the key to Patricia's sense. Shit, how a woman's fantasy can take on a life of its own. Patricia had always seen the best in everyone—way more than herself. But Pinky's East Coast upbringing had helped form a natural skepticism. Patricia was a cock-eyed optimist from the happy land of Seattle.

Maybe, just maybe, Patricia would somehow wake up before she actually went through with it. Maybe she was talking to the wrong person. Paul might be the only one who could bring Patricia back to earth.

"Okay, I have nothing more to offer, Patricia, but I want you to think hard about all this. You are a terrific woman and frankly you deserve better."

"Better than what Brett can offer me? I'll be Mrs. Society Matron. I'll be Myrna Loy."

"Myrna Loy was a brunette," Pinky said sharply. She got up and headed for her room. "And so was Jacqueline Kennedy." It made no sense, but she was too tired to think anymore. She just wanted her flannel pajamas and a glass of port. If she was going to be the bridesmaid from hell, she might as well start drinking early.

* * *

Paul heard a knock at his door. He considered ignoring it and pretending he was asleep. He'd been pacing the room and probably they'd heard that. "Who is it?"

"Pinky."

"Come in."

She came through the door with two glasses of port in her hand. "I want to talk to you."

"Have a seat." He motioned to the bed. Then he saw all the handbags and just swept them off onto the floor with a big angry sweep of his arm. They clunked like dull shoes on his bedside carpet.

"Those are beautiful, Paul, thank you." Pinky didn't comment on his actions. She just flopped herself on one side of his bed. "Come sit next to me." She patted the bed.

For some reason he just did what she said. He couldn't think straight anyhow. He grabbed a clean T-shirt to cover his bare chest, pulled it on, and threw himself on the bed next to Pinky. She handed him the glass of port and he took a stiff swig.

"I know, Paul. I saw the ring. I was being Suzy Snoopy while you were in the shower, and I opened the purse with the ring box in it."

Paul stared at her hard with an angry-but-not-angry-with-*her*-exactly look.

"I assumed it was for Patricia, not Dani, or your Aunt Fanny or anything but what I think it was for, right?"

"You guessed it, snoopy." He slammed his head against the headboard and swigged down the rest of his port. Now he had a headache, too.

"God, I'm so sorry, Paul. I swear that drug didn't just change her hair, it gave her hysterical blondeness, you know? She's gone completely bonkers. Brett is about as right for her as Gene Tierney was right for Cornel Wilde in *Leave Her to Heaven*.

"Don't do film references right now, Pinky. I'm too upset. I'm more than just upset. I'm crazy. I'm just as bad as she is. What was I thinking, waiting all this time? I can't believe the irony of it all. Here I finally figure out I love her, and she's gotten herself engaged to Brett the Barbarian." That's as much as Paul could bring himself to say. He was completely disgusted with everything he knew and loved, or didn't love and hardly knew, at the moment.

"What are you going to do about it, Paul?"

"I'm going to fight back. But I'm not sure what that looks like yet. You know how a kid wants something they can't have more than something you just give them? That's what Patricia reminds me of right now."

Pinky sipped her port. "That's so true. I'm going to help you any way I can, sport. I can't see Patricia becoming Mrs. Martyr Nordquist, you know?"

"Just tell me one thing. Has she slept with him?"

"Nope."

Paul heaved a huge sign of relief. "Thank God for that. So the big rush isn't like . . . she's *got* to get married, right?"

"Right." Pinky sounded cagey.

"What aren't you telling me?"

"It's pretty complicated, but to cut to the chase, Lizbeth Summers is pregnant and got herself engaged to Eric Nordquist. Just between you and me and the fence post I'm not so sure it's Eric's baby, but as she told Patricia while she bought the big fat ring from fine jewelry today, *it's a Nordquist for sure.*"

"Oh my God, my God, what the hell has

Patricia gotten herself into?" Paul slapped his forehead after Pinky finished her twisted tale of Nordquist intrigue.

"I tried to talk some sense into her, but she's on cloud nine and wearing Brett's ring. We have two choices. Bump him off, or do some sort of intervention with her involving duct tape and a therapist."

Paul laughed a bitter laugh. "I'm liking the duct tape so far. Okay, Pinky, I can't take any more tonight. Thanks for the information and the port, but get your fanny out of my bed. I need to be alone and sort out my feelings."

Pinky hauled herself off the bed. "Paul, you are beyond Osgood."

"I'm what?"

"Never mind. Get some rest and we'll figure this thing out in the morning."

"This is something I have to handle myself, Pinky, but I appreciate your support," Paul said. "How's the fine Dr. Bender anyway?"

"He is very fine. We are not getting married in November or anytime this year, but we are enjoying ourselves. Thanks for asking, Paulie."

"Goodnight, Pinky."

She waved goodnight, shutting the door behind her. He finished his port in one more swig. The sharp mellow bite of the wine helped make his head swim into dullness, which was exactly what he wanted. He didn't want to feel or think or figure anything out.

What he'd really like was to go out there into the kitchen where they'd heard Patricia clanging dishes, probably warming herself up some dinner because Brett never fed her, and make her remember their first night together. He wanted to push her up against the refrigerator and kiss her until she stopped thinking she wanted to marry Brett and realized it was him all along.

He knew one thing: he wasn't going to beg her or try and make her see the senselessness of her infatuation with Brett. That would be stupid. He could only wait. He would wait for her to remember who really loved her.

He kept going back to his image of how powerful it was to want what you couldn't have. It applied to him right now as well. And the bottom line was he loved Patricia too much to let her go.

Chapter Sixteen

Expectation is the root of all heartache.
Shakespeare

Patricia was surrounded by diamonds. She ran her fingers over the pretty little stones in their snug little boxes in the fine jewelry display case. *Her* new diamond ring glittered under the case lights like a star that had fallen from the sky.

But her nails were atrocious. She had to make a lunchtime appointment to get them done. What was the use of flashing the ring for all to see if her nails were their usual plain-Jane, clear-polish, clean-but-boring selves? Maybe red would be good.

There was only one thing clouding her shiny bright happy mood, and that was the way Paul had turned without a word and gone into his room without congratulating her. How unlike him.

Paul had been gone a whole week, and she had missed him every morning. She missed his wonderful meals, too. She'd been eating fast food on her trips back and forth from Brett's to home. Yuck. Somehow they'd always already eaten at Brett's and she didn't bother to ask for anything during her visits. It was starting to show on her—a few extra pounds had crept on over the last week.

It wasn't just Paul's great dinners, though; it was the wonderful times they'd had sharing those meals. It was the care Paul took of her. She knew it was going to be hard to break up their little family.

But they couldn't just stay the same way forever. She felt a pang of emotion run through her. She'd probably be feeling like this for quite a while.

"You see what happens when you come to work in fine jewelry?" Madam had come up close beside her and Patricia jumped. "Did I frighten you?"

"I'm sorry, Madam, I was lost in thought."

"About your engagement to Brett Nordquist?"

"How in heaven's name would you know that?" Patricia stared at Madam Gaffer in shock.

"Women always fall for the wealthy man who treats her bad. Why is that?" Madam crossed her arms and shook her head at Patricia.

"Brett doesn't treat me bad, and how did you know?"

"Nordquist's is like small neighborhood. I have ways." Madam shrugged. "So you marry the man who stood and watched when you fell on your face, but you don't marry the man who picks you up off the ground? You young people are so crazy. And I see you have his mother's ring. I sold Lars Nordquist that ring in 1973. He and Gloria have been married more than thirty years. So when is the wedding?"

"Thanksgiving." Patricia was too stunned to defend herself.

"So soon. Be sure and invite me. I wouldn't miss this for the world. And how long do you think you can work here? Because you have much to do to prepare for a wedding in three weeks."

"It's going to be simple."

"Not if Gloria Nordquist has anything to say about it. You'll be married in the family church and your reception will be at the Sons of Norway hall. I know this woman. She's already bribing people to make this happen. Her sons do not marry in city hall. Can you afford a dress?"

"I haven't even thought about it—affording it, anyway. I always thought Pinky would make my dress, but I haven't given her enough time.

"I'll have Virginia in bridal make special arrangements for you. I'm sure Gloria will be happy to pay for the dress. Have you told your parents?"

Patricia thought she might just faint. She steadied herself on the glass counter.

"Tsk-tsk, you'll have to get some Windex and clean off your fingerprints there." Madam shook her head at Patricia.

"Sorry,"

"I think you must take some time off. You are a great little salesgirl, and I'm sorry to lose you, but the future Mrs. Brett Nordquist needs to go talk to her parents, and buy a dress, and for heaven's sakes get your nails done immediately—and your hair, while you are at it. I think you are going to need a touch-up before the wedding, don't you?"

Forgetting the fact that she had just been fired or at least laid off, Patricia ran to the oval countertop mirror. A touch-up? She bent her head back and forth in the light. She moved sections of hair back and forth. No no, *no*! It just couldn't be. The tiniest shadow of her former self was creeping steadily up from her roots. She was going to turn into a brunette again!

Madam came up behind her. "Don't take it so badly, Patricia. Your new life awaits you. Now go get your things and shoosh. I'll make up a paycheck for you, and if you find yourself needing a job for any reason, such as Brett getting cold feet, just let me know. You are welcome back here."

Madam actually spun her around, gave her a quick, rather odd hug, and slapped her on the back with a little push toward the exit.

Patricia opened the lock drawer, left her department keys on the counter, and gathered her belongings. Mandy had apparently been listening in and since she'd already squawked at her about the sale of Lizbeth's engagement ring while she was away, as if it were Patricia's fault, Patricia gave her a smug look. Screw Miss Mandy. She was marrying the boss. It almost looked like Mandy remembered that and kind of slunk off into her corner.

Patricia grabbed her blue wool coat, which she wished she'd bought after acquiring her new, bigger employee discount. But at least she'd used it to buy the matching blue skirt and sweater she had on. She wondered if she had room on her credit card for nails and hair.

She stumbled out of fine jewelry. Oh my God, what just happened? And what just happened to her hair? What about her damn DNA, didn't it alter itself?

Madam was already on the phone chatting away in her interesting accent to someone. Probably talking about her.

She got on the escalator and switchbacked through the entire store all the way up to the crazy fourth floor where the junior departments took up most of the sales area with their driving bass beat and music video screens all over the place. The young men's department rocked a little harder, but the junior women's department wasn't far behind in decibels. Wouldn't it be nice if they played the same thing?

The Pizzazz Salon had its special corner. It wasn't a place she usually came to visit, but she needed to use her employee discount. Good grief, she still had her employee discount, didn't she? Was she fired or just laid off? She'd have to ask Madam for a little more information when she was done here. Surely she'd have a day or two. Or was she on the Nordquist discount now, being Brett's fiancée? Wow. That was a weird thought.

"Hi, I'm Patricia from fine jewelry. I was wondering if you had any openings. I know I need an appointment, but it's sort of an emergency." She held out her hands.

"I'll say. Come right this way, Patricia. We were expecting you. I'm Star." The girl in the pink smock with PIZZAZZ embroidered on it stood up and took her hand. "Wow, Madam was right, it's one stunning ring. Congrats, honey."

Patricia wondered if the entire store would know when she took a pee at this point.

Star the smock girl motioned for her to sit in one of the hairstyling chairs. "We'll do your nails and toes. What else?"

"Um, my hair is sort of a problem."

"Let's see." Star ran her fingers up and around and inside the pathways and byways of Patricia's odd blonde hair. "What a funky color. It almost seems natural, but I see the hint of some other color at the very edge of your scalp. Did you have this done?"

Patricia debated how much to tell Star. If she told her it was a science experiment gone bad it would get all over the store. And after all, every bit of her hair all over her body had turned platinum blonde.

"I used to be a brunette when I was younger, then it turned blonde." She tried that one.

"Wow, that's so unusual. Well, it looks like you're headed back for brunetteville. We could squelch that for a while if you like, but you've got a good week before it starts to be noticeable. Other than that, you've got beautiful hair; a nice natural wave. We can get all thirties and spit-curly or wherever you want to go with it for the wedding. When is the wedding?"

"Thanksgiving."

"Wow." Star's favorite word. "It's okay to use chemicals on you, isn't it? Because, um, well, we could use other products."

"I'm not pregnant." Patricia figured it would help get the news out to the entire store if she just met it head-on.

"Oka-y-y, then! I'd say if you haven't colored your hair in the last six weeks then we can do a double process on you and keep that amazing shade of yours going for at least through the wedding. Wow. You are going to be a stunning bride. Be right back with Marc. He's our colorist."

Patricia had a full-blown bridal fantasy after Star vanished. It was full of white lace and promises and organ music and fat white orchids and Pinky in her chocolate mousse latte dress and brown velvet ribbons and the groom in a brown suit and her in that beaded amber and peach gown with the amazing back detail.

She could see herself walking down the aisle toward Brett, his mother in a light blue silk suit and her mother in brown velvet and the whole amber orange brown vintage blue wedding just like in a movie. She felt a huge rush of excitement.

Oh God, her parents. Thump. She came down like a cartoon anvil landing on the cartoon cat.

Hey, wait They couldn't give her the old why-didn't-you-do-it-like-your-sister? routine because she was going to beat her older sister Carol to the altar! She was going to marry a Nordquist and be rich enough to ignore their put-downs for the rest of her life.

For once in her life she didn't care what they were going to say. She dug in her navy blue Kelly bag and pulled out her cell phone. They weren't on auto-dial but she remembered the number.

"Mom? Hi, Mom. Yes, I'm fine. I have big news. Guess what? . . .

"No, I'm not quitting work, I've actually been promoted to the fine jewelry department, but that's not it. . . .

"No, no, I'm getting married. Yes, really! . . .

"No, not to Paul. I'm getting married to Brett Nordquist. . . .

"Yes, those Nordquist's. Yes. Mom, we've planned a Thanksgiving wedding. . . .

"No, I'm not pregnant." Patricia felt her teeth gritting. "Yes, he just actually wants to marry me this Thanksgiving."

The rest of the conversation was her mother making huge lists in the sky to which Patricia only needed to reply, "I know," and an occasional, "*No*, Mother," to doves or monogrammed napkins or her cousin Sally singing "I Love You Truly."

She looked up to see a young trendy man, who must be Marc, casually listening to her end of the conversation. When she made eye contact with him he just nodded and came over to get a good look at her hair.

"Okay, Mother, I've got to get my nails done and I have a million things to do, so we'll talk later. Yes, brown and amber and vintage blue. Okay, 'bye, now." Patricia clicked off her cell and looked up at Marc.

"Could it get more exciting?" he asked.

"I don't think so. It makes me want to hyperventilate." Patricia leaned back.

Marc leaned toward her and whispered in her ear, "You were in the Feltzengraad study, weren't you?"

Patricia practically fell off her spinny little chair. "How do you know?"

Marc crossed his arms and looked extremely pleased with himself. "You aren't the first, and there is a particularly *totally* blonde thing that you just don't see in real life. May I?" He took her arm and ran his hands over the fine hairs of her forearm. "See? That's like . . . beyond

Scandinavian, you know? And I can tell you aren't a Norski by blood. Are you?"

"There's some Norwegian in there somewhere, but I'm generally a Celtic mutt. Marc, please, please don't tell anyone. Everyone is gossiping about me anyhow and I just don't want that one thing to get around, okay?"

"Think of me as a priest," he said. "After all, I put the color on many heads here at Nordquist's and I can't very well go around talking about it, can I? Notice I didn't say who told me about the Feltzengraad study?" Marc's brown eyes rolled around as if he had a great secret.

"Thank you. I want to keep this color. I *need* to keep this color, you know?"

"I have a French dye called Extreme Beige Blonde that I used on my other friend. Well, actually, we went through a few experiments first, but that was the best match."

"Just do me. Do me Extreme Blonde and make it go away. I don't want to go back to being a brunette." Patricia jumped a little in her chair.

"I just have to warn you that eventually it will get very, very funky all around your body, if you know what I mean, and I'm talking the whole creeping-back-into-brownsville deal here, like eyebrows and little arm hairs and *every*-where hairs, you know?"

"Oh God." Patricia closed her eyes.

"Don't worry, honey, we can do a sort of gradual foil and frost and in a year it will be all anyone can do to remember what your hair color was, and by then you'll be Mrs. Nordquist, so who cares?"

"I'm going to kiss you, Marc."

"Oh, let's not, but I'll give you air cheeks—mwah, mwah, and we're good to go." Marc turned each cheek her way and she blew him kisses.

"While we're at it, I have to show you the Amber Glaze collection because you just won't believe what you'll look like in these lip colors and your nails will love it. Sort of a golden bronzy thing that gives you that blonde goddess look. Isn't being a blonde fun?

"You?"

"Brunette as a chocolate Labrador retriever. I do my eyebrows too."

"I have blue contacts. It took two weeks to get them to stop watering, but now I'm good, and I was a hard-core glasses girl."

"I'd hardly have known. Oh my, I just thought

of something. Have you ever had your hair dyed in your entire life?"

"Never," Patricia answered.

"We'll have to do a patch test. We wouldn't want you to break out in a horrible rash or anything three weeks before your wedding!"

"Three weeks?" Patricia thought she'd break out in a rash just hearing that. Somehow when you hear the deadline out loud it always sounds worse—or better. She was confused, and extremely stressed.

Marc took her to a dressing area and gave her a pink smock to change into. She had the feeling he was a very shrewd dude and she wasn't sure she could trust him completely, but she didn't care. She just loved being able to talk to someone about the entire fiasco of the Feltzengraad study.

Well, not exactly a fiasco. Her last checkup with Dr. Bender had shown significant weight loss despite the "unexpected altered pigmentation," as Dr. Bender put it. Actually, all considered, the results of her mad fling into scientific experimentation had changed her entire life.

Hopefully Marc could keep it that way. Thank God Paulie was back and would put some decent food on the table. If she ever got home in time to have dinner with them. She felt that old feeling creep over her. How she missed her friends and Paul's cooking and curling up on the sofa to watch *Desperate Housewives* on Sunday nights.

Tonight she was dining with the Nordquists, as Mrs. N herself had requested the honor of her presence to go over wedding plans immediately. She'd gotten a written phone message from a runner in the store, hand-delivered earlier this morning. All weekend she'd nursed Brett and watched football with him, but his parents had been away skiing.

Sometimes she felt like she was in a foreign country just starting to learn the language. Worse than that, she felt like she was pretending to be someone she wasn't. But who was she really?

Had she gotten the approval she'd always wanted from her mother just now? Not really, more like, *Oh, what a problem this is all going to be, Patricia, and have you thought this through, and by the way, congratulations.*

She couldn't win with her parents.

But she was winning with Brett.

* * *

"Henri Shreve has retired," Peggy Hanagan told Paul flat out. "He faxed in a letter of resignation from Hawaii."

"I thought he'd been ill."

"He was, poor fellow, and he said he was taking a cure on the Big Island."

Paul sat down in the chair opposite Mrs. Hanagan and rubbed his chin.

"They'll offer the position of head buyer to you, of course. You've been doing the job anyway. You'll get a raise."

"Are you interested in applying?" he asked her.

"Heavens, no. I hate traveling. My husband would have a fit. No, Paul, it's all yours, if you want it."

Of *course* he want the job. He loved going to Milan, New York, and all the other various locations they sent him.

It would get him back to see his grandparents and take more recordings of their history. He'd really worked hard at it this time and made them promise to write things down for him. He wanted to tell their story. He wanted to make it into a historical novel. Being a buyer wasn't a difficult job for him and it would give him the time he'd need to write.

But something was missing. He felt like Edward, King of England, in his abdication speech droning on in a quiet voice over the BBC. *"But you must believe me when I tell you that I have found it impossible to carry the heavy burden of responsibility and to discharge my duties as King as I would wish to do without the help and support of the woman I love."*

The speech that Pinky and Patricia had made him listen to when they were having an English history documentary-a-thon. They'd actually bawled like babies, the gooses. He knew it by heart because they'd rewound it ten times and said it out loud for a week as a reply to every silly thing that came up.

Now he actually knew how King Edward felt. Here he had been offered a great job, a great raise, and without the woman he loved the future seemed like a fog.

"Paul?"

"I'll have to think it over, Peggy. I'm going to sleep on it."

"Okay." She slapped her knees and got up

"What goodies did you bring back from New York for me? I saw a box downstairs you'd shipped. Is it full of fun? You're just like Santa Claus."

"Ho, ho, ho," he said flatly. He pulled out a stack of digital photos he'd snapped at the showrooms and printed up over his painful, soul-searching weekend and spread them like a deck of cards on her desk.

"What's up? Is it the job? Or is it a woman?" Peggy asked.

"Woman."

"You're such a nice guy. Let me give you some advice. Don't waste your time on relationships that are constantly in a state of trouble, Paul. Life shouldn't be so hard. Love can be easy if you pick the right person. Most of the time anyway. You men are kind of thick-headed sometimes."

"Thank you, oh sagely wise Peggy Hanagan," Paul said.

"You're welcome. I hope things work out. Why don't you go retrieve that box from the basement, and I'll study your pictures?"

"Yes, ma'am."

Peggy smiled. "I'm just trying to keep you busy."

"Can you do that for the next three weeks?"

"Want to work on the sales floor?"

"I'll bring the samples up. 'Bye, Peg." Paul made a hasty exit to the sound of his floor manager's laughter. He had worked the selling floor before to get the inside picture of his customers and what they liked and how they went about making a choice. He had nothing but sympathy for the sales staff.

He nodded to each of them as he passed through the department and headed to the back of the store.

He also passed by fine jewelry but didn't see Patricia working the floor. Maybe she was on a break, or in the loft. He'd been sort of a jerk to her all weekend. He'd cooked the most fattening food he could think of, he'd ignored her, and he'd put his Ipod and headphones on and tried to drown out his own thoughts.

He was waiting. But it was killing him.

Not that she was there much anyway; she'd spent the night elsewhere. She'd come and gone quietly, hardly talking to him. He kept reminding himself Brett was in a cast and sex was probably not happening over there at the Nordquist house.

Maybe he should apologize. How could he start figuring out a way to win this woman if they were hardly speaking?

He steered into fine jewelry and caught Mandy straightening pearl strands.

"Is Patricia in the back?"

Mandy was flirty. "No, she got fired or something. Madam sent her to get her hair and nails done and buy a wedding dress." She shifted herself his direction in a sort of invitational manner.

"A trip to the salon doesn't sound like she got fired, Mandy. You might not want to spread rumors like that around," Paul said.

"Whatever." Mandy gave up on him and went back to her pearls.

Every step Paul took today led him in two directions. One step toward giving up on Patricia and taking control of his life again, one step toward finding her and locking her in the attic until she turned back into a sane woman.

Patricia seemed so determined to crash-test-dummy herself into Brett's lifestyles of the rich and self-indulgent. How could he possibly stop her?

As he descended in the freight elevator to

the basement of Nordquist's, he knew he just had to find a way. He slammed his fist on the side of the elevator. There *must* be a way to make Patricia understand what a mistake she was making.

Chapter Seventeen

A rose by any other name
would smell as sweet.
Shakespeare

Patricia had been dreaming about Nordquist's.

Back at the store, Nordquist's was decked out in all its holiday finery from head to toe and from floor to ceiling. Every department, from socks to sheets, looked like a rich woman in a designer formal at the Oscars.

There were gigantic red candles with fake flames, huge gold and red ornaments, and enough wired gold ribbon to circle the entire store five times.

But none of this was enough to take the edge off Patricia's mood, because Marc in Pizzazz had given her the word of doom about hair dye. She was a failed patch test with little blotches of red up and down her neck like hickies. He'd done them all in the back where no one could see, and he promised they'd be healed by the wedding with the cortisone cream he slathered all over her.

He was down to lemon juice and water as a bleaching agent.

Patricia was a blonde time bomb and her fuse was lit. Brunetteness was creeping back over her in tiny millimeters of dullness. She'd actually cried this morning when she looked in the mirror. Last week it was barely noticeable, but this week things were starting to come to light.

She was doomed to actual grow-out, although Marc was still hopeful he'd find a natural product she could tolerate. He said her better bet was to return to her original brunette with some natural-type dye before she turned into two-toned Tessie.

All this stress had made her start hitting the leftover Halloween candy. She knew where Pinky hid it and it was starting to show up on the scale.

That, and every time she opened the fridge for leftovers Paul had made cannelloni or cheese-layered lasagna or something with a million calories. Last night she opened the fridge to find a full two-layer chocolate fudge cake.

Oh, that demon cake. She knew it well. It was one of Paul's specialties. She hadn't touched even a tiny slice of it. Yay for her. Maybe she'd have it for breakfast when she got up.

The stress was more about impending events than to-do lists. It wasn't like she had a million details of her wedding to look after, because with Gloria Nordquist at the wheel apparently all she had to do was show up.

In a dress.

That the Nordquists paid for.

And it *was* her dream dress with the exotically beaded bodice, fit to perfection by Pinky's own hands. She hoped it was anyway.

She had been able to give her future mother-in-law the color scheme, and, amazingly, Gloria had approved. Patricia reveled in her bed. This would be the last time she'd be sleeping alone on a Saturday morning. In twelve days she and Brett would be man and wife.

Brett had seen some specialist and moved

into a sort of walking cast thing so he could hobble down the aisle. And his jaw wiring was being replaced today with some high-tech sort of invisible contraption. He'd still be clenched, but he wouldn't be stainless steel.

Patricia had considered asking him to push the date back, but he and his mother seemed hell-bent on a Thanksgiving wedding. She got the feeling that her wedding was sort of a diversion to throw people off the trail of the Lizbeth and Eric wedding being so fast.

Besides, she'd be completely out of her mind to ask him that. It was now or never for becoming Brett Nordquist's wife.

Today she wanted to do something she hadn't done for months. Go out and photograph life. The autumn leaves were about to vanish into the November bareness. She should capture them before they fell.

"Patricia? Are you awake? It's ten-thirty. Why don't you take a nice shower and dress up pretty and we'll have a special breakfast?" Pinky talked to her through the door.

"Go away. I'm staying in bed all day."

Pinky opened the door. "Now, why would the

little bride-to-be do that? Rise and shine, princess, it's a special day."

"Why is it special?"

"Oh my God, the hair is actually growing in." Pinky ran over to Patricia's bedside and ruffled her fingers through her hair. "What the hell are you going to do?"

"Lemon juice and sun, or a semipermanent natural-based brunette dye are my two options without turning into a blotchy nightmare. I'm allergic to hydrogen peroxide."

"You have to go back to dark hair, Patricia. You can't walk down the aisle with dark roots and platinum tips, can you?"

"I was thinking about a hat. But maybe it's better for Brett to see me as I truly am."

Pinky was dead silent for a moment, then a big smile crossed her freckled face. "Patricia, that's the smartest thing you've said in quite a while. We will lemon-juice you till the big day, then turn you back into yourself for the wedding. You said it yourself—all the colors are brunette colors, and after all, Brett is marrying you, not your hair color, right?"

Patricia thought about that. She pulled the

covers over her head. "I hope so, Pinky. He's been pretty good to me these last few weeks. He's given me presents, and did you know I have an account at Nordquist's now where I can buy anything I want? I've stuck to the basics, but he all but ordered me to buy china and linen and said we were going all-out."

"Are you two going to buy a house?"

"No, there's an entire apartment in the east wing of the house. It's really cute. Mrs. Nordquist, Gloria, showed it to me. She asked me how I wanted it redecorated."

"Holy crap," Pinky muttered. "Well, let me show you the fine art of the headband today and we will get you all prettied up." She flipped back the covers.

"I told you I'm staying in bed today. I want to wallow in self-pity and enjoy my last days as a single woman. Either that or I'm going to dust off my Nikon and go out for a photo shoot." Patricia grabbed her covers back.

"You can't. We're having a freakin' bridal shower for you. It starts at noon. So get out of bed and get your ass prettied up." Pinky smacked her covered-up foot.

"Shit. Are you kidding?"

"No, I'm not kidding. As long as you're no longer surprised, here's more. The guests include your sisters, some friends of yours from college, your mother, your future mother-in-law, and her guest."

"Who is her guest?"

"Lizbeth, your future sister-in-law."

"Who came up with this guest list?"

"It was a snowball kind of deal: sisters to Mom, Mom to Mrs. Nordquist, Mrs. Nordquist to Lizbeth."

Patricia groaned and rolled up into a ball. "Tell them I'm sick."

"Fat chance." Pinky caught her foot under the covers and pulled it. "Get out of bed and face your music, Princess Patti."

Patricia slid almost to the edge of the bed, then screamed—so Pinky let go.

"I brought you home a dress. I knew you weren't thinking that way, so I hit our favorite vintage store and found this dress that they just marked down for a preholiday sale. It just looked like you," Pinky went to Patricia's own closet and pulled out a plastic garment bag Patricia hadn't even notice, not that she was noticing much of anything lately. Inside was a chiffon floral-print day dress that any society matron would look stunning in.

"Pinky, you are so amazing." Patricia sat up. The colors are so autumn and the whole dress is divine. Brown and orange and gold and the whole overjacket thing. What year was it from?"

"Early sixties, and a longer length for that time. I think my grandmother had one like this she used to wear to luncheons."

Patricia wiped away a stray tear that spilled over her cheek. "It's so not Nordquist, you know?"

"Yes, I know." Pinky hung the dress back up and came over to Patricia. She sat with her and gave her a big hug. "Okay, let's get you cleaned up. I'd say this is one day where I'm going to let you swig down a nice glass of flaming rum punch before your guests arrive, but only one, okay?"

"Yes, yes. My overindulgent days are over. Brett's nurse cut off his beer supply and he's been drinking diet cola through a straw. That and a whole lot of milkshakes. He's lost ten pounds, I swear. He's starting to look too thin." Patricia sniffed back her impending breakdown and laughed.

"Wow, we should have just wired your jaw shut and skipped the pigment-altering experimental drugs, I guess."

"I guess. Thank you, Pinky, and I apologize for any relative of mine, current or future, for whatever they say today, because you know one of them will say something stupid."

Patricia got herself out of bed and grabbed her flannel robe. She'd have to find some clean undies. Brett had been having the personal shopper at Nordquist send her piles of lingerie, most of it stuff she'd rather die than wear.

"Did you see that pile of gifts?"

"The never-ending stream of deliveries has been interesting. What's in there?"

"Things with no crotch. I think Brett is feeling better."

"What, no flannel?"

"I'm going to exchange most of it for a couple of amazing French peignoir sets and some more practical things like full-cut spandex underwear." Patricia laughed. She took her towel off the back of the closet door and stopped to talk to Pinky before she went for a shower.

Pinky opened a couple of boxes and pulled

out some stringy items. "Are these all from lingerie?"

"I think so. Why?"

"Well, I was just thinking that's Lizbeth's department. Kind of strange, isn't it?"

"I didn't think about it like that. I'm sure he's just on a lingerie roll, but she'll get some nice commissions from all this, anyhow. That's a nice parting gift to her, I guess, now that she'll be marrying his brother."

"Sure, commissions," Pinky said in a sort of sinister tone.

Patricia was confused, but Pinky had been coming up with out-of-the-blue comments all morning, so she let it go. So Brett had a personal shopper pick lingerie for her. It was just a coincidence that it was Lizbeth's department. It could be any department. It could be china.

"I'm going to get cleaned up and hit the flaming rum punch before noon." She paused and turned back to Pinky from the doorway. "Is Paulie coming?"

"He's our token male. He's also the caterer, so it was the polite thing to do." Pinky smiled a Cheshire cat smile.

* * *

"Oh," was all Patricia said. She left the room and Pinky noticed Patricia seemed to have a whole lot on her mind. Well, she had a lot on her mind, too. Like the continuing coziness of Brett and Lizbeth, and the impending Nordquist heir Lizbeth was carrying, and just exactly how pregnant was she? Had she been seeing Eric for that long?

Rumor had it she'd been toying with both of them for over three months, even with a brief standoff with Brett to try and get him to pop the question, so who knew? Only Lizbeth, and she wasn't telling.

Pinky really liked the idea of Patricia going brunette again. If she and Paul couldn't get Patricia to see daylight and stop this madness, maybe ol' Brett himself could lend a hand. He was pretty skilled at making bad choices. Maybe he'd screw up a few vital things before the wedding and Patricia would regain her senses.

Paul was trying so hard to patiently work his way into Patricia's heart, but the clock was ticking for all of them. Twelve days from now Patricia would be walking down the aisle to marry Brett.

Pinky decided after she lived through this party she was going to go back to work and do some snooping around. Cold hard dirty facts could always be found in the backrooms of Nordquist's department store. And something smelled fishy. Like lutefisk.

In their five years of cohabitation Paul had met Patricia's sisters but never her mother. Poor Paul, Patricia watched him balance trays of crostini with mozzarella, basil and slices of heirloom tomatoes, and melon bites wrapped in prosciutto through the ladies, who acted like none of them had eaten breakfast. They attacked his trays in a very unladylike manner.

They also acted like it was happy hour and were sliding the mimosas down pretty easily. Except Lizbeth, who seemed to be on the wagon like a wise pregnant girl. She looked a little worse for the wear today, for reasons Patricia knew but were not obvious to others at this point.

Patricia's mother Melinda had begun micromanaging every detail of the party from the minute she'd walked in the door. Pinky finally dragged her off and made her a slightly stiffer drink involving orange juice and vodka, which subdued her enough for Paul to finish up in the kitchen.

Paul had outdone himself and fixed a fennel-spiced prawn citrus salad with blood oranges, and an amazing red bell pepper soup. She hoped the only blood by the end of this thing would be blood oranges. And of course the incredible chocolate fudge cake that she was now glad she hadn't eaten last night.

Pinky had done the most creative decorating job on the house she'd ever seen. She'd basically brought fall inside with twigs and scarlet-leaf Virginia creeper twined into the light fixtures and her beloved Japanese maple leaves scattered everywhere. Thick spicy scented candles the color of pumpkins were tucked in all the windowsills, surrounded with maple sprigs and wildly cool pale yellow spider mums.

Patricia's dress looked like all the elements in the room had come together and rested on the sheer, lovely fabric. She fit right in with the décor. Only Pinky could have done that.

Their special table was set for luncheon with another flower arrangement. This arrangement had been picked to death by her mother. Patricia thought Pinky might slap the woman, but it seemed like Pinky made the table bouquet the sacrificial item that Melinda Stillwell could focus on instead.

Her mother's energy sure wasn't focused on her daughter. Her sisters had actually given her big hugs, but could her mother even acknowledge her? Apparently not.

She should be used to this by now. Why did she always think it would be different? If she'd colored in the lines better, did better in school, married the right person, or had the proper grandchildren, would her mother love her then?

"Patricia, these photographs are beautiful." Gloria Nordquist was staring at the framed photo work on the wall. "Whose are they?"

"Mine. I'm a photographer for fun. In my spare time."

"You're very talented, dear," she said. And it was a genuine compliment.

"I didn't know you took pictures, Patti." Her mother let that slip out. Mrs. Nordquist gave Patricia's mother a funny look because, of course, Mrs. Nordquist knew everything about her sons and loved them despite their flaws. Patricia's guts twisted.

Honestly, it could be a convention of Control Freaks Anonymous, but her future mother-in-law was far more used to keeping up a public facade up than her mother.

Carolyn Gangmark and Jan Coleman, her two friends from college, had huddled together for safety. She knew perfectly well her sisters couldn't hunt up any high school chums of hers because no one knew she actually existed in high school. She'd been lost in a sea of blonde and beautiful teenagers.

"I can't get over your hair, Patricia. It's so unlike you, but such a great change. You look like a different person," her sister Carol said.

Thanks, Carol for pointing that out in front of Mrs. Nordquist. The scarf that Pinky had tied strategically around her head kept all the shadow-of-a-doubt roots in check. Patricia didn't know what to say, so she said nothing.

"Where are you and Brett going on your honeymoon?"

Patricia realized she had no idea. She looked at Gloria Nordquist.

"Brett still has a few weeks in his cast, so they're going to delay the honeymoon a bit. They can stay in their little love nest at the other wing of the house for a while," Gloria answered.

More awkwardness.

Pinky saved the day by rounding everyone up to open gifts. Patricia wanted to run into her room and lock the door, but instead she sat down on the leather chair and let everyone gush and hand her gifts.

Her sisters gave her tablecloths and napkins, her mother gave her cookbooks, and her two friends, bless their hearts, gave her a big box of books about things they knew she loved—photography, architecture, art, Paris—the start of a great library.

"This is so wonderful, you two, I can't even tell you." She gushed until her sisters started to look peeved.

"Here," Pinky interrupted. She put a creatively wrapped package in her hand. Patricia peeled back the paper carefully and tied the beautiful leaf and bronze ribbon bow on her wrist. Inside was a boxed DVD set of Alfred Hitchcock movies: *Marnie, Vertigo, Rebecca, North by Northwest, To Catch a Thief, The Lady Vanishes,* all her favorites.

Pinky looked at her and between them passed the secret code of best friends. Patricia knew if Pinky spoke she'd just cry, so she squeezed her hand.

"You and Brett can get started on film festivals," Pinky said in a choked voice.

Paul made a noise from the kitchen.

"Oh, this one is from Paul." Pinky handed her a small package in black paper with a gold ribbon. Interesting wrap choice. She smiled a little smirky smile at him.

She pulled off the wrappings and found a black velvet jewelry box. When she opened the lid she saw a truly lovely vintage necklace with amber and gold formed into leaves and flowers. It was so personal and so perfect. She slipped it around her neck and Pinky automatically helped her with the clasp.

A ripple of oohs went through the ladies. "It matches your dress perfectly," Heather remarked.

"Thank you so much, Paul." She got up and walked into the kitchen. "Thank you," she whispered. She kissed his cheek and left an amber-glaze lip print. A rush of emotion tingled over her.

There was a whole lot of silence from the living room.

Patricia broke the quiet. "Give me a nice hot cider refill, please. Anyone else want a cider refill?"

A little rumble of conversation started back up and Patricia returned to her seat with a cup of hot cider and floating cloves.

Pinky read the tag. "This one is from Lizbeth."

"Thank you, Lizbeth. You shouldn't have." Patricia set her cup down and unwrapped the floral package. It was a black lace bra-and-panties set nestled in white tissue paper. Patricia stared at it for a moment, then lifted it up for the others to see. "How fun." Patricia smiled a fake smile. What was up with the lingerie anyway? She was drowning in the stuff, and no one knew that better than Lizbeth.

The usual round of comedy occurred as she repackaged the set and put the box at her feet.

"One more and we'll have lunch."

"Oh, Patricia, we've forgotten to make your shower bouquet. Here, give me a paper plate and some scissors, Paul, and hand me all the ribbons." Her mother held out her hands to receive the items she'd asked for.

Snip, snip, snip went the scissors, and each little snip made Patricia's nerves jump. While her mother stuffed ribbons in the paper plate, she opened the last gift, from Mrs. Nordquist.

It was from Nordquist's, of course. She sprung the ribbon and handed it to her mother. The box was wrapped the way some people do to let you remove the lid all at once. Patricia gasped. Inside the box was a cup and saucer in the Flora Danica pattern. Her eyes met Mrs. Nordquist's and for a split second there passed between them not the secret language of best friends, but the secret language of women who marry into money. Sort of like . . .sympathy.

Patricia choked up. She put the box carefully on the coffee table and rose to give Gloria Nordquist a small embrace. "How did you know?" she asked softly.

"Believe it or not, Brett mentioned it." Gloria seemed genuinely moved.

Lizbeth glared at Patricia. Oh God, now Lizbeth was going to make this into a daughter-in-law competition.

"Thank you, everyone. These are the most lovely, thoughtful gifts I've ever gotten. She stared at Pinky while she said that. "Now let's do eat. Paul has made us a delicious lunch and if we're good, he'll let us have the chocolate cake I saw earlier." Patricia did hostess with the mostess just to show Gloria Nordquist she had it in her.

The ladies adjourned to the dining nook and seated themselves. Patricia followed Pinky into the kitchen to help Paul.

As they worked together, Patricia notice the seamless team effort the three of them made moving around the kitchen. *This* was her family now.

She loved her sisters and most likely her mother as well, but there was so much baggage there. Carol took up putting Patricia down where her mother left off. Heather was in her own little world, although her baby sister would always be dear to her heart, cute as she was. She seemed to be a wiser girl these days, watching the interactions of Patricia and Mom with a keen eye.

But these two, Pinky and Paul, were the two most important people in her life.

Patricia put her hand over the necklace Paul had given her and felt the intricacy of the beads and gold leaves.

She was in a state of extreme confusion. Maybe she should skip the soup and head straight for chocolate cake.

The three of them sat on the couch of many colors after everyone had left. Paul sat in the center, Patricia was tucked up on one side of him still in her party dress, and Pinky, who had shed her brown and pink dress for flannel pajamas, was curled on the other.

Paul handed Patricia yet another pile of tissues from the box Pinky held. The girls had put *Now Voyager* on the DVD player. It always made the two of them cry, but this time was way worse. Patricia's hysterics slowed to a hiccupping air-gulping stage. She blew her nose again and threw the used Kleenex into the paper bag Pinky had made her breath into earlier. The bridal shower had sent her over the edge.

He'd been feeding them prosciutto and melon with chocolate cake on the side for dinner in between cries.

Paul let the warmth of Patricia soak into him.

This might be the last time he ever got to hold her like this.

Now Voyager was one of their favorites, but the whole part about the main character standing up to her mother at last, well, that hit Patricia's buttons all over again and made stage-two hysterics commence. The whole theme of the movie was how the Bette Davis character transformed from an ugly ducking to a beauty and found true love but the man could never be hers completely.

Kind of like Patricia, because in her heart she must know that Brett would never be her soul mate. He would never give his whole being to her because he was a self-centered spoiled man, even if he did fall off a balcony.

But Paul damn sure as hell didn't want to spend *his* life in a state of noble unrequited love waiting for Patricia to leave her rich husband like Bette Davis did in this movie. If she wanted to marry Brett, he'd have to let go. But letting go was not what he wanted to do.

Why these two always found the movie that hurt the most was really a mystery. Patricia's crying picked up again as Charlotte Vale delivered her final line:

"Oh, Jerry, don't let's ask for the moon. We have the stars."

Pinky on his left began to blubber, too, taking her glasses off to wipe her eyes.

Patricia bawled into a pile of Kleenexes. Between jags she kept staring at the damn teacup Mrs. Nordquist had given her.

She leaned her head on his shoulder and he could feel her wet tears soak into his shirt. Time was running out for them. An intense frustration coursed through him. He gently shifted away from her and got up, leaving the two of them to fend for themselves. He couldn't take it anymore.

Patricia sure as hell had something to cry about. She was marrying the wrong man. He had to stop this wedding.

Chapter Eighteen

Affliction is enamoured of thy parts, and thou art wedded to calamity.

Shakespeare

The harpist was drunk. The groom was on painkillers and champagne. Her beautiful beaded wedding gown had vanished somehow in the alteration stages and been replaced by a rather tight-fitting substitute gown courtesy of Gloria Nordquist, who patted her and said tsk-tsk, she'd put on a few pounds, and, my, my wasn't her hair interesting now?

Her perfect beaded shoes had also vanished and the pumps Pinky foraged up were too tight.

On top of all that, she was a brunette again.

She'd braided pearl strands through her wavy brown hair, she'd tried to maintain her "elegance," but there was no doubt about it, brown was brown.

Last night at the rehearsal Patricia had stepped into the big shiny impressive Episcopal cathedral and Brett had looked her over like a prize filly that had changed colors midrace on him.

"Wat append to eore air?" He'd said through his new no-wire jaw apparatus.

Patricia had made a joke of it and passed it off as a woman's whim. "I decided to go chestnut bronze like the season."

"Av ou gaind eight?" He cocked his cocky head at her.

"A little," she answered. Yes, she had gained a little weight, and thanks for pointing that out.

"Eird," he said, which she took for *weird*.

They'd lived through the mock-ceremony, although she sensed a real change in Brett. He'd held her arm like she was a possession and joked about her with Eric and Lizbeth in garbled phrases that they all thought were so very funny but she didn't really understand anyway.

When she thanked him for the teacup his mother had given her, he said he'd told his mother about what expensive taste Patricia had as a joke, and how well she'd fit into the family, and that she'd better marry into the Nordquist family or all of her measly paycheck would go toward fine china.

And now, in the bride's room, thirty minutes before the wedding, standing here getting trussed up by her best friend, she was nervous as a feral cat. Her tiny little veil kept tipping sideways because it wouldn't hold in her hair. What a stupid veil.

Pinky was worse. Her hands fumbled as she fastened the little buttons on Patricia's fingerless gloves.

"Hold still while I get this last button." She stood back and looked at Patricia. "At least they could have found something that suited you better. Although I do like the sheath look, and the silk is very nice. It's very simple and elegant, don't you think?"

"Honey, *elegant* has become a dirty word in my world. What happened to *your* dress, Pinky, I mean you're wearing peach. Peach is not cocoa." Patricia's hands shook as she held her bouquet of camellias.

"They must have delivered both dresses to

the wrong church." Pinky avoided eye contact with her, but Patricia was too emotionally strung out to wonder why.

"Well, for crying out loud, Pinky, they have to be in this mausoleum somewhere. Let's hunt through these offices!" Patricia felt herself go into a strange angry mode. "Come on." She grabbed Pinky by the hand, her camellia bouquet losing bits of baby's breath as she charged forward. "Come *on,* Pinky." She stamped her foot to Pinky's protesting non-movement.

Pinky didn't say much, but went along with her. They walked down the dark wood-paneled corridors and opened door after door. Her sisters were in one, all happy in peach silk. Patricia briefly nodded to them and shut the heavy door in their faces.

She had to keep up her search. For some reason she just had to know that her perfect dress was not in this building before she'd walk down the aisle in tight silk with a yellow undertone. Yellow. Her dress had a slight pink undertone. Taupe. Beigey pink. *Not yellow,* for Christ's sake. She heard herself muttering, "Taupe," as she walked.

And what had happened to her vintage blue and brown color scheme? Her head jerked back as she passed the sanctuary and saw huge bouquets of peach and white everywhere.

Her father looked more nervous than she did. He waved a scary wave as she passed, and she ignored him. If she stopped, he'd probably criticize her choice of music or something. Not that she'd actually made any choices.

Paul had been staring out the entry hall window watching the rain drizzle down outside for an hour. His insides were raw and his heart actually ached. All he could think about was Patricia pulling him into bed one dark October night not long ago. He moved from image to image of her in his mind.

Paul thought about his grandparents and what they went through and how they stayed together. He thought about how much he loved this woman. He loved her enough to let her follow her crazy dream. But it was killing him to watch.

Earlier he'd noticed Brett pace up and down the front of the sanctuary, which was hard to do in a walking cast. He did look uncomfortable in his gray pinstripe morning suit. Then Brett had walked past Paul about a half hour ago muttering something about getting a drink, and vanished down one of the dark hallways.

Currently, he noticed Patricia was behaving like a deranged bride going in and out of doors one after the other down the opposite hallway. Was she looking for Brett?

She got to his spot in the hallway. "You know it's bad luck to see the groom before the wedding," Paul joked.

Patricia glared at him and passed right by, dragging Pinky in a ghastly peach-colored dress. Pinky looked at him desperately. She obviously needed help.

As he followed them, he noticed Patricia was wearing the necklace he'd bought her in New York. Her hair was now a beautiful rich auburn brown and he wondered why he'd never noticed how lovely it was. He walked a few paces behind and stayed out of the way as Patricia opened and closed doors. They came to a flight of stairs and she headed up.

"I bet they're up here. They always put stuff upstairs," Patricia charged forward.

Pinky lagged behind slightly and caught Paul's arm.

"She's looking for her wedding gown. It didn' arrive at the church and she thinks it's in an other room, but she'll never find it because it' not here."

"How do you know?" Paul asked, climbin stairs.

"I'll tell you later."

A crack of lightning was followed instantly by the rumble of thunder.

"Spooky," Pinky hissed.

"Close," Paul said.

Paul took some huge steps and caught up with his best friend and love of his life that he might never see again, Patricia. She'd opened two doors so far and only found brooms and a Sunday school room, as far as she could see.

"Patricia, what can I do to help you?" he asked.

"Just help me look for my gown. I'm in the wrong gown," she answered, breathless.

No kidding she was in the wrong gown. Her hair was tangled in pearls and tousled, her veil was crooked; she was one crazy bride. He stood back and let the spark of hope that she might call this off fan into a full-fledged fire.

Patricia flung open a door and yet another dark room greeted them. Pinky stood behind Paul and sighed loudly.

As Patricia stood in the doorway, a blinding flash of lightning illuminated the entire room through its multicolored stained-glass gothic window. She saw sofas, a desk . . .

And on that desk sat Lizbeth. She twisted around at the sound of the door and screamed when the lightning flashed. Her blonde hair lit up like gold.

And so did Brett's.

At first Paul had trouble making out the actual scene, but then it all became clear. Brett had Lizbeth on the desk and Lizbeth's dress was temporarily pushed up to her waist. Brett was engaged in Lizbeth.

Brett was so engaged he didn't actually hear the door open, and he continued his engaging behavior, letting out the distinctive sounds of a man engaged in having sex. Brett had his hands on Lizbeth's bare behind and had just given her a quick pull his direction, with the appropriate groan of male pleasure muffled through a mouth brace.

* * *

Patricia slowly closed the dark wooden door and turned to face her two friends. She could actually *feel* the color drain out of her face. This must be what people who get hanged feel like. All of a sudden the trap drops, whoosh, and you're in midair with nothing to hold you up, then, snap, your neck is sideways.

She sucked in a breath.

Pinky rushed to her, but Patricia pushed her away.

"You *can't* go through with this," Pinky yelled.

"Leave me alone. Get out of here, both of you. Go downstairs."

Paul took Pinky by the hand. "Let her go. I'll take care of this," he said. They turned away from her and started back down the stairs.

All along he'd known one thing. Patricia had to come to him on her own. She had to wake up from her dream world and realize deep in her heart that *he,* her best friend, was what she'd been searching for.

He couldn't pick her up and throw her over his shoulder and drag her out of here, she had to wake up and see the light. Well, the light was cracking through the sky in shocking bolts at this point!

Now was the moment. There was no way he'd let her marry Brett Nordquist, even if he had to stop the wedding himself.

"She can't do this, she wouldn't. Would she?" Pinky tried to catch her breath and talk at the same time.

"We're going to have to see just how far she will go, Pinky. But I promise you something. There is no way this wedding is going to take place today or any other day.

"I like the sound of that. Shall I lock her in the bridal room? Got duct tape?"

"No, we're going to let Patricia have a little rope, but we won't let her hang herself, okay?"

"Okay, Paulie, just let me know if you need anything." Pinky touched his hand.

"I might need a few hours alone at home tonight. Watch for the sign."

Pinky elbowed him in the ribs. "I'll watch. Now I have somewhere to go when you need privacy. Dr. Jimmy Bender will save me from the storm."

* * *

The thunder and lightning continued to punctuate her spinning thoughts. Patricia held her hand against her temple and tried to stop the pounding.

In the shadows of the dark hallway she found a corner to shield her. Minutes ticked by and finally Brett emerged from the room she'd barged into. He turned to Lizbeth and patted her hip. She straightened his tie. Then he left her there, grabbed the rails of the stairway, and swung down the stairs jolly as you please.

Lizbeth stood in the hall and powdered her nose with a pretty gold compact full of pressed powder—expensive powder, no doubt. She smoothed her smooth blonde hair and calmly walked down the stairs.

Patricia emerged from the shadows. This was her life now. This was what rich, spoiled husbands did. They kept a mistress and a wife. The wife got the Flora Danica china and the mistress got diamond bracelets.

Lizbeth was a perfect mistress. Even if she *was* going to be his brother's wife. She'd fixed it so she'd gotten *both* brothers. But that made it so handy. So *in the family.* Every holiday, brother Brett and Lizbeth could sneak off and find a quiet spot in the attic to screw their brains out while Patricia and brother Eric drank eggnog with the folks downstairs.

Brett didn't even care that Lizbeth might be carrying his *baby*. Or maybe that turned him on even more. Maybe he figured that was the perfect way to stick it to his brother Eric for stealing Lizbeth out from under his nose.

It was perfectly clear to Patricia that Brett Nordquist needed to be removed from the planet. He was an amoral, evil man. She considered her options.

She could marry him and kill him later, which would make her his widow and entitled to his money. She started walking down the stairs slowly. At each step her dark side grew darker. She was a dark-haired woman. Darkness filled her like an inky blackness.

She could just stab him right at the altar. She'd put Pinky's sharp-as-death scissors in her bouquet and stick it to him in one swift movement instead of saying, *I do.* That was it, she'd bend forward just slightly, lean in, and slice his innards open. Or maybe she should go for his black, evil heart.

Oh, wait, he didn't have one.

Patricia staggered down the stairs carrying her bridal bouquet. As she approached the opening to the sanctuary, she saw Lizbeth take her place next to Eric on the groom's side. Oh, *that* was completely sickening. Maybe after she stabbed Brett she'd stab Lizbeth, too. Just to do a favor for Eric.

No, Lizbeth deserved to live because she was pregnant and karma would get her in the end anyway.

Far away in her mind she heard organ music. It was the old classic "Here Comes the Bride." Like she'd have that played at her wedding.

Her father took her arm and pulled her toward the red-carpeted aisle. Patricia had a flashback of *Father of the Bride* and the aisle turning to rubber as Spencer Tracy walked toward the altar. That made her laugh. Here she was, walking to her doom, with old movie scenes flashing in her head.

She could see Pinky on her left with her sisters. She could see Brett to the right, smiling like the gigantic *fesso* he was, fresh from sex with Lizbeth. My, he'd limped down here quickly.

No, she was the *fesso*. She had been a complete

idiot for so long it had actually become second nature to her.

Damn, she forgot to put the scissors in her bouquet. Why was she here? She didn't want to marry Brett. She didn't want to raise his little towheaded children and have them running all over the lawn of the estate while he screwed his sister-in-law in the pool house.

Patricia noticed everyone had stood up.

Lightning flashed like the crack of a whip.

Thunder rumbled outside.

Patricia kept walking. She walked all the way up to the front of the sanctuary and let her father give her to Brett.

Pinky stood beside her, tears streaming down her face. Her makeup smeared down her cheeks. Poor Pinky. Have some faith, girl!

"Sorry, babe, wild oats," Brett whispered in her ear. It came out pretty clearly for once.

He *knew* she'd seen him.

Blah blah blah, the man in the white satin nightgown at the front of the church droned on. He might as well be speaking Klingon. *Wild oats.* His words rang in her ear. Patricia felt rage rush through her like a fever.

While the minister was talking, Patricia handed her bouquet to Pinky. She heard a little rustle of commentary, as it just *wasn't* the right time to do that, but she couldn't get her glove off properly if she had the damned camellias in her hand. She pulled the glove with her teeth and finally got the damned thing off.

It took more self-control than Paul had ever possessed to stand at the back of the church and wait for Patricia to remember who she was.

He couldn't believe she'd gone all the way to the front of the church. Twice on the way down she'd stopped dead in her tracks. Her veil was sideways, her face looked like hell.

But Paul stayed planted like an oak tree in front of the double doors. The moment would come. He believed in her. He believed that whatever had possessed her was wearing off. With the loss of her blondeness came the fading of her confused alter ego and the revival of her true self. He loved that true self. He wanted to shout that out to the entire congregation. But not yet.

She handed Pinky the bouquet and struggled with her glove. He saw her begin to unravel. The Nordquist family shifted in their pews.

How he wished he could save her from this, but this was nature's consequence, just like Pinky had said.

Her glove dropped to the floor. A rumble of thunder drowned out the minister, but then, faster than lightning, a sharp crack echoed throughout the church.

She pulled back her arm and let it fly, flat-handed, right in his busted jaw, right on his pale Nordic cheek.

Patricia felt the sting from the tip of her fingers to the top of her head. It was the best sting she'd ever felt. She saw a bright red welt exactly the shape of her hand form on Brett's surprised face. From his expression she thought perhaps she'd just rebroken his jaw. What a pity. He'd have to be rewired.

The entire congregation sucked in a collective gasp. She twisted the ring off her finger and threw it on the floor at Brett's feet.

And then, only then, did Patricia turn around. Her eyes sought his and when she saw him standing there she screamed out loud. *"Paul!"*

Brett grabbed her by the wrist. Pinky punched

Brett in the stomach with her best Brooklyn right hook. Brett let go fast and crumpled in a very pained pile of groom.

Paul strode forward and Patricia ran. She ran down the aisle, past the very rich Mrs. Nordquist, past evil Lizbeth and poor Eric, past her disapproving mother and father. Boy, wouldn't she be the bad daughter now? She ripped off the stupid veil and flew like an angel, wings outstretched.

And Paul held out his arms and caught her. He spun her around one time as she covered his face with kisses.

He swept her up, kicked open the double doors, and carried her out of the church. As he ran down the stairs, he hear Pinky's voice cheering, *"Waaaa-Hooooo!"*

"Do it," she screamed. They were home now and she *had* to get out of this dress.

Paul carefully positioned Pinky's sewing scissors at the bottom of Patricia's hem and started cutting. He opened the dress from top to bottom in a long, shivering slice of silk.

When it was done, she grabbed both sides and ripped it off of her body, stamping her feet and screaming like a crazy woman until it was a cut-up pile of silk on the floor. She stamped on it ten times. She counted. Then she took off her dreadful shoes and threw them across the room one at a time. Paul ducked.

"Now do *me*," she screamed.

In less than a minute, Paul was down to his tight knit boxers. He took off his glasses and pulled her close. He reached around behind her and in one quick second he'd unzipped the crazy petticoat she had on. She stepped out of it like a reverse Cinderella. The less gown she had on, the better, she felt.

Underneath she had on her silk tap pants. Not anything Brett or Lizbeth had sent over, which no doubt Lizbeth had a matching set of, but a special set of vintage undies she and Pinky had collected.

Oddly she felt like she'd put them on for Paul this morning. She sure as hell hadn't put them on for Brett.

"You are beautiful, Patricia. You are my beautiful brunette." He smoothed his hands over her push-up-bra'd breasts and let his mouth trail behind. He continued down across her full waist with its little ripple of pudginess that had recently returned, and knelt down to run his mouth across her silky tap pants, heating her to a boil with his hot breath. She trembled and held on to his hair, screaming every few seconds.

"Ow." He came up laughing and pulled her against him. "Are you going to kick and scream all night?"

"All *night*," she screamed. She needed to scream, she needed to let loose of all the horrible days and days of what she'd done.

"Okay, then scream away." He kissed her and teased his tongue in her mouth gently and playfully. She screamed into his mouth and let him play in her mouth until her scream turned into a burn of desire for him.

"Now wash me off, Paul. Take me into the shower and wash off all my sins. Wash away all my stupidity and all my blondeness and all my elegance. *I don't ever want to be elegant again.*" She'd started out soft, but she ended in another scream.

He picked her up and carried her from the living room to his bedroom and through to the master bathroom. She kissed his arm and bit him a couple of times on the way. He kissed her twice in the hall and once as he set her down to turn on the shower.

While they waited, his fingers traveled her. He lightly moved across her breasts with his two index fingers and down each side, following the bottom edges of her tap pants, and then he slid his thumb across her hottest spot and made her weak. He pressed. She screamed and put her arms around his neck, pulling him to her, crushing her body into his.

He opened the shower with one hand and moved them inside, clothing and all. It was hot and good and she stood in the water until her whole face and hair and bra and tap pants were slippery wet.

She reached over to stroke the huge erection that Paul had now revealed as he stripped off his boxers. She'd never seen him in the light. He was a beautiful man. She pinned him back against the tiled wall of the shower and touched him everywhere. She explored and kissed and ran her mouth over him until he groaned and closed his eyes and couldn't speak anymore.

She rose up and he unfastened the hooks of

her bra, throwing it over the shower door. Next he slid her tap pants off. He slid his mouth with the slippery streams of water until he found the perfect spot to stop with his tongue.

Patricia screamed as he moved his fingers into her and pressed his mouth against her. She loved screaming. She wanted to scream herself hoarse. He didn't stop until she throbbed against him and screamed, *"Paul!"* a dozen times, pulling his hair as she called his name.

He rose up like a water god, full of passion and ready to give her whatever she needed. He kissed her over and over again, their wet mouths moving together like lovemaking.

"Patricia." He whispered her name slowly against her ear and down her neck until he reached her breast and pulled her already hot and throbbing nipple into his mouth. He was savoring her, she could tell. He was taking her to slow sexual places she'd never been before. She didn't even know what lovemaking was until Paul showed her. He had to make love to her like this a thousand more times.

She had no thought of preventing him from making her pregnant. She couldn't think of anything she would love more than to have his child.

"Come inside me," she demanded, but not with a scream, just her mouth against his ear softly. He straightened to look at her fully, his eyes piercing through all the twisted crazy misplaced dreams she was having him wash away. He held her face in his hands for a full minute, reading her, kissing her, pausing.

Then his kisses increased in intensity, as if he had made up his mind. He drove her to the edge of reason with his kisses, then picked her up and held her perfectly, slowly, and moved himself into her. She leaned her head back and screamed, shaking her head, feeling her long brown hair against her own back, feeling him inside her.

He was strong and he moved with deliberate pleasure as she continued to scream whenever a wave of heat moved its way from her center to her throat and out into the air, emerging as a deep, animal scream. Her screams had changed and she clung to him hard and pushed against him till she felt a shudder climb through him that she devoured with her own body. "Oh, *Paul,*" she cried, and then she cried out again as they both came together, his yell as he released at last, her screams and his mouth finding hers as they both trembled from the emotion.

"Marry me," he whispered,

"Oh yes, oh yes, Paul, I love you, I love you, my best and most lovely Paul," she answered. His very beautiful words wove around her and she started to cry.

He rocked her. He let her pour over him. She cried a brokenhearted cry, that she had betrayed his love and let him suffer so long. Every touch and move and word Paul gave her was a touch of love, a move of love, a word of love. How could he ever have waited for her? Her eyes could not stop crying and her heart could not stop hurting.

He shut off the water and, without letting her go, opened the door and pulled a towel from the hook. He wrapped her in the towel and carried her to his bed.

She had never cried this cry in her life of tears. It was a well so deep she wondered if she would cry this way forever. He held her close and stroked her wet hair for hours. The half-moon shone over the water outside and caught her like a fish in a golden net. Her tears slowed down.

She watched the shimmer of water reflect the moon through Paul's window. She drifted, drifted somewhere. But now she knew that Paul would be there by her side forever, so she let herself drift away.

Chapter Nineteen

But here's the joy, my friend and I are one . . . that she loves but me alone!
Shakespeare

"Don't even speak of it." Patricia put her finger over her best friend Pinky's lips for a moment. "You were the wisest and most faithful friend I will ever know, to keep this gown away from me on that day. Just think, I would have spoiled it for its true purpose by having it paid for by you-know-who.

"Did I tell you when I tried it on the very first time and closed my eyes and dreamed of my wedding—which, by the way, did not include a drunken harpist or an organ playing 'Here

Comes the Bride'—that I saw Paul waiting for me in that vision? Even my visions were smarter than I was."

Patricia looked down at her beautiful antique art deco ring. She brought it to her lips and kissed it. It had been on her finger since she awoke to find it there the morning after Paul saved her life. He had slipped it on her while she slept. And he had knelt beside the bed when her eyes fluttered open to the light of that new morning and asked her again to marry him, holding her hand with the ring that was his grandmother's. The only other ring she needed now was a plain gold band.

He'd called her his amber-eyed, brown-haired girl and sang the Van Morrison song to her for the rest of that day. It was enough to make her shed her blue contacts forever and be content being quite a strudel in her new stylish glasses.

"Pinky, you are a vision." Patricia looked at her friend standing beside her in the mirror.

Pinky turned around. "It suits me, doesn't it? I'm glad I didn't end up in the cocoa latte dress. Being a bride is always better than being a bridesmaid," Pinky said. Patricia straightened the lovely rolled collar on the jacket of Pinky's pale beige silk wedding suit.

"The shoes are fabulous, aren't they?" Patricia said. Pinky's tiny feet were clad in completely beaded slides with a plump little heel in all the colors they loved, beige and green and amber and gold.

Patricia felt the necklace at her throat. "Look how Paul's necklace matches this dress. I can't believe it. It's like a perfect match. It's like he was there in a shop in New York and knew that someday he'd marry me and I'd wear a beaded gown that matched this necklace. He is definitely beyond Osgood.

"Life is good, my Pinkster. A double wedding, in our own home, to two wonderful men. Who would have even thought we'd be so happy at the same time? Now if we can just get the people next door to sell you and Dr. Jim their house, we'll be all set." Patricia took in a breath.

"We're only ten minutes away, darling Patricia. Oh God, we're just blathering." Pinky moaned. "Can't they just call us out there and get it over with?" Pinky sat down hard in the wooden chair next to Paul's bed.

The sound of the little musical group with

their mandolin, violin, and concertina in the background actually soothed Patricia. She and Paul had found an old Italian folk song that his grandparents had loved as children.

A knock came at the door and scared both of them out of their wits. "Good grief, you'd think we were nervous!" Pinky got up quickly.

"Here, grab your orchids, let's get married."

"Can't we take our Christmas Birken bags with us?" Pinky smiled. "Or my Christmas Barbie lunch box?"

"No, and no, they stay in the closet till later. Now march," Patricia ordered.

"You are so bossy." Pinky started toward the door.

"I'm recapturing my inner blonde."

"Oh no, you don't, as God is my witness, you'll never go blonde again!" Pinky declared.

Patricia opened the door and pointed with her flowers. She let Pinky go first, then took a soft whiff of her Cattleya orchid bouquet.

Pinky's Dr. Bender had definitely outdone himself when he'd found them these. They were most unusual, with their golden colors and intense fragrance. He was right. It was handy to have botanist friends.

She'd even forgiven him for letting her participate in the Feltzengraad study and becoming emotionally impaired along with her platinum transformation and weight loss. Paul promised he'd never let her near another scientific study as long as they both shall live.

Patricia had mixed the orchids up with forget-me-nots for vintage blue and pink cherry blossoms for spring and tied them in a little bundle with thin gold ribbons. She liked the one orchid in her pretty brown hair. No veils this time.

Suddenly Patricia wasn't a bit nervous. She was here in Paul's house, their house now, with the people who loved her. Paul, who loved her the best, and Pinky and Jim Bender, whose love had blossomed into a full-blown romance, were all here together.

She walked toward the living room and joined Pinky. Paul and Jim were waiting, looking very handsome in their suits. Asta the cat was on her mother's lap sporting a gold bow. Her mother must be going nuts. Maybe Asta would bite her.

They'd moved all the furniture for the wedding and the boys had created a canopy of willow branches with their new leaves budding out. For a couple of guys, they'd done pretty well

Pinky had woven in cherry blossom branches and forsythia and bellflowers.

Last night she'd heard Paul and his brothers hammering and swearing and laughing, and today his entire family had gathered to watch the wedding. There'd been a steady stream of great Italian food for at least a week.

Jim Bender's parents were there and so were Patricia's sisters and even both her parents, whom she'd told in no uncertain terms that if they had nothing good to say, they could cram it up last winter's Christmas goose. She'd done her Charlotte Vale imitation.

She and Pinky walked down a little aisle of flowers and gold ribbons and as she looked around she saw Paul's grandparents take each other's hand. The four of them gathered in the bay window under the willow canopy.

Paul had to hand it to Pinky for altering that beautiful beaded wedding dress to fit around Patricia's new roundness. It was about time he made an honest woman of her, and he would have married her months ago, but she was determined she should show as much as possible and be the most pregnant bride ever. She'd settled for a spring wedding. His Patricia had definitely turned into a nonconforming rebel.

So here they were on a soft April evening surrounded with candles and flowers and family having the double wedding Patricia and Pinky dreamed up.

Actually they'd all dreamed it up that night that Jim Bender had spelled "Will you marry me Pinky" on the scrabble board. He'd gotten double points, too. It was a good thing Paul and Patricia had slipped him all the extra letters.

Paul still couldn't figure out how he'd managed to keep his job after November's drama. True, Patricia had lost her job at Nordquist's forever according to that very creative pink slip handwritten by Brett just before they sent him away to open the new Alaska store.

But Paul had a feeling Henri Shreve reached out and pulled some strings with his old friend Lars Nordquist regarding Paul's new position as head handbag buyer, complete with a raise.

Being unemployed had made his wife-to-be bloom as far as he could see, and her photographs had turned into a true artistic pursuit.

How lucky he was that she had turned around

and realized he was waiting for her. Since that moment she had never left his side or his bed.

And since they'd found out she was pregnant, she'd never stopped eating pickled cauliflower and cannoli with chocolate ricotta filling.

Pinky stepped next to Jim, and Patricia put her hand in Paul's.

Patricia had never felt as much love in one room as when the four of them took their vows together.

For where you go I will go, and where you stay I will stay. Your people shall be my people. . . . To love and to cherish; from this day forward.

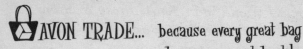